A MUMBAI MURDER MYSTERY

A completely unputdownable must-read crime mystery

MEETI SHROFF-SHAH

A Temple Hill Mystery Book 1

JOFFE BOOKS

Joffe Books, London
www.joffebooks.com

First published in Great Britain in 2021

This book is a work of fiction. Names, characters, businesses, organisations, places and events are either the product of the author's imagination or are used fictitiously. Any resemblance to actual persons, living or dead, events or locales is entirely coincidental. The spelling used is British English except where fidelity to the author's rendering of accent or dialect supersedes this.

Cover art by Jarmila Takač

ISBN: 978-1-80405-003-3

For my Meeru Peeru,
for always remembering to ask me
that most important of all questions.

CHAPTER 1

Among the Gujaratis on the quiet, sun-dappled slopes of Mumbai's posh Temple Hill, the fear of God is a mere second to the fear of what people will say. Reputations are prized. Appearances are vital. And keeping them up is a life skill, passed down through generations, alongside the family trade. There exists a code of conduct, unarticulated yet palpable in the power it exerts. Everything is as it should be — at least on the face of it. The actual messy business of living is conducted behind the gilded doors and silk-draped windows of plush, sea-facing apartments. On Temple Hill, being happy is not quite as important as *seeming* happy.

As she darkened her lipstick, Radhika Zaveri thought about the world she'd returned to. In a few minutes, she'd enter the welcome-back party her sister and brother-in-law were hosting for her. She'd be surrounded by family and friends. Some would be here because they cared for her, but most would attend out of curiosity. She couldn't blame them. They were sure to have heard the rumours.

Radhi had been abroad for more than a decade, but the Gujaratis of Temple Hill were many tentacled, with uncles and aunts and cousins across the world. Snatches of her life, or some warped version of it, would have got back to them.

She inhaled deeply. She couldn't afford to appear weak. Most of them would be delighted if they thought she was suffering. It would validate their own approach to life, their narrow, rigid world view. It served her right. She'd been one of them but hadn't minded their ways. For anyone else, the community of Temple Hill would have long cut the cord. But her family was too well connected and Radhi herself almost frightfully rich. For her, they'd made an exception. But it would be good to see her down. And she was damned if she gave them that pleasure.

She could deal with their probing questions. The whispers behind her back. The stories they told each other, which often made their way to her, twisted so much that she hardly recognized herself in them. What she couldn't bear was their pity. In a way, she was still one of them. It was essential to her that they thought she was fine.

She gave herself one last look in the mirror. She was dressed in white cigarette pants and a nude-coloured sheer top through which you could see her black lace bra and flat stomach. Regardless of how she felt, she looked good. And that was the important thing.

Taking another deep breath, she walked into the bright, chandelier-lit living room. A hush descended for a nanosecond, then a woman's voice squealed, 'Radhika *dikra*!'

Wincing as she recognized the voice, Radhi turned to see a chubby, sari-clad woman waddle up, her jiggling arms outstretched, large sweat stains beneath her armpits, despite the heavy air-conditioning. She pressed Radhi into a hug long enough for her to gag at the strong smell of garlic on the woman's breath.

'Hello, *kaki*,' she said, pulling herself free after what she felt was a reasonable amount of time.

'How skinny you've become! Just look at those hollow cheeks! It's that terrible business with what's his name . . . McDonald . . . no, Mackinzey, no? Lost your appetite because of that, I suppose. Perfectly understandable, of course . . . but never you mind, you are back now . . . among your own family . . . you can trust us to feed you well.'

'Oh? And then pay Sonali Kulkarni to lose all that weight again? Come now *kaki*, that's hardly a sound plan,' said Radhi, referring to her aunt's long-standing dietician.

Radhi knew she'd been blunt, even by her standards, but she hadn't expected her aunt to bring up Mackinzey's name quite so soon. It had come as a bit of a shock. She hadn't heard his name out loud in over a year now. This, she supposed though, was Ila *kaki*'s speciality. She had a sixth sense for being able to sniff out where people were hurting most.

Before Ila could answer, she was joined by her husband, Pankaj Zaveri, 'Hello, *beta*.' He gave Radhi a hug.

'Hello, *kaka*,' said Radhi with genuine pleasure.

Mild-mannered and kind to a fault, Radhi's only grouse with her father's brother was that he'd married Ila *kaki*. That, and the fact that he *never* spoke up when she behaved badly.

'I'm so glad you decided to move back. We hear you're opening up the old apartment again?' He was referring to Radhika's childhood home.

'Yes.' Radhika smiled. 'Though it's not going to look like the old place much longer . . . I'm changing all the furniture.'

'That's good. Make a fresh start . . . India has changed so much in the last decade. The publishing scene here is booming—'

'Oh, you are still writing then?' Ila *kaki*'s voice was like a *pepsicola*: ice cold and dripping with sugar. 'I had no idea! We live under a rock, here in India. Can't believe we missed your new book. What's it called?'

Radhika's cheeks burned. It had been three years since her last novel came out. She wasn't working on anything new. In fact, she hadn't opened a Word document in over a year. Her aunt probably knew all this. There'd been an article in the *Post* about how writers these days were starting young but burning out early, and they had cited Radhi as an example. It had been circulated widely in their circles on WhatsApp.

'It's top secret, *kaki*,' Radhi returned brightly. Then, leaning towards her conspiratorially, 'The thing is, I've got a three-book deal. Can't really have the first one out, without knowing where the other two are headed, no?'

Her aunt gave her a cold smile. She hadn't expected Radhi to lie so bald-facedly. But she couldn't very well call her out on it, not without revealing that she'd known about Radhi's dry spell to begin with.

'How lovely. We want our signed copies as usual, of course.'

'Of course.'

Madhavi, Radhika's elder sister, suddenly materialized by her side. '*Kaka-kaki*, I'm just going to snatch Radhi away for a minute.'

'Couldn't you have come sooner, *di*?' hissed Radhi when they were out of earshot. She swiped a chilled mojito from the tray of a nearby server. 'I've only just gone and told her I'm working on three books at once!'

Madhavi grinned. 'Good! Whatever it takes.'

Radhi made a face as she took a sip of her mint-flavoured drink. 'When will we start serving alcohol at family gatherings?'

Madhavi laughed. 'Ha! Fat chance of that.'

'It's not like *they* don't drink.' Radhi waved at some cousins. 'So, why can't we all drink together?'

'Come now . . . good *Gujju* children don't drink in front of their elders, you know that. In any case, do you *really* want to do shots with Ila *kaki*?'

Radhi grinned. 'Not particularly. Though she is the reason one needs the drink in the first place!'

As the sisters made their way across the room, Radhi stopped to greet an assortment of uncles, aunts and family friends.

'Seems like we have a full house,' she muttered to Madhavi.

'Are you kidding me? You're like the most scandalous person they know. They wouldn't miss it for the world,' said Madhavi, as they stepped out on to the balcony, where a tall, bespectacled man, with salt-and-pepper hair and tired brown eyes, turned to look at them.

'Hrishi!' Radhi gazed at him in surprise. 'How wonderful to see you here!'

The man's eyes lit up when he smiled. He immediately looked a decade younger. 'Sorry, I asked your sister to drag you here. I wanted to say hi, before I left.'

'What? Already?'

'Neha is expecting me back. On school nights she . . . uh. She likes both of us to be home, to tuck Anoushka into bed.'

Hrishi and Radhi had been close in college. One of those intense friendships, where everything was always deeply felt and dramatic. Their friends had been sure they'd end up together. And the idea hadn't seemed so terrible. But life had got in the way and, apart from the occasional birthday wish on Facebook, they'd hardly spoken over the past few years. Now he was married, with a daughter.

'Well . . . I'm glad you came,' she said.

'Me too. I'll call you once you've settled in a bit. I want to meet you properly over chai.'

Radhi smiled. 'Sounds good.'

As she watched his retreating back, she turned to her sister. 'Is it me, or was that a little off?'

'Definitely off,' Madhavi agreed. 'From what Sanjana tells me, his wife is a . . . shall we say . . . a bit of a character.'

'Oh? I had no idea—'

'It was Sanjana's idea to invite him today.' Madhavi checked the slim Rolex on her wrist. 'Speaking of, where is that girl? She called me this morning, asking if I needed help with this party. She's been so excited about you moving back.'

Radhi smiled fondly. Sanjana was one of her oldest and closest friends. They'd attended the same school, lived in the same building and, for almost eighteen years, shared everything — toys, clothes and secrets.

'Let me call her and check.' Radhi patted her pockets for her phone.

'Later Radhi, there are a lot of people who've been waiting to meet you. See, there's Vrinda *fia*.'

Radhi turned to see her favourite aunt walking towards them. Vrinda was their dad's sister and had been like a second mother to the girls after the death of their parents. Last year, when Radhi was at her lowest, Vrinda had flown to the US just to be with her. A professor of psychology, with a master's from Oxford, Vrinda had a refreshing perspective on most of life's problems. In fact, it was she who'd first suggested Radhi move back.

'*Fia*!' Radhi hugged her aunt happily.

'Looking stunning, darling,' Vrinda whispered in her ear.

The two had barely greeted each other when Radhi was surrounded by some cousins, followed by a gaggle of aunts. Most of the evening passed by in a blur of answering the same questions over and over again.

How had she been? *Fabulous.*

How was the writing coming along? *Fantastically.*

Was she here for good? *Hopefully.*

Had she kept her apartment in New York? *Yes.*

Would she now consider joining her sister in the family's diamond business? *No.*

Was she thinking of getting married again? *Hell, no.*

As the evening progressed, Radhi's guests appeared to be losing interest in her. Maybe the stories they'd heard about her depression, the therapist and the torrid affair with said therapist were just stories after all. She didn't *seem* depressed. A little too skinny, maybe, but certainly not suicidal, as some of the nastier whispers had suggested. They were disappointed and probably would have considered the evening a bit of a let-down had it not been for the fabulous dinner. For food was the other great preoccupation on Temple Hill.

Radhi watched as the guests moved towards the dining table, which was groaning under the weight of a startlingly inventive pan-Asian spread. There was a fresh Burmese tea-leaf salad set up beside a chunky water-chestnut soup and crusty, herbed bread. Vietnamese spring rolls stuffed with julienned carrots, red peppers, cabbage and vermicelli were lined up beside a platter of garlicky tofu and mushroom-stuffed dim sum, both to be enjoyed with a spicy peanut sauce. For the mains, there was *khow suey*, a Burmese stew with a creamy, coconut-milk base. Surrounding it were bowls of caramelized onions, lime wedges, finely chopped coriander, roasted peanuts and almost half-a-dozen other condiments. At the other end of the table was a Jain version of every dish for the more conventionally religious members of her family, who didn't eat root vegetables like carrots and onions.

'*This caterer is simply outstanding, Madhavi—*'

'*Oh, is this Noritake dinnerware? From your Sri Lankan trip? Nice!*'

'*What's this flavour in the chestnut soup? Lemongrass? No! No! It tastes like mint and something else—*'

'*I'm going to try this tea-leaf salad at home. Did I tell you I'm on this new keto diet adapted for vegetarian Indians?*'

'*Speaking of diets . . . have you seen Vanita recently? She has put on SO MUCH weight!*'

Snatches of conversation reached Radhi as she stood in a corner, a steaming bowl of soup in her hand, grateful that the food was now the centre of attention.

There were so many, many rules around food. What could be consumed. In what season. *No leafy greens in the monsoon.* In what combinations. *No mixing lentils with dairy.* Till what time of the day. *Nothing after sunset.* The residents of Temple Hill were essentially clean eaters who ate no meat or seafood. And yet, every now and then, they polished off entire reputations before lunch. The irony never failed to amaze her.

As Radhi took a spoonful of soup, she grimaced. Ever since she landed, there had been a burning sensation in her stomach, which she knew she couldn't completely blame on the terrible airline food. Some of it was nerves.

'You're craving a cigarette, aren't you?' Anshul, Madhavi's husband, had come to stand beside her. She'd always enjoyed an easy camaraderie with her brother-in-law and was grateful he was in her sister's life.

Radhi closed her eyes and sighed deeply to indicate just how much.

'Pity you told Madhavi you've quit!'

Radhi sighed again, watching her sister, who was making sure her guests took seconds. She would be very disappointed to know that Radhi was back to smoking a pack a day.

'The next best thing, then?' Anshul raised an eyebrow, nodding towards the platters of mango panna cotta and dark-chocolate mousse, which the servers had just brought out.

'The next best thing,' Radhi agreed, smiling, and together they made their way towards the dining area.

A brief silence had descended on the room, punctured only by the sound of fork against glass, as everyone focused on the dessert in front of them. Radhi looked about her, relishing the sudden quiet. Life on Temple Hill was predictable. And that would be good for a change.

CHAPTER 2

Radhika awoke the next morning unrested. She was still jet-lagged and she'd had that old dream about her parents again. But that wasn't what had been niggling at her all night. She couldn't quite remember what, just that it was something pressing.

She reached for her pack of cigarettes, then cursed silently — they were hidden in her purse inside her cupboard, away from the sharp eyes of her sister and nieces. Her hand found her phone and she cursed again, vowing for the hundredth time to change her wallpaper. It was a photograph of her and Mackinzey at a party. She was sitting on his knee, a glass of white wine in her hand, her head thrown back, laughing at something he'd just said. Mackinzey's hand firmly on her waist, his grey eyes smiling down at her. Radhi sighed, willing herself to look away, when suddenly it came to her — what was bugging her.

She sat up, now wide awake, and quickly scrolled through her messages. There was still nothing from Sanjana. They'd been on the phone every day this past week, talking about Radhi's move back. It was unlike her friend not to show up, and Sanjana wouldn't have missed the party unless there'd been an emergency. That was possible — Sanjana was a paediatric surgeon after all. But she'd have called or at least messaged. Unless . . . unless the emergency involved her. Sanjana was five months pregnant and had a history of miscarriages.

Horrified at the thought, Radhi checked the time. 7 a.m. A bit early to call, but she didn't care. Sanjana's phone just rang and rang. Radhi jumped out of bed, phone under chin, trying again. Still no answer. What to do? The Sea Mist Apartments, where they'd both grown up and Sanjana still lived, was only a fifteen-minute walk away. Quickly pulling on a T-shirt, jeans and sneakers, she dropped her sister a message to let her know where she was going and hurried out of the apartment. She just had to see Sanjana.

* * *

In the mornings, the air on Temple Hill always smelled the same. Saffron, sandalwood and divinity. It rose from the ancient Jain temples that dotted the neighbourhood as casually as coffee shops and permeated the world with the nectar-sweet fragrance of the Tirthankaras. Radhi walked down the slope, breathing it all in, the cigarette in her hand unlit and forgotten, as a more powerful emotion filled her head and heart. This was another reason she'd returned to Temple Hill. There was no other place on earth where she felt closer to God. Or angrier.

The ground was strewn with hundreds of flaming yellow and orange flowers from the gulmohar trees. A carpet for the devout who were hurrying up the steep slope to the temples, choosing to approach them barefoot. Not out of respect for God but rather for the life of the ants they'd inevitably step on. On Temple Hill, where *ahimsa* was a critical tenet of living, all forms of life were considered precious.

Mornings suited Temple Hill. People were up and about early. Some with yoga mats tucked under their arms, others with sneakers on, heading for the park. Young children waited at the gates of their buildings for their school buses. Cooks and maids rushed to their first jobs of the day. Tiny florist stalls were already set up, their lilies, orchids and chrysanthemums magnificent in spite of the cheap, plastic buckets that held them.

A tea vendor was starting to make his first batch of the morning. He was surrounded by drivers, newspaper boys, security guards — all those who started their day early, so that the residents of Temple Hill could begin theirs on time. Radhi craved a cup of tea. She hoped she and Sanjana could have one together.

* * *

Sea Mist Apartments had got a fresh coat of pastel-green paint since Radhi was last there, eleven years ago, and the font of the white, hand-painted lettering announcing its name was bolder and larger. Other than that, it was exactly like she remembered it: eight storeys high, with a large, leafy compound between its A and B Wings, where children played hide-and-seek, cops and robbers and any other game that could be manoeuvred around the long row of expensive cars parked along its edge. It was also perennially restful, face turned towards the Arabian Sea, perpetually enjoying the sun and the cool sea breeze. Radhi's heart lurched at the sight of the familiar swing set in the garden situated at the start of the compound. The little sandpit in the corner had been replaced by a new jungle gym. But the rest of it, the crooked red slide and the yellow-and-black-striped seesaw were the same. She turned towards the B Wing of the building. Sanjana and Jayesh, her husband, had bought an apartment here after their wedding, to be close to the family.

The old watchman at the front of the lobby watched the young woman as she approached. There was something familiar about her and yet he was almost certain he hadn't seen her before. But why was she smiling at him?

She stopped at his desk, smiling. 'And *chaacha*? All well?'

He recognized her then. Or rather, her voice which had pestered him to get her ball out from under a car a thousand times.

He gave her a big smile. '*Aare* baby, after many years you've remembered us!'

Radhi smiled at his use of the word "baby" and this habit among servants of referring to the children of their employers as "baby" or "baba", long after the said babies and babas had grown up and had babies of their own.

'Is Sanjana at home?'

His smile fell away instantly. 'Yes, yes. Of course. Third floor.'

As she stood in the lift, Radhika pondered the sudden change in expression on the watchman's face. Her sense of uneasiness intensified.

On the third floor, she exited the lift, making her way to Sanjana's door. It flew open the second she rang the doorbell. Dishevelled, her eye make-up smudged, her hair wild, Sanjana looked at Radhi blankly, then flung herself, sobbing, into her arms.

'What's the matter?' Radhi cried. 'What's happened?'

'Papa! It's Papa!'

In-between Sanjana's sobs, Radhi learned that Kirti Kadakia, Sanjana's father, had passed away the day before. His wife, Manjula, had come home at around 5 p.m. to find him lying slumped over his desk in the study. There was a plastic bag over his head and empty strips of sleeping pills scattered on the table in front of him.

'The police think it is suicide. But it can't be! It just can't be!'

'Shh.' Radhi stroked her friend's hair as she tried to make sense of what Sanjana was saying.

'I spoke to him just that morning! He told me he couldn't wait to hold my baby in his arms! And now they're saying he's killed himself! How can that be?'

'What about your mother? Your brothers? Do they believe it? Do any of them have any idea why he'd do something like that?

'No, everyone's just shocked! You know how he was, Radhi. He was tough. It's just not like him to do this—'

‘I know,’ Radhi said softly. ‘I know.’

Mr Kadakia was more than tough. He was one of the most cantankerous people Radhi knew. He argued with everyone and complained about everything. Over the years, he’d fought with the Patels on the third floor because they had too many parties with too many guests whose cars were always blocking the building’s driveway. He’d argued with the Dholakias on the second floor because they kept their dustbin outside their apartment, near the stairs, an unseemly sight for anyone passing by in the lift. When the building security guard was leaving his post to run errands for Mrs Ghadiyali, the powerful BMC bureaucrat on the fourth floor, the building looked to Mr Kadakia to raise the matter with her. If his car was parked in its usual spot, the young boys who played cricket in the compound after school would put away their bats and stumps and play chor-police instead. Sanjana was right. It wasn’t in Mr Kadakia’s nature to go quietly, to give up or give in. And yet, he’d committed suicide. It didn’t make any sense.

‘Where is Jayesh?’

‘He is in the US, trying to get the earliest flight out . . . I’ve just come home to change . . . the police will be coming again . . . I can’t believe this is happening . . .’ Sanjana was jumping from one thought to another. She started to cry again.

‘Hush, darling,’ Radhi soothed. ‘Go get ready. I’ll come with you.’

While Sanjana freshened up, Radhi thought back to her brief interactions with Mr Kadakia over the years. When her parents had died suddenly in a car crash, he had taken to watching over Radhi and her sister in his own gruff way. He’d dealt with their new driver, who’d been stealing petrol from their car and, while he found them a trustworthy replacement, he’d lent them his own car and driver whenever they required. That summer, he’d sent his mango seller to the siblings’ house after negotiating and fixing the price of mangos with him to make sure the siblings weren’t cheated.

And once, soon after the accident, when he'd found Radhi crying on a bench in their local park, he'd sat beside her silently, keeping her company. And now, he'd killed himself? It made Radhi sad to think how desperate and alone he must have felt.

Sanjana came out of her room wearing white for mourning. 'Let's go. I want to find out what happened.' She seemed calmer. Her eyes were still bloodshot from lack of sleep and crying, but her voice had a new, determined quality to it.

Sanjana's family lived on the fifth floor of the building's other wing, the A Wing. Radhi and Madhavi's childhood home lay two floors above, on the seventh. This was where Radhi planned to move into in a day or two. As they crossed the compound and walked towards the building, she was spared a fierce attack of nostalgia by the arrival of a police jeep.

A man with a large belly and a heavily pockmarked face got out of the vehicle and walked towards them. 'That is the investigating officer on the case, Mr Shinde,' Sanjana murmured to Radhi, before turning to greet the inspector. 'Hello, Shinde*ji*.'

'Good morning, ma'am.'

'Has the coroner submitted his report?'

'Not yet.'

'But what are they thinking? Any preliminary thoughts? Can you tell us anything at all?'

'Well.' The inspector hesitated, looking at Radhi.

'Please, it's all right,' said Sanjana. 'This is Radhika Zaveri. She's a close family friend.'

'It was most likely suffocation . . . He seems to have taken an overdose of sleeping pills and then slipped a plastic bag over his head.'

'Oh.' Sanjana's lower lip trembled from the effort of trying not to cry. Radhi knew she'd really been hoping there was some other explanation. Suicide was just too terrible to contemplate.

'He didn't suffer. It's a painless way to go,' the inspector continued, perhaps in the hope that it would make Sanjana feel better. 'We are going up to talk to all the family members.

Please.' He gestured towards the building, indicating that they should join him.

Sanjana nodded and silently they all made their way to the lift.

On the fifth floor, a young maid with a tear-stained face opened the door to the Kadakia home. Radhi followed her friend down a short passage, turning right into a large drawing room with high ceilings and heavy, old-fashioned mahogany furniture. Arranged in the shape of an L were two sofas with maroon velvet upholstery and intricately carved wooden arms. On the opposite wall, a broad TV cabinet was flanked on either side by glass showcases stuffed with souvenirs, bronze figurines, ceramic flower vases, Buddha statues and photo frames. The room had the cared-for but unloved appearance so common to many joint family homes. Everything was comfortable and tidy and well-maintained and yet, it struck Radhi, it didn't look like any one person took pride or joy in it. Radhi had been to this house hundreds of times as a child, but children are happily oblivious to the things that occur to adults.

Sanjana's brothers, Ranjan and Amit, sat on one sofa, while a wide-hipped woman, with thick, black hair and a sullen expression on her face, sat on an armchair near the window. Both Ranjan and Amit were bespectacled and reedy like their father. But while Ranjan had gone soft around the middle, Amit was gym-toned, his chest strong and broad on an otherwise lean frame.

Amit acknowledged Radhi with a tense nod, while Ranjan ignored her, addressing the inspector instead.

'Has the coroner's report come in, Shinde*ji*? When will you release my father's body? When can we have the funeral?'

'Not yet . . . another day or two I think . . . but before that we have a few more questions for everybody in the family. If you can give us one room? Then we will speak to you one by one.'

'I'll go first.' Amit got up to lead the way out of the room.

Sanjana waited until they'd left, before asking Ranjan, 'Where's Mummy?'

'Resting in her room.'

'How's she holding up?'

'She's okay, but she isn't eating much. No dinner last night, nor breakfast this morning. Just a cup of tea. We sent in a plate of mango slices, but it came back untouched. She told Hetal she's given up mangoes.'

Sanjana sighed and nodded. 'Papa's favourite fruit . . .' Then addressing the woman on the armchair, who was looking at Radhi curiously, 'This is Radhi, my childhood friend. She used to stay above us on the seventh floor. She knew Papa well.' And then to Radhi, 'This is Hetal, Ranjan's wife.'

The woman nodded as Radhi and Sanjana took seats on the empty sofa opposite the armchair.

The young maid came out of the kitchen, carrying a tray with cups of tea. Her eyes were swollen and she had the petrified look of a child who has just spotted the needle of the injection she is about to be given.

Sanjana tilted her head towards the maid who was setting the tray on the centre table. 'Kamal was the only one at home when this happened'.

'Oh, I'd assumed Uncle was alone,' said Radhi.

'She was in the servant room. Taking her afternoon nap.'

'She didn't hear anything?'

'She was sleeping. And in any case, even if she'd heard something, she'd have assumed it was my father pottering about, or the TV. She wouldn't have heeded it. It was her time off.

'He was found in there,' Sanjana added softly, pointing in the direction of the study at the far end of a passage that led deeper into the apartment from the living room.

'Did you—?'

'No, I was in a surgery, by the time they got through to me and I managed to get here, the police had already removed Papa—'

'It's just as well,' Radhi interrupted. 'It would've disturbed you even more.'

'No . . . I think I'd have wanted to see him . . . It would've made it easier to believe it. This way, it just doesn't feel real—' She broke off as Amit came back into the room.

Amit seemed relieved his meeting with the inspector was over. He looked at Ranjan and his sister-in-law.

'You or Hetal can go in next. They are in my room.'

'I'll go.' Ranjan rose, quickly leaving the room.

'What did they want?' Sanjana asked her brother.

Amit picked up a glass of water from a tray on the side table between the two sofas and took a long gulp before answering.

'A detailed account of what I did yesterday.'

'Why do they want to know about us?' Hetal asked.

'Police formalities, I guess. I told them I was on the road, on my way to a meeting in Nariman Point when Ranjan called me. Then they wanted to know how long it took me to get home and what I saw when I got here. They also wanted to know if Papa was in any kind of trouble. If he was depressed or if he'd fought with anyone. That sort of thing.'

'What did you say?' Hetal wanted to know.

'I told them, I've never seen him depressed in my life and that he fought with everybody.' Amit finished his water, putting the glass down before taking his seat on the sofa. He seemed preoccupied, Radhi thought. As if his father's death wasn't his only problem.

'God, the scandal this is going to cause,' Hetal fretted. 'What in the world are we going to say to everyone? The neighbours, the relatives, our friends — people will have a thousand questions. And if we don't answer them, they'll make up a thousand ridiculous stories!

'My poor parents! When word gets out among our relatives . . . it's going to be a nightmare for them. Oh, and when my Rotaract friends hear of it . . . dear God . . .' She shuddered, horrified at the prospect of facing the exceptionally catty group of ladies who she lunched with every Friday.

'Why would Papa do something like this?' Hetal continued.

Beside Radhi, Sanjana had gone very still. Radhika could sense that her friend was about to say something, which she'd probably regret later.

'Where is Sonal?' she interjected, inquiring after Amit's wife whom she'd known briefly at college.

It took Amit a moment to realize that Radhi was talking to him. 'Oh, she's gone to her parents' home to drop off some things for the kids. They were visiting when this happened. We've decided they should continue staying there for a few days—'

'Oh, don't even remind me about the children!' Hetal wailed. 'Mine will be back from summer camp next week. What will I tell them? Their teachers? Their friends?'

'We'll help you figure it all out, Hetal,' said a strong female voice, which though weary held an unmistakable hint of steel.

Radhi turned around to see Mrs Kadakia emerging from a corridor to the far left of the living room.

Hetal shot her mother-in-law a look of pure hatred, but the older woman ignored her.

'Are the police here again?' Mrs Kadakia asked, as she approached them. She was a tall, fair, heavyset woman in her sixties, with piercing black eyes and crinkly white hair, which she currently wore pulled back in a severe bun. Even in a crumpled cotton sari, her face devoid of make-up, she looked distinguished.

'Yes, Mummy,' Amit replied.

'Manju Aunty.' Radhi rose from the sofa as she greeted her. 'I am so sorry for your loss.'

'Thank you, *beta*.' Mrs Kadakia nodded at Radhi distractedly, 'Where is Ranjan?'

'I am here, Mummy,' Ranjan said as he came out of Amit's room. 'Hetal, you're next.'

'What more do they need from us?' Mrs Kadakia asked her son.

'They wanted to know where I was between two and three.'

'Why you?'

'They're asking everybody, Mummy. Because that's when Papa passed. They've also made a list of all the people he called or received calls from that day. They want to know if he met anybody before . . . before, you know—'

'I don't understand the point of all these questions. Anyway, let me know when they need me. I'll be in my room,' said Mrs Kadakia.

'Who did he call that morning?' Sanjana asked Ranjan.

'As far as I can remember, there was Mummy, you, Vinod *bhai*, his broker, someone called Hemendra *bhai*,' Ranjan replied. 'And me.'

'What did he want to speak to you about?' Sanjana asked curiously.

'He couldn't find his chequebook and he wanted to know if I'd seen it.'

'That's it?'

'Yeah,' Ranjan confirmed, but Rahdi noticed he had hesitated for just a nanosecond before replying. She wondered why.

The doorbell rang. Radhi watched Kamal go down the short passage to open the door. She came back, followed by a stout, fair-skinned man, carrying a large cloth bag of what looked like groceries. He turned left to go towards the kitchen.

'Bhawani, one minute please,' Ranjan called out to him.

'Ji *bhai*?' Closer up Bhawani had a wet nose and shifty, light brown eyes.

'The police will want to speak with you.'

'Again?' An unmistakable flash of fear rippled through his face, before he got a hold of himself.

'There's nothing to be afraid of, they just want to make sure they haven't missed anything. Sometimes people forget things in all the excitement, things they may remember when they are calmer.'

'*Ji*,' Bhawani said, before proceeding to the kitchen, which lay opposite the corridor that led to Manjula's and Ranjan's bedrooms.

'That's Bhawani Lal. He does most of our cooking and a few odd jobs for others in the building,' Sanjana explained to Radhi.

Hetal appeared in the doorway to Amit's room. 'Where is Mummy? They want her.'

'I'll go and fetch her,' Amit replied.

Sanjana looked at Hetal inquiringly.

'I was asked the same as everyone else, I suppose,' the woman shrugged. 'Where was I yesterday? Did Papa seem different over the last few days? What did I know about Papa's finances—?'

'Why finances? What has that got to do with his death?' Sanjana interrupted.

'How should I know? I made it very clear to them that I am not in the habit of poking my nose into my in-laws' affairs. My parents have given me enough to last me a lifetime. Besides, I have my own source of income.' She was referring to her jewellery-designing business.

'You were at your studio all day?'

'Till about 2.30 p.m. Then I locked up and went to Worli Naka to pick up some fruit and vegetables. There's this new diet I am on where I've to eat eight oranges in a day — in fact, I've already lost four kilos.' She glanced at her husband, who was busy on his phone, oblivious to his wife. 'Anyways, after that, at about 4 p.m., I went to my tailor to get some clothes altered — all my kurtas have become a little loose now with this diet — I had to get them tightened. I was there when Ranjan called and asked me to hurry home.'

The doorbell sounded again. This time, Radhi noticed, it was Bhawani who answered the door. A few moments later, he reappeared in the living room.

Hetal glanced at him inquiringly.

'The vegetables fellow. I told him we don't need any today.' He headed for the kitchen again.

Ranjan got up, his eyes still glued to his phone. 'I'll be in my room. I need to make a few work calls.' He glanced at Hetal. 'Come and get me if the police need anything else.'

Radhi's phone buzzed. It was Madhavi. She declined the call, instead quickly messaging her sister to tell her what had happened.

Mrs Kadakia walked into the room again. 'You are next, Sanjana,' she said to her daughter, before heading towards the dining area where she seated herself at the table with a paper and pen.

Sanjana got up to go talk to the police, and Radhika rose too, crossing the room to join Mrs Kadakia at the table.

At Radhi's approach, the older woman looked up. She gave Radhika a small smile. 'His obituary.' She gestured to the handwritten words on the paper in front of her. They were in Gujarati and Radhi felt the familiar embarrassment that she could barely read or write her own mother tongue. 'It needs to appear in the paper tomorrow.'

'Can't someone else write it for you?'

'I prefer to do it. It'll keep my mind off . . . this.' She glanced around the room and the people in it.

'Sanjana told me it was you who found him. It must've been a terrible shock.'

Mrs Kadakia shook her head. 'No, I'm not shocked . . . I feel . . . betrayed.'

'I can only imagi—'

'You can't.' The older woman cut her off. 'I don't think anyone can.' She stared at the paper in front of her with unseeing eyes.

'How is the school?' Radhi asked, after some moments of silence.

Mrs Kadakia ran a prestigious high school for girls. She'd been a teacher and a principal for most of her forty-year career, but about ten years ago, she had started Aspire High Girls' School.

'It's going well, thanks.' She continued to stare blankly at the page in front of her.

Radhi sat silently for a few minutes before speaking again. 'Sanjana thinks Kirti Uncle would've never done something like that.'

Mrs Kadakia sighed. 'Yes, it'll be especially hard on her. She was terribly attached to her father. Especially after her mother passed away.'

It was only then that Radhi remembered that Mrs Kadakia wasn't Sanjana's birth mother. She was her *maasi*, Sanjana's mother's sister. Sanjana's own mother had passed away from a rare heart condition when she was six and Amit, four. A year after her death, after watching Mr Kadakia struggle, his in-laws had advised him to remarry. Preferably to Manjula, their eldest (and much to their distress) unmarried daughter. So, Manjula had become the second Mrs Kadakia, and Ranjan was born to the couple a year later.

Sanjana, Amit and Ranjan, despite the age differences, had always been so close that no one recalled they had different mothers. And while Radhi didn't remember Mrs Kadakia as being particularly motherly or warm, she'd always taken a keen interest in their education and disciplined the three children with equal firmness.

'You stay with her tonight if you can,' Mrs Kadakia requested. 'I don't want her all alone in her home. Once Jayesh comes back, it should be OK.'

Radhi nodded. Mrs Kadakia patted her hand, got up and returned to her room.

Radhi sighed, and checked the time on her phone, suddenly aware that she hadn't eaten in ages. She'd barely had dinner at the party the previous evening or breakfast that morning and was now feeling distinctly uncomfortable. The all too familiar burning in her stomach had begun to ascend to her chest.

She got up and went towards the kitchen, in search of a banana or a glass of water and an antacid. But at the doorway, the sound of hushed voices made her stop.

CHAPTER 3

'Stop it!' Bhawani hissed. 'Stop crying, you fool!'

'You're lying,' Kamal sobbed.

'Why would I lie?'

'I just know you are!' Kamal dissolved into fresh tears.

Radhika waited a few seconds to see if either of them would say more, but all she could hear were Kamal's sniffles, then the sound of a mixer grinder. When she entered the kitchen it was to find Kamal sitting on a stool, her face in her hands, while Bhawani was standing with his back to her, grinding chutney.

At the sound of her footsteps, they both started guiltily.

'It's been a great shock for her.' Bhawani gestured to the girl. 'She won't stop crying.'

'Have you worked here long?' Radhika asked the maid, kindly.

'Five years.'

'The servant's room is in there, isn't it?' Radhika pointed to a door to the left of the kitchen.

Kamal nodded.

'It's not your fault. You couldn't have heard anything. It's too far from the study.'

The maid peered at Radhika gratefully through her tears.

Radhika wanted to stay and talk to her, but Bhawani was hovering around them nervously.

'Did you want anything, *didi*?' he asked. 'More tea?'

'Some water, please.'

'Radhi?' Sanjana entered the kitchen. She was clutching a large photograph.

'I begged the police to give me a copy.' Her eyes filled again. 'I wanted to . . . I had to see for myself.' She handed a twelve-by-eight-inch picture to Radhi.

People who were used to live-in servants in their homes could sometimes forget that they were there and carry on their most personal conversations in front of them. Radhi, who'd lived on her own for more than a decade now, could acutely feel Bhawani's prying eyes on them. She smiled at him, before steering Sanjana out of the kitchen and back towards the empty dining area, away from the others. Once they were both seated at the table, she turned her attention to the photograph in her hand. It was of the tragic scene.

Mr Kadakia lay back on his armchair, his eyes closed, mouth partly open, a polythene bag tied tight around his face. On the cluttered study table in front of him there was an almost full purple Tupperware bottle and about half a dozen empty strips of sleeping pills scattered haphazardly. There was also a pair of spectacles, three newspapers with one clearly open on the stock page, a mobile phone, a weekly pill organizer with the Thursday, Friday and Saturday compartments full, a stout transparent vase with yellow plastic sunflowers, a notepad attached to a decorative penholder shaped like a baby elephant, and a little tray with four glass bottles of mouth-fresheners: fennel seeds, betel-leaf crumble, dried dates and *jeeragoli*, a digestive aid with a sweet-and-sour powdery coating. On the far right corner of the table there was a palm-sized idol of Ganpati, the Elephant God, and a smaller idol of Laxmi, the Goddess of Wealth, both facing Mr Kadakia, and seemingly indifferent to the very end.

Shaken, Radhi handed the disturbing photograph back to Sanjana. 'That notepad in the picture . . . was there anything on it? A suicide note? Or a goodbye message? Something to give an idea of what was on his mind.'

Sanjana shook her head. 'There was no note . . . The police have taken the notepad along with everything else on that table to examine it further.' She stared at the photograph, then started to cry again.

'Sanjana?' Mrs Kadakia's voice travelled to them from her bedroom doorway. 'That's enough now, darling. Come, let's have some lunch.'

Sanjana wiped her cheeks with her palms and put the photograph away. Then she rose, hand on stomach, gingerly making her way to the bathroom, her five-month pregnancy suddenly seeming to catch up with her.

'Stay for lunch, Radhika.' Mrs Kadakia gestured to the dining table, where Kamal had already begun laying out the plates. 'The police have just about finished talking to everyone now. They're about to leave.'

At the thought of lunch, Radhika's stomach growled fiercely. But the burning sensation in her stomach had travelled up to her throat now. And she could sense a nasty headache coming on. 'Thank you, Aunty, but no lunch. I've a few things I need to take care of. But I'll come back this evening and spend the night with Sanjana.'

* * *

Manjula Kadakia retired to her room immediately after lunch. There was something she had to do but hadn't had a chance until now. The previous evening the house had been crawling with the police. And at night, Sanjana had insisted on staying with her. Now, it could no longer be put off.

Ever since Manjula had seen her husband's face, the mouth open in one last gasp for breath, the transparent plastic sticking to him like a grotesque cling wrap, she'd been waiting for a moment alone.

Lunch had been interminable. She couldn't recollect what she'd eaten, if anything at all. But she must have or they would have made a fuss about it. They'd all been silent for the most part, with the exception of the empty chair at the table, which had all but shrieked for attention. Amit had asked her a question, but she'd found it difficult to follow what he'd said. Her mind was only on one thing now. She pushed up the metal stopper and locked the door behind her. She wanted to be absolutely alone for this. Alone, unwitnessed and undisturbed.

She brought out the bunch of keys attached to a peacock made from pure silver, which she always wore at her waist. It contained the key to every single door, cupboard and drawer in the house. With a practised eye, she selected the familiar scuffed key and slid it into the keyhole of her husband's cupboard. Then braced herself.

Just as she'd expected, Kirti's rosewood perfume filled the room as soon as she opened the door. A neat row of crisply bleached and ironed white shirts, identical in every fashion, hung before her. Roughly she pushed them aside. Sticking her hand inside, she felt around the back, searching for what she was looking for. The jacket, which he'd refused to take to the dry-cleaner's because they were too expensive.

With trembling hands, Manjula brought it to her face. It smelled of sweat and perfume. And him. Now she did what she'd been wanting to do ever since she'd laid eyes on his dead face. She cried. Gently at first, and then in great big shuddering gasps. Waves of intense regret washing over her with such force that she almost bent double in pain. How very, very sorry she was, for all those lost years, for the way things had been and for the terrible way they'd ended.

* * *

By the time Radhi returned home, her sister and brother-in-law had left for work and her nieces were at school. Madhavi's housekeeper, Palak*ben*, let her in.

Only servants who'd proved their loyalty and value over decades could afford to behave as obnoxiously as Palak*ben* and get away with it. In the absence of Madhavi's mother-in-law, who lived in Delhi, Palak*ben* considered it her job to look after "Anshul baba's" house and ensure that everything was up to her mistress's standards. And by mistress, she didn't mean Madhavi.

Palak*ben* ran the kitchen, managed the servants and made weekly calls to Madhavi's mother-in-law to report on all the comings and goings at her son's house. She did not like Radhika one bit. She considered her to be a bad influence on her sister. The last three times that Radhika had visited Madhavi from the US, it had been with three different men. The last had been Mackinzey, a man twenty years her senior. Palak*ben* had been horrified and had shown her disapproval in a myriad of little annoying ways. But Radhi didn't care. She'd just taken to tipping the other servants even more generously, so that her needs were always taken care of.

'The new servants are coming to meet you between 4 and 5 p.m.,' Palak*ben* announced, with a forced smile on her face.

Madhavi had arranged for Radhika to interview the new staff for her apartment, today. Radhi glanced at her watch. It was already 2 p.m.

'Where's your medicine box, Palak*ben*? I need antacids. Also, a banana would be great.'

'Oh, so sorry, we don't have any bananas at home,' Palak*ben* responded, her tone making it clear she wasn't sorry at all.

Radhi knew that Madhavi only tolerated Palak*ben* because having her around kept Anshul's mother at bay. But personally, Radhi didn't have any patience for the judgy old woman. 'Please call for them then. Send one of the servants. You have those, don't you?'

Palak*ben* visibly bristled. 'Of course.' She left the room in a huff.

By 4 p.m., Radhi had showered, dressed and consumed a simple lunch of curd and rice. The banana and the antacid had helped settle her stomach. Marginally.

She checked her phone. She'd received messages from Hrishi, Vrinda and Preeti, an old college friend who'd been unable to attend the dinner the night before. Hrishi wanted to know if she was free to meet for tea that week, while Vrinda wanted Radhi to have dinner with her that weekend. There was also an email from her literary agent, George Samuels, telling her to please return his calls. Radhi sighed. George had been so patient with her that she was embarrassed about the way she was behaving. She resolved to write to him soon.

The doorbell rang and, moments later, Palak*ben* showed a stout, plump woman with twinkling eyes into the living room.

'Lila!' said Radhi surprised, her delight obvious. '*Didi* didn't tell me that she'd hired you!'

Lila giggled. 'Yes, it was supposed to be a *shurprise* for you.'

'Come sit!' Radhi patted the seat next to her on the sofa.

Palak*ben* gasped, giving Lila a look of warning. Sofas were not for servants! In all her thirty-three years of service, Palak*ben* had not once, *not one single time*, sat on the sofa. And now Madhavi's crazy sister was inviting a maid to sit on it. Lila grinned at Palak*ben* and squatted on the rug on the floor in front of Radhi. Palak*ben* gave an audible sigh of relief. Still, she made a mental note to mention it in her weekly telephone report to her mistress.

In the normal course of things, Radhi would have challenged Palak*ben*. She hated the way servants were treated in most Indian households. But she wasn't feeling too great and she was weary after the events of the day. She contented herself by asking Palak*ben* to organize a cup of tea for Lila. And Palak*ben*, relieved that a major disaster had been averted, bustled away to the kitchen.

Lila had grown up with Radhika and her sister. Her parents had worked for the Zaveris. Lila's father had been a peon at their office, while her mother did the cleaning at their home. During the summer holidays, when she didn't have anyone to watch her, Lila's mum would bring Lila to

Radhi's house. Lila was just a year younger than Radhika, and the two girls would play together, while Lila's mother finished her work.

'How long has it been? Twenty years?'

'Eighteen, *didi*,' Lila corrected.

'Last I heard, you had a husband, a kid and a job at a school.'

'I only have the kid now. I left my husband because he used to beat me black and blue. Then my school job, because I got fed up of washing the bottoms of those brats! I was working at a designer's studio doing odd jobs for them when your sister called and asked me if I would manage the house for you.'

'Well, will you?'

Lila nodded happily.

The two women spent the next half an hour talking to the driver, the cleaning lady and the cook. The driver, Ramzan *bhai*, came across as a sober and sensible fellow. And the cleaning lady, Savita, though painfully shy, seemed a good sort. But Radhi wasn't too sure about the cook. He went on and on about being a high-caste Brahmin and managed to put both the women off. When Radhi expressed her reservations, Lila suggested, 'Let me do the cooking, *didi*. I grew up eating the food my mum brought home from your house. I know exactly how to cook for you.'

Radhika, who enjoyed cooking herself, agreed. Between the two of them, they'd manage just fine.

* * *

The sight of the olive green, paisley-printed sofa filled Radhi with such a deep and crushing longing that she stood rooted to the spot.

Radhi and Lila had driven to Sea Mist Apartments where Radhi had just opened up her parents' flat, hoping to move in over the next couple of days. But this was the first time she'd seen it in more than a decade. Over the years, it was her sister who'd maintained it, getting it cleaned regularly and ensuring there weren't any leakages of any kind. Radhi had avoided it. She'd been scared of coming here. Fearful of feeling too many things. And she'd been right to be afraid.

Just the sight of her parents' sofa had transfixed her. This was where they'd sit together, watching TV, having tea, talking on the phone, reading the paper, playing bridge with their friends. Any moment now, Radhi expected her mother to walk out of the kitchen, smelling of the coriander she'd used to make her famous chutney. She'd settle herself on the sofa, her feet crossed on the centre table, flipping through a *Femina*.

'*Didi . . . Didi?*'

Radhika could hear Lila but she couldn't answer. She could taste her mother's chutney in her mouth and she was afraid if she said anything, it would disappear. Ever since her parents had passed away, seventeen years ago, Radhi had been in search of a chutney just like her mum used to make. At restaurants, at weddings and dinner parties, she made it a point to ask for the green chutney, but she'd never found one with the familiar mint and gingery flavours. Once she'd come close. At a homestay in Dharamshala, the owner's wife had made a green chutney that reminded Radhika of her mother's. She'd promptly taken down the recipe, but she'd been disappointed to see that it contained nothing new, no secret ingredient she didn't know about.

'*Didi?*' Lila tried again, this time a little louder.

Radhi forced herself back into the present. She turned and stepped back out of the apartment.

'The movers are coming tomorrow to shift everything to my apartment in Cuffe. I would like this apartment to be completely empty. Everything that can go, goes. You'll supervise it, won't you?'

Lila just nodded. She didn't need to ask Radhika why she was doing this.

Radhika left Lila to lock up the apartment and made her way to Sanjana's home in the next building. She wondered if she'd made the right decision in deciding to move back here. She could have stayed at her apartment in Cuffe Parade, an equally affluent neighbourhood in South Mumbai. Her parents had purchased it along with one for her sister. The two apartments were supposed to be their wedding gifts but her parents had died before either girl was married and neither apartment had ever been lived in. Radhi knew that staying in Cuffe would've been a fresh start for her. But it was Sanjana who had convinced her to stay here at the Sea Mist and confront the past. To reclaim the happiness she'd experienced here with her parents. To separate the pain and guilt associated with the tragedy from every memory associated with her childhood. At the time, it had seemed like a good idea. Now, she wasn't so sure.

CHAPTER 4

Sanjana was in the shower when Radhika rang the bell. The maid let her in and offered her a glass of water.

In contrast to the Kadakia home, Sanjana's living room was smaller but airier, with sheer white drapes, modern furniture with silk and velvet upholstery and a wooden swing surrounded by a dozen potted plants by the window. While Radhi waited, she noticed Sanjana had left the crime scene photograph of Mr Kadakia, which the police had given her, on the centre table in front of the sofa. Radhi picked it up and studied it again. She hadn't noticed the photo frames on the side wall of his study before. There were pictures of Mrs Kadakia and the children taken on holidays when the kids were young. And more recent ones of the grandchildren taken at various festivals and school events.

There were none of Mr Kadakia himself, except for one on his wedding day. A closer look revealed that he was with Sanjana's and Amit's mother, the late Mrs Urmila Kadakia. Radhi wondered who had taken the trouble to choose these pictures, print them and get them framed. At first she had assumed it was Manjula but now, looking at it, Radhi didn't think she would have picked that particular wedding photo to frame, even though the woman in question was her own sister.

Radhika wondered how it had been for Manjula Kadakia, expected to step into her younger sister's life and take over her household, her children and even her marriage. To have to transform suddenly from sister-in-law to wife. To know that her husband would invariably end up comparing the two of them, even if he didn't mean to. To know that her sister would always fare better, even if it was only by virtue of being dead.

In the photograph, the late Urmila Kadakia was petite and fair, a large diamond pin in her delicate nose. Manjula had the same skin tone but that was where the similarities ended. She was a large woman, with a broad forehead and a button nose. She had an intelligent face and, over time, Mr Kadakia might have grown to love it. But had he? And what about her? Had Manjula experienced love in the way one was meant to? The heady rush of it, the butterflies, the romance? Maybe not at first, but had it happened for her eventually? Radhi wondered whether she had married of her own free will or if she had given in to that bane for women living in India — societal pressure. Manjula's younger sister had two children when she died, while she, the older, was yet unmarried. Thirty years ago that wasn't something that would be taken lightly. There must've been talk. Manjula was a strong woman and she might've have been able to disregard the taunts of "well-meaning" aunts, but would she have been able to bear their pity? Was that why she'd agreed?

Radhi was still thinking about Manjula Kadakia when something made her stop and study the photo more closely. The pillbox on the desk. It had the Thursday, Friday and Saturday pockets full. It gave her pause. So, on Wednesday, just before Mr Kadakia took his own life, he had bothered to take his medication? Radhi thought this, this act of self-preservation mere hours before committing suicide, was a curious thing to do. Of course, he could've just done it out of habit. Taken his pills at the prescribed hour without giving it any thought. But what if he hadn't planned to kill himself that day? What if something or someone had triggered it?

Everybody in the family, including the servants, maintained that there'd been nothing out of the ordinary about

Kirti Kadakia's behaviour that day. He'd gone for his morning walk. Done his daily prayer rituals. Spent the morning working and making phone calls. Eaten a full lunch. Nothing about his actions suggested a mind disturbed enough to take such an extreme step. But how sure could any of these people really be? The family members had all left for work before or by 10 a.m. So they couldn't really vouch for Mr Kadakia's state of mind post that. And the two servants would've been busy in the kitchen, or even in and out of the house, running errands. How much of their statements was based on observation and how much on assumptions? If one of those phone calls had upset him, or if he'd received a visitor or left the house for a short meeting, would they have known?

Sanjana came out of her room. It was clear she'd been crying; her eyes were swollen. But she looked calmer than this morning.

'Hi.' Her eyes dropped to the photograph Radhi was holding. 'What is it?'

'I was just wondering about Kirti Uncle's phone conversations. What they were about. Was there anything important or upsetting in them? Or if he'd perhaps met someone? Anything that might give us an idea of why he'd do this.'

'The police think that maybe Papa had financial troubles. They've asked for his bank statements and other papers. But I don't think it was money related. Papa has made huge losses before. Twice, in fact, he had to start from scratch. But he came out of them okay. He was a fighter.'

Sanjana's eyes were brimming with tears again. She frowned, then shaking her head murmured, 'He did meet someone. Kamal said that he asked her to make two cups of tea before she left for the laundry.'

'Oh, for whom?'

'She doesn't know. Papa told her to leave a tray on the dining table. And when she came back, the cups were empty.'

'I wonder who it could be,' Radhika mused.

'The police said that they'd check with the watchman and look at his register.'

'*Didi*, dinner is ready,' the young maid announced.

At the thought of food, the burning in Radhika's chest intensified. And the headache, which had been threatening to come all day, finally made its glorious appearance. She winced. 'Do you have any ice cream? Or even chilled plain milk? I don't think I can have dinner.'

Sanjana studied Radhika. 'Acidity?'

She nodded. 'I think I had better go see a doctor tomorrow.'

* * *

Radhi wiped away the bead of perspiration on her upper lip as she waited in the building lobby for Ramzan *bhai* to bring her car around. She'd forgotten how oppressive the heat could be here in early June. The sun had burned incessantly all of May. The earth, scorched and thirsty, suffering wordlessly, as if aware that it was only a matter of time, that it was on the verge of sweet relief, that patience would see it through. Any day now, the monsoon winds would bring mercy to the city with showers of cooling rain. But until then, the air was heavy and the weather hot, humid and unbearable.

Radhi threw her half-finished cigarette to the ground, grinding it out with a heel, before stepping into the air-conditioned interior of her sister's Jaguar. The last thing she needed was for the car to smell of smoke and for her sister to realize that Radhi had been lying to her about giving up. She made a mental note to go car shopping as soon as she was settled in. Her phone rang. It was her sister. She had some sort of freakish sixth sense when it came to Radhika.

'How are you feeling?' Madhavi asked as soon as Radhi answered.

'I'm on my way to Dr Bihari now.'

'That bad, huh? Did you eat something?'

'Yes, a banana.'

'You can't survive on bananas, Radhi . . . What about sleep? Did you sleep okay?'

'No, but that's just jet lag.'

For months now, Radhi had been suffering from anxiety. The only way she could get some sleep was with the help of a sedative. She'd forgotten to take the pill bottle with her when she left for India. But she had a note from Ms Daniels, her therapist in America, which she planned to give the doctor here and get a local prescription. Radhi felt no compulsion to share this information with her sister, however. She worried too much already.

'Well . . . your kitchen will be completely stocked by the end of today. I've given Lila a set of keys along with a list of everything you'll need.'

'Thanks, *di*! You're the best.'

'How's Sanjana coping?'

'She's very shaken up.'

'You know, I would've never thought him capable of it.'

'Yeah . . . me neither.'

There was a short pause before Madhavi began to talk about the apartment and what Radhika would need to get. She rang off, after giving Radhi the names of a few home stores to check out for furniture and upholstery.

At Dr Avinash Bihari's clinic, there was already a long line of patients waiting for the elderly physician.

The receptionist looked at Radhi's midriff-baring crop top with barely concealed disapproval. 'Do you have an appointment?'

'No. But you can give him this.' Radhi tore a piece of paper from the receptionist's rough pad and scribbled her name, being careful to include her father's in the middle.

Reluctantly, the receptionist took her note to the doctor. She came out of his office a few seconds later, indicating, with a stiff nod, that Radhi could go in.

Dr Bihari had been their family doctor and, over the years, he'd developed a close friendship with Radhi's father.

He beamed at her. 'Hello, *beta*. So wonderful to see you after so many years.'

'Thank you, Uncle. It's good to see you, too.'

'How is the husband?'

'Long divorced.'

'Oh. Excellent. Marriage, in my opinion, is overrated.'

'Does Aunty know?'

'No, thank God, or she'd have long divorced *me*!' He laughed loudly at his own joke. 'So, tell me, what brings you here?'

Radhi told him about the severe acidity, the headaches, the lack of appetite and finally, about the anxiety. Looking at the note from her therapist, he raised his eyebrows. He went on to ask her a few more pointed questions about her health before prescribing her medication for her various problems.

'Check in with me in about two weeks, okay? Mental health shouldn't be neglected. Also, here's the number for Dr Sudha Nanal. An excellent therapist. Please consider continuing your therapy here.'

Radhi nodded. After thanking him again for seeing her on such short notice, she left the clinic. Her next stop was one of the home stores her sister had recommended.

Earth Lover was a gorgeous jumble of period pieces and modern, contemporary furniture. There were restored temple bells, large teak *almirahs* and doors belonging to hundred-year-old *havelis* placed next to sleek console tables and TV units in clean Scandinavian design. A whole section was lined from floor to ceiling with rolls of rich upholstery fabrics in exquisite-sounding shades like "sienna summer", "amber romance", "rowan red" and "sage green".

Radhi had already decided to purchase only the essentials. The rest of her home would be a work in progress, just like her New York apartment. She'd do it up slowly, picking up pieces from her travels and from little-known markets, as and when something caught her eye. She placed an order for a L-shaped, mango-wood bookcase; a four-poster bed in a white distressed-wood finish; a deep wingchair with bottle-green upholstery; a luxurious, linen tuxedo sofa in a beige, herringbone print; a rectangular, glass dining table with a set of six chairs in the same herringbone linen as the sofa but in a contrasting cobalt blue; and some jute curtains in fresh floral prints, all of which would be delivered over the next day or two.

Radhi had promised Sanjana she'd drop by after running her errands, but first she wanted to get a bite to eat. She hadn't eaten any breakfast that morning nor dinner the night before, and the doctor had told her clearly that she needed to eat more frequently. She asked Ramzan *bhai* to drive to her favourite dosa place, a street-side vendor on Hughes Road who served the most delicious South Indian fare.

'Here, *didi*? Are you sure?' Ramzan *bhai* looked uncertainly at the garage-turned-food-joint Radhi had directed him to.

'Quite sure.' Radhi really hoped the food hadn't changed much in the decade since she'd been here.

Ramzan *bhai* honked, and the waiter came to their car to take Radhi's order. She hadn't come here for the dosa though. Anyone could master a crisp, buttery crêpe. No, it was the chutney that was the draw, it set one dosa joint apart from another. Some places made it purely from coconut, adding just enough water, so that the chutney was crumbly. Others added a spoon or two of sour yogurt to give it just a hint of tartness. Still others mixed the coconut with green chillies and coriander, making it green and spicy. And then there were the ones that served a dollop of a tomato garlic chutney or offered a spicy peanut powder alongside their coconut chutney. All the joints served *sambhar*, a thick, lentil soup-like accompaniment. Regardless of what came with it, the coconut chutney, with its strong seasoning of mustard seeds, skinned black gram and curry leaves, was the real draw of a dosa place.

After consuming one deliciously large butter dosa, Radhi returned, satisfied, to Sea Mist Apartments and her friend.

* * *

A delivery boy carrying a brown-paper parcel hurried into the lift, just as it was about to shut. He rode up to the fifth floor with Radhi and stood beside her while she rang the bell.

Kamal opened the door and gave Radhi a small smile of recognition. While Radhi paused to loosen the straps of her heels so that she could leave them at the door, Kamal took the parcel from the boy's hand, examined its contents and asked him for the bill. As the boy handed it over, Radhi could see written in black ink at the top of the list was "latex gloves", followed by "eucalyptus oil", "paracetamol", "coconut oil", and "Threptin biscuits" written in blue. Kamal checked off the items in the parcel before carrying it inside. Radhi followed her.

In the living room, all the furniture had been pushed to the sides, and in the area that had been cleared, multiple large mattresses, covered with white cotton sheets, had been spread out. Sanjana's brothers, Amit and Ranjan, sat at one end of the room, along with a few other men, presumably friends and relatives. Sanjana sat with Manjula and her sisters-in-law, Hetal and Sonal, on the other side, along with the other women. Everyone was dressed in white, the official colour of mourning among Hindus, and Radhi cursed herself for not having paid more attention to what she was wearing. The eyes of both men and women followed her as she made her way towards Sanjana.

Kamal offered the package to Manjula. '*Bhabhi*, from the chemist.'

'That'll be mine.' Hetal intercepted the brown-paper bag before it reached Manjula's outstretched hand.

Radhi took the empty seat next to Sonal, who smiled at her in recognition. Radhi smiled back, marvelling at how the woman hadn't aged a day since Radhi had last seen her in college. Slender and petite, Sonal had the figure of a thirteen-year-old girl, one of those bodies that go through childbirth and come out without a single extra curve or crease.

Radhi was about to greet her, when Manjula called out, 'Sonal? Did you call the pundit*ji*?'

'Yes, Mummy.'

'Did he give you a list of all the items he'll need for the funeral?'

'Yes.'

'Did he tell you where we'll get everything?'

The younger woman blushed furiously. 'Uh, no. I didn't ask.'

'Well, could you please? I haven't planned many funerals, and I don't want to be scrambling at the last minute.'

'Yes, Mummy.'

While Manjula turned her attention back to her visitors, Radhi's eyes followed Sonal as she got up, making her way across the room to place the call to the pundit. It seemed Sonal really hadn't changed since their college days. She was still jittery and jumpy, unsure of her place in the world.

The doorbell rang, and two women in white saris entered and, on cue, the three women sitting on one of the mattresses rose to take their leave. Radhi recognized the older of the two newcomers, Mrs Maniar, the Kadakias' immediate neighbour. She had lived in the building for over three decades.

'So sad.' She clucked her tongue, as soon as she sat down beside Manjula. 'I was so shocked when I heard. Came home from the *satsang* and my cook told me that something was wrong at your house. But who would have imagined this? Such a good man! So helpful, so active in the building committee. Such a tragic end!'

Manjula's face was devoid of any expression. 'Yes, it was quite a shock.'

Radhi studied Sanjana's mother. Back ramrod straight, white hair pulled severely back in a proud bun, her face unmarked by a single tear stain, she was the school principal, even in grief. Radhi could tell that she was loathing every minute of this, the morbid delight of the visitors, masked, half-heartedly, by profuse expressions of sympathy. Radhi knew from her friend that Manjula had never mingled with the neighbouring women, even when she was young and newly married. She'd found their Housie groups and pedicure parties frivolous, their pressing concerns about uppity maids, drivers' rising salaries and dominating mothers-in-law tedious. Or at least that's what the ladies of the Sea Mist

Society seemed to conclude after a few initial attempts at befriending her.

Radhi wondered how much of it was due to Manjula Kadakia's inherently reserved nature and how much due to the difficulty of the situation she found herself in. It couldn't have been easy being the second Mrs Kadakia. Her younger sister had been a traditional beauty with an ever-ready smile, by all accounts perfectly happy raising her children and managing her home, content with a life that had been kind. Manjula didn't have her sister's easy charm or her easy life. She preferred the company of her books to that of human beings. Radhi remembered playing with Sanjana at the Kadakia home — they always had to keep their voices low and play sit-down games, because Mrs Kadakia would be at the dining table reading or working and was not to be disturbed. Surrounded by papers, marking essays or spelling tests, which she'd brought home for correction, or reading and making notes from thick books, she'd sit there for hours, looking up only to remove her spectacles every now and then to rub her tired eyes, the children well aware that if they disturbed her, they'd lose their garden playtime. Their *ayah* organized their meals and snacks, sending them straight into their rooms to eat them, because the dining table was occupied by Mrs Kadakia and her things. It was very different to how things were at Radhi's house. She'd never realized the kind of ruckus they must've created for her family and servants, trying to climb into laundry baskets and cupboards while playing hide-and-seek. Or pestering the cook in the kitchen for dry beans and lentils and pulses, which they could "prepare" in their miniature vessels and serve as grand feasts for the grown-ups.

'Don't mind my asking, Manjula, but do you think he suffered from depression?' Mrs Maniar continued. 'Depressed people can be quite moody and irritable, you know . . . Was Kirti *bhai* behaving any differently?'

'Not that we could tell.' Manjula seemed to be keeping her answers as short as she politely could.

'A cousin of mine would just sleep all day and when she was awake she'd cry. Turns out that's also depression,' Mrs Maniar's companion, a Mrs Gandhi, interjected.

'Yes.' Manjula turned her attention to the woman. 'I'm aware of the common symptoms. If he was depressed, I'd have been able to spot it.'

While Manjula concentrated on Mrs Gandhi, Mrs Maniar took the opportunity to talk to Radhi.

'I hear you are moving back into your old home?'

'Yes.'

'Good, good . . . very happy to hear it. I miss your parents . . . such wonderful people they were. Come have tea with me tomorrow. Give an old woman some news of the world.'

'Tomorrow evening . . . uh . . . I've some errands to run for the house.'

'Morning then. For breakfast. You do eat breakfast, don't you?'

'Yes, but—'

'Good then. Come however early you like. I am up at 5 a.m.,' said Mrs Maniar firmly.

Radhi had forgotten how persistent the old aunties could be. She was embarrassed to be receiving a breakfast invitation in the middle of this tragedy. So to cut the conversation short, she reluctantly agreed to visit the old woman the next morning.

The doorbell rang again, and Radhi watched as Kamal went down the passage to open the door.

'It is the vegetable seller, *bhabhi.* Do we need anything?' She came back into the room to ask Manjula.

'Nothing right now,' Manjula replied distractedly.

The phone rang and Bhawani approached Manjula with a cordless phone in his outstretched hand. '*Bhabhi*, for you.'

Manjula took the instrument from him and rose to take the call in another room.

'The calls have been relentless.' Hetal watched her mother-in-law's receding back. 'Everyone wants to know what happened. Why he did it. How he did it. When the funeral is. When the prayer meeting is. People have a thousand questions.'

'Yes.' Mrs Maniar nodded encouragingly. 'People will talk. It's what they do. But how insensitive that they are bothering the family at a time like this . . . How would *you* know why he did it . . . No?'

'Yes, exactly! Who knows why he did it? Why did he ever do anything? It's not like my in-laws were in the habit of asking for *my* opinion. Take for instance, the dinner they were planning to host next month. Did anyone ask me if I was available? No. My father-in-law just asked for my wedding silver. Said he wanted to get it polished, so that we could use it at the dinner. And then he goes and kills himself. You tell me, what sense does it make? And on top of th—'

'Did you give it to him?' Manjula was suddenly there beside the women.

'What?' asked Hetal, startled.

'Did you give him the silver?' repeated Manjula.

'Yes . . . last Wednesday . . . And now I have no idea where it is!'

Manjula's jaw tightened, her lips settling into a grim line. 'It will turn up, Hetal. We'll find a receipt for it or something, once we've had a chance to look through his things.'

Ranjan joined them, saying, 'Mummy, I need to step out for some work.'

'Work? Today?' Manjula looked surprised.

'It's a patient . . . He's in pain. It won't take more than half an hour.'

Manjula nodded absently. 'Come back soon.'

Just as Ranjan turned to go, Hetal asked her husband, 'Can't Mahesh or one of the other therapists cover for you?'

Ranjan's irritation was obvious. 'Each therapist has a different technique and approach. And you know I don't like my patients to consult other therapists if I can help it. And a break of even one or two days can set a patient back by a week.'

Radhi could see that Hetal wanted to say something more. Instead she bit her lip, perhaps mindful of all the other people present. It was telling that Ranjan had chosen to inform his mother rather than his wife that he was leaving, and Radhi suspected that this was not the first time. She wondered how Hetal felt about that.

'We'd better be going.' Mrs Maniar got up to leave, mainly Radhi suspected, because she was aware that she wouldn't be able to extract any juicy titbits from Hetal now that Manjula was present. Mrs Gandhi rose with her.

Sanjana said her goodbyes, then waited until the women had shut the door behind them, before turning to her mother. 'What dinner was this, Mummy? What was Papa planning?'

'I don't know,' Manjula responded softly, lost in thought. 'I just don't know.

CHAPTER 5

Ranjan lit a third cigarette and took a deep breath. The nicotine had finally managed to spread a false sense of well-being within him, and he found that he could think again. He was sitting at White, a new café at the bottom of Temple Hill. He'd chosen this spot because there was little chance of running into anyone here. The place was jinxed. Had been for the last thirty years that he knew of, and maybe longer if the stories were to be believed. It had already been an art gallery, an ice-cream parlour, a laundry, a men's salon and a video library at one point or another. But none of these had ever turned a profit, usually shutting within months of opening. In the same row as White, there were half a dozen other shops and joints. A chemist, a confectioner, a high-end fabric store for men's suits and office wear, and a popular fast-food restaurant. All of these had remained constant for over two decades, while this space changed name and colour every year. Passing it by on his way to work each day, Ranjan had always been amazed at how the owner managed to lease it with such regularity, when everyone on Temple Hill knew how ill-fated it was.

Today, he was just grateful to have a place where he wasn't likely to be spotted. Close friends and relatives were flocking to his home to console his family. It wouldn't do to be seen sitting at a café, smoking and nibbling on a samosa. And yet he couldn't help himself. It was impossible to sit there while visitors shared stories of his father. He felt suffocated with guilt. Nauseous with the shame of it. He couldn't bear to look at his mother. What would she think, if she knew?

Ranjan knew his mother had the highest expectations of him of all her children. She'd tried never to distinguish between the three children, but she was human, after all. He'd always felt the difference — not in anything she said or did, but just in the way she looked at him. Ever since he was a child, he'd noticed how his mother's eyes lit up at the sight of him. Him. Not the others. He was aware that he was the one responsible for her happiness. And God knows he'd tried. It was for her that he'd pursued medicine and become a physiotherapist. Left to his own devices, he'd probably have gotten into advertising. Or photography. He didn't know for sure. He hadn't had the chance to explore. It was on her advice that he'd married Hetal. She hadn't forced him. No, that wasn't her style. She'd simply suggested that a girl from a cultured, well-connected family like Hetal's would be a good fit for their home. And he'd agreed. He'd been quite the model son. Up until recently.

* * *

That afternoon, back home at her apartment in Sea Mist, Radhi was surprised at how different it seemed. Devoid of most of the furniture, it seemed younger somehow. Not weighed down by a lifetime of memories, it seemed breezier, brighter.

'Tea, *didi*?' Lila offered.

Radhi shook her head. The burning sensation in her chest, which had abated a little after the dosa, was back in full swing now. She'd forgotten to pick up the medicines. They would've helped matters by now. She handed Lila the doctor's prescription.

'Could you call the chemist and order these, please? Also, do we have any bananas?'

'I'll send Ramzan *bhai* for the medicines, *didi*, it will be quicker than waiting for the delivery.'

Lila left the room, returning a few minutes later with a plate of bananas, which she placed in front of Radhi.

Radhi thanked her distractedly. She was sitting on the floor in her old room, with a suitcase open in front of her. She had started putting things away in the built-in cupboards — clothes, bags, shoes, jewellery, make-up — but there were more than eleven suitcases to go through. She marvelled at how much she had accumulated in the last decade. She estimated that even if she used both her own cupboard and her sister's, there'd still be about four suitcases left. And these bags didn't include her books, fourteen boxes of which were on their way to India in a shipping container, along with other assorted items like tennis racquets, picture frames and wall art. Lila could have helped her with it all, but Radhi preferred to work alone.

The act of arranging her things was helping Radhi order her thoughts. As she hung the dresses up on hangers and stacked T-shirts in neat piles, she thought about the day she'd finally cleared Mackinzey's cupboard out. How devastated she had been. How final it had seemed. What a gaping hole that man had left in her life.

Lila entered the room with a small knock on the open door.

'Your medicines, *didi*.' She placed a tray with a glass of water in front of Radhi.

'Thank you, Lila.'

Radhika checked the medicines. There was Gaviscon for acidity, activated charcoal for her stomach, aspirin for her headaches and calcium, B12 and some multivitamin tablets, which Dr Bihari had insisted she take. In all, Radhi had eight pills in her hand. She started to take them one by one, sipping the water each time. By the time she came to the fifth pill, the glass was empty.

Radhi got up, opened the door and called out in the direction of the kitchen, 'Lila, may I please have more water?'

Returning to her spot in front of the suitcase, Radhi sat on the floor with a thump, struck by the most sickening thought.

'God!' She shook her head as if the action could dislodge the picture that was forming in her head and send it back to where it had come from. 'Dear God . . . It can't be.'

'Everything all right, *didi*?' Lila paused in the doorway, glass of water in hand.

'I don't know, Lila.' She got up again. 'I need to see Sanjana.'

* * *

Sanjana opened the door to her apartment herself.

'Radhi, I just—'

'Sanjana, may I look at the picture again?'

Sanjana didn't need to ask what her friend meant. Silently, she went to her room, returning with the last photograph of Mr Kadakia in her hand.

Radhika glanced at it with a sinking feeling. Yes, she'd remembered it correctly.

'Sanjana, what time did the police say Uncle consumed the pills?'

'Between 1 and 2 p.m.'

'So it could've been during lunch or immediately after that?' Radhi frowned. 'Bhawani was in the kitchen during that time. Can you call him here?'

'Yes . . . but why? What are—?'

'It may be nothing. I'll tell you in a minute,' Radhi assured her friend. 'First, I need to ask Bhawani something.'

Sanjana called the Kadakia apartment. Speaking to Hetal, she asked if Bhawani could be spared for a few minutes. She nodded at Radhi. 'He's coming.'

'How many pills did they say he'd had in his system?'

Sanjana looked at Radhi curiously. 'Thirty to forty, approximately.'

Radhika frowned again as another thought occurred to her. 'How did Uncle have access to so many sedatives? Did he have a prescription?'

'I'm not sure. The police were asking that as well,' Sanjana admitted.

The doorbell rang. Moments later, Sanjana's maid led Bhawani inside.

Radhika saw the wandering leer Bhawani bestowed on the maid and disliked him immediately for it.

'Yes, *didi*?' Bhawani greeted Sanjana. 'How can I help?' He probably thought he'd been summoned to do one of the odd jobs Sanjana usually assigned him when her maid couldn't do it.

'Bhawani, how many times did Kirti Uncle ask you for water during lunch?' Radhi asked directly.

Bhawani seemed taken aback. He clearly hadn't expected this to be about his employer's death. Immediately, his expression tightened, and his guard came up. 'Water? He didn't ask for any. Kirti *bhai* wasn't in the habit of having water with his lunch. He'd usually have a glass or two of thin buttermilk.'

Buttermilk! Of course, that explained it! Radhi was relieved. The alternative would have been dreadful.

But Bhawani continued, 'And on the days when there was *aamras*, like on that day, not even that.'

Radhi tensed up again. 'So, he didn't ask for any extra water or *nimbu paani,* or anything else to drink with lunch, that day?'

'No.'

'And what about the bottle in his study? Who filled that and when?'

'What is this about, *didi*?' Bhawani looked at Sanjana. 'Why am I being asked so many questions?'

'This is not about you, Bhawani. Please just answer the questions.' Sanjana's tone was unusually sharp.

'Kamal usually fills the bottles in the morning.' Bhawani was now staring at Radhika with barely concealed hostility. 'And then refills them around noon when she goes in to clean the room.'

'OK. Thank you, Bhawani. You may go now.' Radhi dismissed him.

'I have to tell you, *didi.*' Bhawani ignored Radhi, again addressing Sanjana. 'After ten years of service, I don't appreciate the way I am being treated by this family. First Kirti *bhai* and now you—'

'Oh, for heaven's sake, Bhawani!' Sanjana interrupted him impatiently. 'It's just a few questions! Why do you have to make such a fuss over it?'

Bhawani glowered at the two women in silence.

Sanjana sighed. 'Thank you, Bhawani. You may go now.'

She watched Bhawani leave the room, waiting until the door had closed behind him, then, unable to contain herself any longer, she cried, 'What is it, Radhi? What are you thinking?'

Radhi inhaled deeply, then took a seat beside her friend. She wasn't sure how Sanjana would react to what she had to say. She didn't even know if she should be saying anything given Sanjana's delicate condition. But how could she not? She reached forward, picked up the photograph from the centre table and held it out in front of Sanjana.

'Do you see that Tupperware bottle of water on the table? Do you have one like that here?'

Sanjana nodded. 'Yes, but what—?'

'In there?' Radhi was already walking towards the kitchen.

Sanjana nodded again and rose to follow her.

On the counter, Radhi found a full Tupperware bottle and an empty glass. Carefully, she emptied around a quarter of the bottle's water into the glass and handed it to Sanjana.

'This is the amount of water Kirti Uncle consumed from noon that day, till the time he died, between 3 and 4 p.m.'

Sanjana looked at the glass blankly. It was about three-quarters full. 'So?'

'It is not possible to consume thirty pills with that little water.'

Sanjana continued to stare at her friend uncomprehendingly.

'What he could've had — and which I think he did — are the four or five pills that were probably in the Wednesday compartment of his medicine box. But it would be very difficult to consume thirty to forty sleeping pills, no matter how small they were, with such a little amount of water. And also it's very unlikely that he'd try to, when there was more than enough water in the bottle beside him.'

Sanjana's mind refused to grasp the full import of what Radhi was saying. 'But the coroner found the drugs in his system—'

'I called Bhawani because I wondered if Kirti Uncle had asked for more water at lunchtime. He didn't.'

'What are you saying, Radhi?'

Radhi watched Sanjana carefully. 'What if he didn't swallow the pills? What if they were crushed and put into something he ate?'

'But why would he do that?'

'*He* wouldn't.'

Sanjana's expression began to change, bewilderment turning to horror as she finally registered what Radhi meant. She opened her mouth to speak, then shut it again. Tears began to stream down her face.

'I knew he wouldn't commit suicide! It was just not in his nature. But murder? That is just too awful! Who would kill Papa?'

CHAPTER 6

Hetal stared at herself in the mirror with a little less self-loathing than usual. Not because she'd managed to lose a few kilos, though that always cheered her up, but because she'd finally shed the self-pity that had permeated her entire existence and taken a terrifying step towards shaping her own future. It wasn't something she'd imagined herself capable of, but strangely, when she'd got down to it, it hadn't been too hard.

It all started with the conversation she'd overheard when she passed her father-in-law's study one night. Oh, if only she hadn't heard anything! If only she hadn't gone to the study looking for a stapler. If only the children had kept theirs safe. If only their project wasn't due the next day. But she had and they hadn't and it was. She had. She'd heard every single word. And she'd been shaken to the core. It had roused something within her, something that she hadn't known existed. Setting her on a path from which there was no coming back.

She looked at the picture frame on her dresser of Ranjan and herself on their honeymoon in Turkey. Short-tempered, self-involved Ranjan, who hadn't looked at her properly ever since her thyroid acted up and she began putting on oodles of weight. She'd never been beautiful. No, that was a word people used to describe her younger sister. Short and stout,

Hetal had been passable at best. Her luxuriously thick hair, probably her best feature. But her parents had managed to arrange a match for her with Ranjan, at twenty-two, when she was endowed with the fickle glow that the gods bestow on the young. She knew why Manjula had agreed to it, although she'd never admit it. Hetal's parents had offered to help Ranjan buy an office space to set up his own practice. It wasn't a dowry, no — the "progressive-minded" Manjula would never stoop as low as that. But if Hetal's parents wanted to discreetly help their future son-in-law, then she wouldn't stand in their way.

You would've thought that a swanky 1,500-square-foot clinic on Temple Hill would've bought her some respect within her new family. But things hadn't quite worked out like that. In some perverse way, having accepted Hetal's parents' generosity, Manjula had seemed to hold it against her. In the beginning, she had tried to win her mother-in-law's affection and, failing that, she'd hoped for a relationship based on some sort of mutual respect. But Manjula hadn't thawed towards her.

Well, it didn't matter now. None of them did.

* * *

Radhi and Sanjana had spent all afternoon talking about Radhi's theory. Examining it from this way and that, to see if there could be any other explanation. Murder seemed laughable, unreal, like something out of a Bollywood film. Yet, even if they hadn't yet admitted it to each other out loud, there was a part of both women that believed it could've happened. They had decided to keep it to themselves for the time being. At least, until they could gather more information or, better still, find a more palatable explanation for Kirti Kadakia's death.

Now, they were back at the Kadakia home, where the family was receiving more visitors, but Sanjana was too disturbed and physically too uncomfortable to sit for long. The two friends retreated to Manjula's room so that Sanjana could lie down.

Manjula's room was like the living room, full of things she'd acquired on her many holidays, all arranged precisely. The walls had pictures and posters and wall plates, while the shelves had curios, coffee mugs and a clock. A chest of drawers, Rajasthani in origin by the look of it, proudly displayed artworks made by her grandchildren. A card that read "For the best Grandma in the world" had been given the place of privilege. The dresser had all manner of perfumes and creams and a big wad of bindi strips in all shapes and colours.

Radhi had just propped up a few pillows behind Sanjana, when Kamal walked in with a bucket of soapy water and a mop.

'Oh, I didn't realize . . .'

She made as if to leave, but Radhi stopped her. 'No, no. Finish up. We don't mind.'

'I will do it quickly, *didi*.' Kamal squatted down on her haunches and dipped the mop into the bucket, wringing it completely, before spreading it out to wipe the floor.'

After watching her for a few moments, Radhi asked, 'Kamal, did you speak to Kirti Uncle at all that day?

Then, seeing Kamal's frightened face, she added, 'We are just trying to see if he was upset about something.'

'I wouldn't know, *didi*. I hardly interacted with him. In the morning I was busy heating the milk, filling the water bottles, making the teas and coffees for everyone, while Bhawani was making the breakfast.'

'So you were in the kitchen all morning?'

'Yes. No. I mean, yes . . . We were in and out of the kitchen but we didn't really talk to Kirti *bhai*. At one point, Manju *bhabhi* sent me downstairs because she couldn't find a blouse and she thought that maybe it had blown off while it had been hung out to dry. She asked me to check with the watchman. And Bhawani came down to wash the car and also because Ranjan *bhai* had asked Bhawani to buy his . . . his . . .'

She looked nervously at Sanjana, who filled in, 'His cigarettes?'

Kamal nodded, relieved that she hadn't said more than she should have.

'When I went upstairs, Manju *bhabhi* had just finished preparing *aamras* for Kirti *bhai* and was putting the mixer away. Soon after, she left for work, which is when Hetal *bhabhi* came to the kitchen and created a bit of a ruckus.'

'Why?'

'She couldn't find a glass from her new set of glasses. She began searching in all the cupboards and drawers and sent me to look for it in all the rooms and when I couldn't find it, she insisted that I had broken it while washing vessels! I promised her that I hadn't, but she wouldn't believe me. She kept saying it was all right if I had broken it as long as I admitted my mistake. But why would I, when I had not broken anything? She only left when Kirti *bhai* called her into his study.'

'What did Kirti Uncle want?'

'I don't know, *didi*, I was only glad that she had left me in peace.'

'And after that?'

'After that Sonal *bhabhi* came into the kitchen. She usually waits for everyone to finish their work in the kitchen, then she makes two hot cups of ginger tea for herself and Amit *bhai*, which they have alone in their room, before heading to work. She always leaves me half a cup also, because she knows I really like her tea.

'By the time I went into the living room to begin the sweeping, all of them had left for work and Kirti *bhai* was in his study. I finished sweeping the whole house and entered his study last. He was talking on the phone that time.'

Sanjana leaned forward. 'Did you happen to hear what he was saying? Did he seem angry or upset?'

'I don't know, *didi* . . . He was talking in a loud voice, but he always spoke loudly and quickly. It wasn't unusual. And most of it was in Gujarati, which I don't understand very well. I didn't pay any attention to what he was saying. I just swept the floor and left the room.'

Kamal was Maharashtrian and like many servants in Mumbai had come to work in the city from the small villages that dotted the Western Ghats. She spoke only Marathi and a smattering of Hindi.

'And when did you see him again, after that?' Radhi asked.

'Half an hour . . . no, maybe an hour later, when I went to tell him I was leaving for the laundry. He told me to make two cups of tea and leave them on a tray on the dining table.'

'Who was the other one for?'

'I don't know. I left immediately.'

'What about Bhawani? Did he see who came?' Bhawani had answered this already, but Radhi wanted to check.

'We asked him,' Sanjana interjected. 'He said Papa had sent him for some bank work. He didn't see who came either. By the time he came back around 12.30 p.m., the teacups were empty. He cooked Papa's rotis, then served lunch to him at 1 p.m. and left around 1.30 p.m. after eating his own lunch.'

Radhi wished that Sanjana hadn't answered for Kamal. She gave her friend a meaningful look before turning back to the maid. 'And when you returned from the laundry?'

'I came back when Bhawani was leaving. I met him in the lobby. I have the keys to the servant room so I entered through that. I looked into the living room. It was empty. Kirti *bhai*'s lunch tray was lying on the dining table. I cleared it up, washed the vessels, had my lunch and went back to my room for my nap.'

'Kamal! There you are.' Manjula entered the room. 'Can you please go sweep the living room now, while there are no guests.'

The frightened-rabbit expression was back on Kamal's face. 'Yes, *bhabhi*.' She swiftly left the bedroom.

'Now where did I put it?' Manjula murmured, half to herself. She made her way to her wardrobe, searching inside, before bringing out her handbag.

'What is it, Mummy?' Sanjana asked.

'That obituary I wrote yesterday . . .' Manjula was now rummaging through her bag.

'Amit is going to drop it off at the newspaper office right now . . . and I can't seem to remember where I put it . . .'

She sat on the bed and began to remove the contents of her handbag, laying everything down in front of her. Radhi watched the small and neat collection of items grow. There was an orange, Hermès leather purse, a hairbrush, a compact, a slim embroidered case for spectacles, an aubergine-coloured Paper Clip diary, a single black Uniball pen, two little plastic bags of cashews and raisins, two sets of keys, one attached to a thick cluster of shells, the other to a keychain made with colourful pieces of glass and wool, and, finally, a single Mac lipstick. There was nothing extraneous in Manjula's bag.

Radhi had once read that a woman's handbag was the surest reflection of her state of mind. It was on a lazily edited listicle of a fashion magazine about "Things to change about yourself in the New Year", but it was true. Radhi was a hoarder. She had lost too much too early in life. And now she found it difficult to throw things away. Her handbag always carried a great jumble of things. There were bills, receipts, rubber bands, programmes from Broadway shows, metro maps of the cities she'd last travelled to, sweets and wrappers, loose change, often in different currencies and, most importantly, scraps of paper and tissue with hurriedly scribbled notes and ideas for articles and stories. Things languished in her handbag for months, sometimes even years.

When Radhika had read the piece, she'd decided to clean up her handbag to see if it helped declutter her mind. It had. Almost miraculously. But she had found it hard to keep it up. Now, as she watched Mrs Kadakia put her things back in her handbag, she resolved that this new phase of her life in India would include a lighter handbag.

'Where could it be? I am sure I kept it safely,' Manjula muttered to herself as she got up to check the bedside drawer.

'There!' She removed a folded piece of white paper from the drawer. She scanned what she'd written once and nodded to herself.

'Mummy,' Sanjana murmured softly. 'I can't believe he would do this.'

Manjula looked at her for a long second, her expression bitter. 'There's a lot about your father you wouldn't believe.' Then as if to soften her words, she patted Sanjana gently on her head before leaving the room.

Radhi raised her eyebrows at Sanjana.

Sanjana sighed. 'They haven't had the best relationship for years now. In fact, from what Amit tells me, they were fighting even more than usual of late.'

'What about?'

'Honestly, anything could set them off. How he drove. How he dealt with the servants. How her books and papers were always all over the dining table. Just the other day, they were arguing about the price he'd paid for custard apples! She thought he always overpaid for everything. And he thought she was always treating him like one of her pupils at school. And you know how stubborn Papa can be — he hates losing an argument, he . . .' Sanjana broke off, as if suddenly aware that she was speaking about her father in the present tense. Her eyes began to well up again.

'But what do you think she meant by that last statement?' Radhi spoke less out of curiosity and more to distract Sanjana from thoughts of her father.

'Who knows? Neither of them is really the type to chat about their "feelings".' She made quote marks in the air. 'But it wasn't like this when we were younger. You remember, don't you?'

Radhi nodded.

'I think in the beginning, they really did try to make things work. He was supportive about her teaching, fought with granny, who didn't want a "working" daughter-in-law, to make sure that she got the career she wanted. And God knows she tried her best to raise us. It couldn't have been easy. Sure she was our *maasi* . . . but to suddenly go from aunt to mother? I don't think I could do it.

'I mean, I love Amit's and Ranjan's kids to bits. But to take up all the responsibilities and angst of motherhood? Must've been so bloody hard. I think my father saw the effort she made and respected that, but I don't think that ever transformed to love. Not the kind he had for my mother, anyway. And I think this really rankled her.

Sanjana grimaced, then fussed with the pillow behind her. 'At first, she probably thought that things would change, that given enough time, their relationship might be able come out of the shadow of his previous marriage. But my father never got over my mother and that's made Mummy very bitter.'

Radhika watched her friend with concern until she settled. 'Well, I don't blame her. How long were they married? Twenty-five, thirty years? That's a long time to be second best.'

'Yeah, I know. But I don't blame my father either. He really did try to love her. And when he didn't succeed, he felt very guilty. But I think the guiltier he got, the angrier Mummy became. And Papa, doesn't — didn't,' Sanjana corrected herself, 'respond well to anger. If you yelled at him, he just yelled back louder. Hence, the shouting matches.'

Radhi frowned. 'I'm sorry. I didn't know things were rough at home. Why didn't you ever tell me?'

'Because they weren't like this in the early years. By the time things deteriorated, we were pretty grown up and busy with our own lives . . . also, you had your parents' deaths to deal with.'

Sanjana was fiddling with the pillow again, moving it this way and that, as she tried to find a comfortable position. 'What are we going to do, Radhi? I keep forgetting and then remembering! And every time I remember, it's as horrible as finding out that first time!'

Radhi stayed quiet, unsure of what to say to make her friend feel better.

Sanjana removed the pillows from behind her back and threw them on the floor, attempting now to lie down flat on her back.

'A hot-water bag will help your back,' observed Radhi, rising. 'Let me ask Kamal to make you one.'

Sanjana nodded gratefully, and Radhi left the room. In the living room, Manjula was sitting, surrounded by a few visitors. Not wanting to disturb her, Radhi walked quietly to the kitchen. It was empty.

The door to the servant room was ajar, and Radhi called out for Kamal. There was no answer. She left the kitchen and knocked on the first bedroom, diagonally opposite the study. Amit opened the door.

'Oh, hi.' He looked surprised and stepped out of the room, shutting the door behind him.

'Hey, is Sonal free? Sanjana's back is hurting and I wanted to make her a hot-water bag.'

'Sonal's, uhm . . . not feeling too well. Aren't either of the servants around?' He led the way to the kitchen. Then seeing that it was empty, he said, 'Wait, let me just do it for you.'

'What's happened to Sonal?' Radhi watched as Amit opened a couple of drawers before finding a steel pot large enough to boil water in.

'She's got . . . a headache. I've told her to lie down.' He filled the pot with water and then opened a couple of other drawers in search of a lighter.

'And, how are you? You were close to your father.'

Amit appeared to consider her question, before answering. 'Yes, in our own way we were.'

Radhi waited. Finally, he continued, 'My relationship with Papa wasn't an easy one. Honestly, neither Ranjan nor I had that. Ranjan, as you know, is too much like the old man. Hot-tempered and impulsive. They clashed every chance they got. I, on the other hand, rarely got into an argument with my father. Not because we thought alike or agreed on everything. Far from it.' He laughed at the absurdity of the thought. 'I don't like confrontation. I can't stomach it. Never could.'

Radhi smiled, nodding. She remembered Amit as a quiet boy, his face always hidden behind his video games, ears covered by headphones. Constantly kicking and punching and fighting, but always through his on-screen avatar. Never in real life.

'Papa didn't understand this about me for the longest time. Ranjan, he got. Sanjana, as well. You know how *didi* is. She doesn't mince her words. And she's stubborn like Papa. But me, he kept thinking he needed to toughen me up. And I hated it! Hated knowing that he thought I was soft. That I wasn't like my siblings. You know, I actually began going to the gym and working out just to win his approval. Yeah,' he added at Radhika's expression, 'I'm not sure of that logic either.'

The water on the stove had come to a boil now. Amit reached up and got out a pink rubber hot-water bag from a cupboard. He unscrewed it and carefully poured the water into the bag, before shutting it tight.

He handed it to Radhi. 'Things *had* changed between us in the last few years. Not me, so much. But him. He had mellowed a little. I think he had come to understand that there are different kinds of tough. Do you know, we'd even started playing chess of late?'

'Really?' Radhi smiled. 'That must've been nice! So who'd win?'

Amit's eyes flashed with some unfathomable emotion. 'I did! . . . And how the old man hated it!'

Radhi clutched the hot water bottle to her. 'I'd better get this to Sanjana . . . Thanks.'

She made her way walked back to the kitchen entrance. Had she looked back, she would have been surprised by the expression on Amit's face. He was thinking about his last conversation with his father.

* * *

'What happened?' Sonal was sitting on the bed, her laptop in front of her. Her face was puffy, her nose red.

'*Didi* needed a hot-water bag and Radhi couldn't find the servants.'

'That's right. When they need something done, they come to me. Otherwise who cares if I am dead or alive?'

'Oh, come now . . . you can't still be that upset?'

'Why not?' Sonal's resentment was obvious. 'I am so, so sick of always being an afterthought. Your father was planning a grand dinner. But did anyone think of telling me? I know my parents didn't give me a lot of silver that can be polished, but don't I deserve to know about anything at all?'

Amit sat beside his wife and put an arm around her shoulders. 'Sonal, come on! You know it's not intentional. Nobody means any harm—'

'I know!' Sonal flung his arm aside. 'And that's what makes it worse, don't you see? If these snubs were on purpose, it would mean they'd spent thought, time and energy to think up ways of hurting me. I think in a way it would make me feel better!'

'Okay. Now you're beginning to sound crazy.'

'Am I, Amit? I have spent eight fucking years trying to fit into this family. Trying to fit into your precious Temple Hill! Honestly, when we got married, I didn't think it would be so hard. I thought if I could just look the part, I'd get the part.

'To think of all those ludicrously priced designers and salons I went to! Why just last month, I spent half my monthly salary on a tiny clutch bag! A clutch bag, Amit! God, what a fool I have been!' Sonal covered her face with her hands as she began to cry.

'Shh . . . hush now.' Amit gathered his wife in his arms. 'You know I don't care for any of that? You know I love you, right? Seriously, Sonal, all of this doesn't matter.'

* * *

'These bloody food-obsessed Gujaratis!' Bhawani cursed under his breath as he cooked. 'There's been a fucking death in the family. You'd think that one day, they'd have a simple *khichdi*, if not out of grief then for the sake of propriety. But no, every day it needs to be a feast!'

His mind was working as furiously as his hands. How did some people have so much and some, so little? And why did they think that made them better than him? He was so angry, for the most part at himself and his lot in life. For the choices it had forced him to make. And for the consequences that now confronted him. He needed a proper plan. Sooner or later these idiots were going to start asking him questions. The right kind of questions, instead of the nonsense they were going on about now. And when they did, he needed to have believable answers. So far, he had none.

The knife in Bhawani's hand moved expertly across the chopping board, swiftly slicing red and yellow bell peppers into fine, almost identical crescent moons. On the stove in front of him, a pan sizzled with vegetable cutlets bound together with raw bananas. On the burner beside that was a pan in which he was simultaneously searing the herbed paneer cubes that would go into the soup he was about to start making on the third burner.

Bhawani worked quickly. The soup and the stir-fry were for Hetal and Ranjan. For Manjula and Amit, he would have to make a separate meal. They preferred more traditional Gujarati fare. For them, he was going to make rotis made out of a mixed-millet flour and a bottle-gourd-and-pea vegetable curry. If the children were here, there'd most likely be a third meal just for them, like a white sauce pasta, unless he could slap the cutlets in the middle of two slices of bread and cheese and convince them that they were burgers. Usually, Bhawani didn't mind the multiple meals. This was why the Kadakias had hired a live-in cook, to deal with their demands. But today, Bhawani was stressed.

'*Fuck*!' A hot mustard seed crackled, flying out of the seasoning he'd just prepared for the curry, right into his eye.

Kamal glanced at Bhawani. She was roasting the leftover rotis from lunch into crisp wafer-thin *khakhras*. For the umpteenth time, she wondered what was wrong with him. Ever since the old man had died, he'd been acting strangely. She'd tried asking but he'd refused to say. Now Kamal was worried that this stupid man had gotten himself into trouble. And she was terrified that might lead to her own secret being found out.

CHAPTER 7

The next morning, Radhi hurried to get ready for her breakfast at Mrs Maniar's.

'I'll see you in about an hour at your dad's house?'

Sanjana nodded grimly. She looked drawn and tense.

Radhi crossed the living room to give her friend a hug. 'Try not to worry. We'll get to the bottom of this. Just promise to take care of yourself.' This really wasn't the kind of pregnancy Sanjana deserved.

Sanjana smiled weakly as she hugged her back. 'Thanks, Radhi.'

Radhika's phone rang, as she made her way to Mrs Maniar's house in the A Wing.

'I feel we spoke more often when you were in the US!' Madhavi complained in her ear.

'Sorry, *di*. I've just been spending some time with Sanjana . . . Haven't had a chance to finish unpacking either.'

'I know. I know.' Madhavi sighed. 'I hope she is doing better.'

'Yes. Jayesh gets back today, so that should help.'

'Good. Good. So listen — dinner. Day after. My place.'

'No, *didi*. Please, no socializing . . . I'm kind of just hoping to settle into the apartment over the next few days. I'm not really up to meeting people.'

'Please, Radhi, don't say no. My mother-in-law is in town. She's invited her friend, Parul Aunty, and her son for dinner, along with Ila *kaki* and Prachi. She hopes to set them up.' Prachi was their cousin, Ila *kaki*'s daughter. 'They're bad enough on their own but imagine having to tackle both of them together!' Radhi knew Madhavi meant their aunt and her mother-in-law. Anshul's mother was an obnoxious tyrant with an inflated sense of self-worth and a variety of health problems — most of them imagined.

'That does sound like fun!' Radhi grinned.

'If you come, it will be!' Madhavi's tone was bright. 'Besides, Parul Aunty's son, Nishant, is pretty nice. I've met him before. Oh, and I have invited Vrinda *fia* as well!' She knew Radhi adored the aunt who had all but brought them up.

'All right, all right, I'll come. You don't have to sell it to me. Your sweet mother-in-law is motivation enough.'

Madhavi groaned. 'Please Radhika. You have to promise to behave yourself.'

'Of course, *di*.' Radhi's tone was saccharin sweet. 'Bye for now.'

Now at Mrs Maniar's apartment, Radhi rang the doorbell. Immediately an eye appeared at the keyhole. Then the door flew open and Mrs Maniar embraced Radhika in a hug that smelled of talcum powder and Parachute coconut oil.

'I'm so glad to see you.' She watched Radhi as she removed her shoes before entering the house.

'You are right on time. I like it when people are punctual. I've asked the cook to make *idli-sambhar*. I hope you haven't become like those desis who live abroad for too long and then spend the rest of their lives complaining about how nothing ever comes close to Starbucks' bagels and chai lattes!

'My younger son is like that. And it always amazes me. I didn't think any offspring of mine would ever say no to *jalebis*. Imagine! *Jalebis*!' She smacked her lips at the thought of the deep-fried, sugar-soaked, pretzel-like sweets.

'"How can you have such greasy food in the morning?" he asks me. Well, better morning than at night, no? Besides, aren't his pizzas twice as greasy? But you seem like a sensible girl. You don't speak much, do you?'

Radhika smiled. As if it were possible to get a word in.

A maid had entered the room to announce that the food was ready.

'Come, let's eat.' Mrs Maniar ushered Radhi towards the dining area, where a vase of fresh tube roses stood tall on the table, and the food had been laid out around it, in what looked like brand new CorningWare bowls and platters.

'Aunty, this is too much!' Radhi was surprised to see the peppery, deep-fried *medu vadas* and the cardamom-scented semolina *sheera* that had been placed alongside the *idli-sambhar*.

'Pssh . . . It's nothing.' Mrs Maniar beamed with pleasure as the two women took their seats.

'So, now tell me. How have you been? And how is your sister? Madhavi, right? She has two little girls, no?' Mrs Maniar served Radhi two *idlis*. The savoury steamed rice cakes were fluffy and almost impossibly soft.

Radhika nodded as she helped herself to a bowlful of piping hot *sambhar*. Then dipping her *idli* into the spicy lentil-based preparation, she took a big bite. The medicines she'd taken the night before seemed to have helped and she actually felt hungry.

'And what about your friend, Sanjana? She's going to be all right, I hope? But to tell you the truth, it's not Sanjana I was thinking about. It's Ranjan. I can't even imagine how he must be feeling.'

'Why?' Radhi paused mid bite.

'Oh, I thought you'd know!' Mrs Maniar was trying, unsuccessfully, to mask the pleasure she'd derived at Radhika's obvious surprise.

She put two donut-shaped *medu vadas* on Radhi's plate. 'See, it is not in my nature to talk. I don't like to poke my nose where it doesn't belong. Or make idle gossip. *No way*. I have my Krishna to pay attention to. If I don't turn to religion now, there's going to be no place for me in heaven! I wouldn't even have said anything right now. But seeing as you are such a good friend of Sanjana, I just assumed you'd know about it. I sometimes thank my stars that my children live separately and not with me. Oh, it gets a little lonely sometimes, but there's so much love and respect between all of us . . . really, I feel most blessed. In fact, just the other day I was telling—'

'Aunty, please,' Radhi interrupted gently. 'What happened?'

'Oh, sorry, *beta*. Sorry. I do have a way of rambling on. But honestly, I don't know whether I should be saying anything. This is such a terrible time for them and one word misspoken or misunderstood would just add fuel to the fire. You know what I mean?'

She took a sip of her ginger tea, the food on her own plate lying untouched. The gossip she was in possession of seemed far juicier than anything her cook could rustle up. She was clearly dying to talk, but Radhi could see that she would need a slightly different approach to coax the information out.

'No, of course, I understand. I wouldn't dream of encouraging talk about my friend or her family,' she assured. 'I just hope Ranjan's OK. His mother really needs him to be strong . . . Mmm, this *sambhar* is really delicious. What do you use to get this slightly tangy taste? Tamarind or lemon?'

As Radhi had guessed, Mrs Maniar didn't want the topic changed. She watched, amused, as the old lady hurried to bring the conversation back to what they'd been discussing.

'We use both. Tamarind and lemon! They give it a distinctly tart flavour, no? My elder one, Pratik, loves *sambhar*. Growing up, Pratik and Ranjan were great friends, you remember?'

Radhi nodded as Mrs Maniar continued. 'I must tell Pratik to call Ranjan and offer his condolences. Poor boy. I do feel sorry for him.'

'What happened, Aunty?' Radhi asked, sure that this time Mrs Maniar wouldn't let the opportunity pass.

The old lady paused dramatically, as if she was still uncertain if she should speak. Then she sighed. 'What often happens with grown sons and fathers. Ranjan got into a massive fight with his father. And you know what a loud voice Ranjan has. It was terrible. There was some name-calling and, at one point, Ranjan even pounded the wall with his fist . . . *dhud-dhud*.' She mimicked the noise, one palm splayed on her chest. 'As you can imagine, I was quite shocked!'

'When was this?'

She put a spoonful of sweet *sheera* on Radhi's plate. 'On Tuesday . . . no, wait, was it Tuesday? When did Kirti *bhai* pass away?'

'Wednesday.'

'So, yes, it was Tuesday then. Tuesday morning.

Radhika leaned forward, the piece of *idli* on her fork forgotten. 'What were they fighting about? Did you happen to hear?'

'No, *baba*. I immediately left the living room and went for my bath. I couldn't possibly eavesdrop like that. These are their personal family matters. I had no business listening to them. Of course, one couldn't help but overhear a few words . . . but nothing that I could string together.'

Mrs Maniar leaned back on her chair, hugging her teacup to her chest. Radhi could see that probing further would be useless. Mrs Maniar might love to gossip but she loved her own idea of herself even more. She wasn't going to admit that she'd stuck around to listen to the whole fight, and Radhi was certain that she had.

'So you can imagine why I thought of Ranjan when I heard the news,' Mrs Maniar continued. 'He must feel terrible. What an awful way to part with one's father. It will probably haunt him all his life.' The grim relish in her voice was unmistakeable.

'You are probably right, Aunty.' Radhi finished her food in a few quick bites.

Mrs Maniar tried to give her another *idli* but Radhi immediately covered her plate with both hands.

'No more! I'm stuffed, Aunty!' She pushed her chair back.

The maid, who'd been standing within earshot, came forward to take her plate and offered her a box of tissues.

Radhi wiped her hands and stood up. 'Thank you so much for breakfast, Aunty. It was much more delicious than any bagel I've ever had.'

'What, going already?' Mrs Maniar looked disappointed. 'Have a second cup of tea, at least?'

'No, no . . . I really must be going. I have some furniture being delivered today.' It wasn't exactly untrue, as her furniture *would* be delivered later that day.

Reluctantly, Mrs Maniar walked Radhi to the door. 'In that case, promise to come again soon.'

Radhika smiled. 'Of course.'

Mrs Maniar waited while Radhi put on her shoes. She continued to stand watching as she walked the short distance across the lobby to ring the doorbell to the Kadakia home. Radhika ignored the inquisitive eyes on her back, her mind mulling over what she'd just been told.

When Bhawani opened the door, he seemed annoyed to see her. He hadn't liked her questions the night before, that much was clear. It was too bad though, thought Radhika, as he let her into the apartment. She had a couple more things to ask him later.

Inside, Sanjana and Manjula were busy in the living room with a few visitors who had come to offer their condolences. Radhika gave Sanjana a little wave, before turning towards the kitchen. It was time to take the second dose of her medicines, and she needed some water. She found Hetal in there, making tea.

'Do you need help with that?' Radhi pointed towards the tray, where Hetal was arranging empty teacups on a tray.

Hetal acknowledged Radhi with a smile. 'No, I'm almost done . . . Sanjana *ben*'s in-laws have come. Would you like some tea?'

Radhi shook her head. 'No, thanks, I've just had some . . . Where is everyone?'

'They are releasing the body today. Amit *bhai* and Ranjan have gone to the police station to complete the formalities.'

'So, when will the last rites be held?' Radhi asked, watching the woman.

'Tomorrow morning, most likely. Hopefully, Jayesh *bhai*'s flight is on time. Would you like some coffee instead? I am going to make a cup for myself once I've given them their tea.'

Radhi really didn't. Her acidity was finally under control and she wanted to avoid caffeine, but a cup of coffee seemed like the perfect way to linger a little and talk to Hetal. She'd been planning on asking Sanjana if she knew anything about Ranjan's fight, but Hetal was even more likely to know. If only she would open up to Radhi.

'Coffee would be lovely, Hetal. Thanks.'

Hetal picked up the tray and walked out of the kitchen, while Radhi got herself a glass of water and sat on a kitchen stool to take her pills. It occurred to her that it would've been easy for literally anyone to mix something into Kirti Uncle's food. The kitchen was located towards the far end of the living room and completely out of sight from any of the bedrooms. Unless you were standing right at its entrance, there was absolutely no way to see what was going on in the kitchen. Of course, it was entirely possible that the pills were put in something else he'd consumed that day. Even the mystery person who came to see him that morning could've mixed them into Uncle's tea. Yet the timing didn't make sense. If they were in the tea, he'd have been completely knocked out by lunchtime.

Radhi was still thinking about how, if at all, the pills had been administered, when Hetal returned.

'It's always nice to have coffee with someone.' Hetal cleaned the filter of the coffee machine and loaded it up with beans as she spoke. 'Everybody here drinks tea, except me.'

'Oh, I love Jamaican roast!' Radhi exclaimed, when she saw the pack of coffee beans that Hetal was holding.

'Do you know, when I got married, they didn't even have a coffee machine? My mother-in-law asked me to make do with instant. Buying a machine for one person was not "practical" she said. Instant coffee! Can you imagine?' Hetal made a face.

Radhi smiled sympathetically.

'I asked Ranjan to intervene, but he refused. Didn't want to get in the middle of all our "kitchen politics", he said. Typical of him.' Hetal shook her head, as she put a mug below the spout to collect the coffee. 'Always taking the easy way out. And in those days, I was too new, didn't want to take my mother-in-law head-on by buying a machine myself and putting it in her kitchen. So for six whole months, I began my day with instant coffee.' She shuddered as she removed the mugs, wiping the bottoms. 'Sugar?'

'Yes, please. One.'

'Then for Diwali, I did a smart thing.' Hetal stirred sugar into Radhi's mug. 'I asked my parents to gift me a coffee machine. They were going to give me gold earrings since it was my first Diwali after marriage, but I said, "No, thank you. There would be plenty of occasions to get those earrings, but I can't cope without my morning coffee."

'Once the machine was in the house, my mother-in-law couldn't very well forbid me from using it.' Hetal's satisfaction was unmistakeable. 'She grumbled a bit about how it occupied too much space. And was cumbersome for the servants to maintain. And the beans were too expensive for daily use. But beyond that, she couldn't do much. Not making space for the machine in the kitchen would've been disrespectful of my parents' gift. And my mother-in-law wouldn't do that. She is very proper that way.' Hetal grinned. She took an appreciative sip of her coffee.

Radhi grinned back. 'Living in joint families can be tricky.'

'Oh that's an understatement! Adjusting to everyone's temperaments and moods, likes and dislikes . . . God, I had the toughest time in the beginning.'

'Yeah . . . Kirti Uncle must've been a hard nut to crack.'

'Oh, don't get me started! He was so finicky and stubborn and awfully impatient. If you left your room with the fan still on or if one of the kids' clothes had a stain on it, he'd be sure to tell you off about it. Once, when I was newly married, we were all supposed to go to an aunt's house for lunch and I was late getting ready. You should've seen him pacing in the living room. He was furious. He didn't say a word to me. Seeing as I was new to the family, his silence was even scarier. I remember nobody spoke a single word in the car. They were all afraid to set him off!'

Radhika smiled sympathetically, knowing that this was enough. Most people didn't really need a reaction to their story. Not really. They just wanted to know that they'd been heard. That someone had seen things from their perspective and understood how they felt. This intuitive quality to know when to say nothing had stood Radhi in good stead when she interviewed people for her articles and stories.

Hetal turned to open a cupboard behind her, reaching in to get a steel cannister of spicy fenugreek puris. She offered the flatbreads to Radhi before taking a couple herself. 'I always need something crunchy with my coffee. Don't worry, these are low fat,' she added, when Radhi declined. 'Not that you need to worry about calories.'

She took a bite and continued speaking, this time with her mouth half-full. 'My father-in-law did have one redeeming quality though. He was the only one in the house who could stand up to my mother-in-law. And she *really* does need standing up to. I shouldn't be saying this, but the one good thing that may come out of this awful scandal is that it may force her down from her high horse. You know, initially, I couldn't give the servants a single instruction without first checking with her . . . She was just so territorial!'

She offered Radhi a puri again, and this time Radhi took one.

'You know if it was only the kitchen, I wouldn't have minded her being bossy about it. But she has a view on everything! Which schools our children should go to, what extracurricular classes they should join, even where we should host their birthday parties! I mean, c'mon, I understand that academia is her forte but these are *my* kids. Of course, I can't say any of this to Ranjan. He hero-worships his mother. Thinks she is the sun, moon and stars!'

She sounded so bitter that Radhi felt sorry for her. It must've been hard for Hetal to always compete with Manjula for Ranjan's attention. This was the opening Radhi had been waiting for. For Hetal to talk about Ranjan, so that Radhi could ask about the fight.

'Ranjan wasn't as close to his father, though, was he?'

Hetal shook her head. 'No. I think they were too similar, too stubborn to get along.'

'He must feel bad about his fight with his father though?' Radhi prompted gently.

Hetal had been rinsing one of the coffee mugs and for a split second, her hands stilled.

'Fight? You could hardly call it that! Have the servants been talking about it? Really, how they love to gossip! And how much they exaggerate! It was just a small argument. One of those things between fathers and sons . . . a difference of opinion. Hardly a fight. I was right there!'

Radhi was puzzled. Mrs Maniar wasn't the most reliable source and she could have easily exaggerated what happened to make the story more entertaining. But Radhi could tell that the question had ruffled Hetal, and she had a feeling that the young woman wasn't being forthright about something.

'Of course, I get it. These things happen in families all the time.' Radhi was purposely encouraging, hoping Hetal would say more. But it seemed Hetal was done sharing.

'Listen,' Hetal's voice had dropped to an undertone, 'I would appreciate it if you didn't tell anyone in the family about this figh — uh . . . argument. It is just such a sad time for everybody. This would just make a mountain out of a molehill.'

'Don't worry, there's nothing to tell.'

Hetal smiled at Radhi gratefully.

The doorbell sounded outside the room.

'Must be Kamal.' Hetal wiped her hands with the dishcloth hanging beside the fridge. 'We sent her down to organize a few plastic chairs in the lobby for the older guests who are attending the last rites.'

Radhika followed Hetal out of the kitchen and into the living room. While Hetal opened the door to let Kamal in, Radhi said her hellos to Sanjana's in-laws who were just getting ready to leave.

The doorbell rang again, and this time Radhi noticed Kamal went to answer it. It was the *dhobi* who did the ironing. Kamal came back with a bundle of pressed clothes from him and asked him to wait while she went to the laundry area to bring out the newly washed clothes that needed pressing. Moments later, the woman returned, holding out a red blouse to Manjula. 'Here it is, *bhabhi*! Your blouse.'

Manjula, who'd been talking to Sanjana's mother-in-law, paused. She looked at Kamal blankly.

'Remember, the one you sent me to find? On that . . . that day.' Kamal faltered, realizing that the day in question, was the day of her employer's death.

Manjula's jaw tightened. As a widow, bright reds and greens would now be considered inappropriate for her to wear. 'What use are these colours to me now?'

Sanjana put her arm around Manjula's shoulders, squeezing them gently. Her mother-in-law, a slight but fit woman, with a thick mop of curly white hair, took Manjula's hand in hers, and patted it. Then sombrely, she said her goodbyes.

'I'll be in my room if someone needs me,' Manjula said after Sanjana's in-laws had left. 'Hetal, can you please check if Bhawani has prepared the study? Hetal nodded and left the room. Soon after, Manjula followed.

When they were alone, Sanjana turned to Radhi. 'I need to go home to get some incense sticks for the study. They'll be laying out Papa's body there tonight.' Her voice cracked. 'Oh Radhi, I just have to find out what happened that day. It is driving me mad!'

'Hush,' Radhika soothed. 'We will find out . . . Let's first make a list and talk to everyone he spoke to that day.'

Sanjana nodded slowly. Radhi had decided against telling Sanjana about Ranjan's fight with their father, at least for the time being. She decided to wait until she found out more. If Hetal was telling the truth and it was all just some fanciful concoction, it wasn't worth worrying her already overwrought friend about.

'Listen,' Radhi checked her phone, scanning a text, 'I have to go. My furniture is being delivered right now, I'll see you in a couple of hours, okay?'

Sanjana nodded again.

Radhi paused beside the door. 'Whose keys are these?' She pointed at an elephant-shaped keyholder on the wall, where there were three sets of keys hanging by the elephant's trunk.

Sanjana came forward to take a closer look.

'This one is a spare set to my place.' She pointed first to a pair of keys on a brass metal ring, then to a single key with a woollen clown keychain. 'While this is for the main door here. Bhawani or Kamal use it when they are running errands, in case there's no one at home to answer the door.' And this last one here,' she gestured to a single key attached to a silver "S", 'this is for the Solankis above us. They both work and they keep their key here for emergencies.'

'Isn't it risky? To keep the keys lying around like this? I know, growing up, Mummy used to keep our keys by the door for the driver to wash the cars etc., but it means anyone who gets their hands on the spare key has access to the house, no? And I've seen how many people come to the door every day. The vegetable guy, the ironing fellow, courier delivery guys . . .'

Sanjana frowned, 'I suppose you're right . . . though I've never really thought about it. We've been hanging keys here for years.'

The two women stared at each other. Worried. Scared. The sudden implications of what a key in the wrong pair of hands could mean was not lost on either.

CHAPTER 8

Radhi stood in what used to be her parents' room looking at an exquisitely embroidered depiction, framed on the wall, of Trishala Mata, the mother of Lord Mahavira, the twenty-fourth and last Jain Tirthankara.

She'd told Lila that everything had to go and yet, when it came to parting with something her mother had so painstakingly hand-embroidered over eight months, Radhi hadn't been able to get rid of it.

The frame showed the queen mother in her royal chambers, lying in bed surrounded by her attendants. Above her, in little golden clouds were the fourteen auspicious dreams that she'd had when she was pregnant with Lord Mahavira. An elephant, a bull, a golden urn filled with water, a lake of lotuses, a lion, the moon, the sun, a celestial plane of swans, a heap of jewels, a pair of garlands descending from heaven, a large flag, an ocean, the Goddess Laxmi and, finally, a smokeless fire. It was a mystical combination prophesizing that her son would be the greatest of all spiritual leaders, a Tirthankara.

As a child, Radhi had spent hours on her parents' bed studying the bliss on the queen mother's face as she dreamed her dreams. Now that Radhi had converted this room into her study, she planned to place her writing desk below the frame. Hoping that she'd be able to find a shadow of that joy in her writing, like she'd once been able to. When her heart wasn't in tatters like it was today. When Mackinzey was still a part of her life.

At the thought of Mackinzey, Radhi's chest constricted in that familiar aching way, and it was difficult to breathe. How utterly livid she was with him. And yet, the few years she'd spent with him had been the most transformative of her life.

After her parents' death, she'd shut off parts of herself, corners in her mind effectively cordoned off like a crime scene. She didn't dare to duck under the red tape to investigate how she really felt, as if the memories could be willed out of existence by simply skirting around them. There was a space within her that was so heavy with guilt that she always left it in the dark, drapes drawn, windows shut, doors locked, the key hidden. She'd gone about the daily business of living in the bright, illuminated parts, hosting parties, making friends and even falling in love — without people ever stumbling into the dark room, even by mistake. The only time during her marriage that the drapes had shifted and her ex-husband had come close to getting a glimpse within was during an argument. But Radhika had reacted with a vicious comment, and the drapes had fallen back into place swiftly and for ever.

With Mackinzey it had been different. From the very beginning he had sensed the darkness and accepted it. But he hadn't circled around it, looking for cracks from which he could peep in. He had flung the crime-scene tape aside and walked right into the restricted area, torch in hand, shining light on cobweb-ridden shadows. Prodding here, poking there, despite Radhi's outraged protests, he'd gotten the story out of her in tortured bits and pieces at first, and then in one huge, relieved gush. She remembered that afternoon well, and the tender, anguished look on his face as he'd wiped away her tears. They'd never spoken of it again. There had been no need. And while the darkness still existed, it wasn't as dense as before.

'*Didi*?' Lila's voice drifted in from the living room, where she had been supervising the furniture's assembling. 'They're almost done in here.'

With an effort, Radhi brought herself back to the present and walked out into the living room. The sight that met her made her happy. All the furniture had fitted into the space naturally. Already the room looked transformed.

'*Didi*, what about the curtains?' Lila had come to stand beside Radhi.

'They'll come later today. Listen, do me a favour? Will you tell Ramzan *bhai* to bring the car around? I need to buy a couple of white *kurtas*. I really can't keep showing up at the Kadakias' like this.' She gestured to her white crop top and jeans.

'*Ji, didi*,' Lila grinned.

* * *

That afternoon, when she got to the Kadakias' apartment, Radhi found the family in the living room, talking to visitors. There were more than a dozen new faces and Radhi was glad she'd worn an appropriate white Lucknowi *kurta*. Sanjana got up when she saw Radhi and led her down the corridor to Manjula's room.

'Don't worry about me,' Radhi protested. 'Finish greeting your guests.'

'No, no. I need to lie down anyway.' Sanjana propped some pillows up and sat on the bed with her legs outstretched. 'Besides,' she continued in hushed tones, 'they're going on and on about what a shock it was. And how he wasn't the type to take his own life. And I feel like getting up and screaming that Papa didn't. So, all things considered, it's best if I stay here.'

'Did they bring Kirti Uncle home?'

'Yes, he's in the study. They'll take him to the crematorium tomorrow morning. Everyone will be here by then, including Jayesh and the children.'

The doorbell sounded.

'Listen, could you please check if it's the coconut vendor? I asked the watchman to send him up. My gynaecologist has told me to have coconut water daily.'

Radhi emerged from the passage into the living room in time to see Kamal walking away from the main door, a basket of tomatoes in hand. She returned to the room and took her seat next to Sanjana. 'Vegetable seller, I think. Did you manage to find out who your father spoke to that morning?'

'Better, in fact. We have his phone.' Sanjana got up carefully and went to Manjula's dressing table. She took a Samsung Galaxy S7 from the first drawer and handed it to Radhika. 'The police gave it back when they released his body.' 'The password's "Urmila".'

Radhi raised an eyebrow quizzically.

'I know. My mother's name.'

'How did you know?'

'Amit. He helped Papa set it.'

Radhi wondered if Manjula knew and how she felt about it. She switched on the phone. The wallpaper was a picture of Kirti Uncle's four grandchildren at the youngest's birthday party. The little boy was standing in front of a blue fondant, monster-truck cake with a number four candle. The three older children had smeared cake all over his laughing face. Radhika pressed the call log.

'Here, make a note of this.' She handed Sanjana her own phone and waited until her friend was ready.

'There's a call to you in the morning. Then a missed call from a Hemendra *bhai* at 10.07 a.m., another missed call from an unknown landline immediately after that . . . Then an outgoing call to a Vinod Shah at 10.10 a.m. for thirteen minutes, then to Ranjan at 10.24 a.m. for ten minutes twenty-five seconds, after that to a K. Poddar at 10.43 a.m. for twenty seconds.' She waited as Sanjana tapped away.

'Then there's an incoming call from the same unknown number as before, again for less than a minute . . . Then another incoming call from a different unknown number for twenty-seven seconds . . . Finally, there's an incoming call at 1.10 p.m. for thirty-two seconds from Manjula Aunty.

'Mummy was probably the last one to speak to him then,' Sanjana mused as she looked up from the phone, where she'd diligently jotted down the names and timings of all the calls.

Radhika nodded. 'Who's Vinod Shah?'

'Papa's broker, I think.'

Radhika looked back at the call log. 'And is this K. Poddar the one who lives in our building?'

'Yeah, I think so. They are — *were* part of the Sea Mist Society Committee and often spoke to each other.

There was a brief rapping at the door, before Amit poked his head inside.

'Did you order this, *didi*?'

'Oh, thanks, Amit. Come in, will you, I wanted to speak with you.'

Amit pushed the door open, walking across to his sister to hand her a tall glass of coconut water. Then he settled back against the wardrobe, waiting expectantly.

Sanjana sipped the water. 'Papa's broker's name is Vinod Shah, right?'

'Yes, wh—'

'And who is Hemendra *bhai*?' Sanjana interrupted.

Amit looked at her curiously. 'I don't know, *didi* . . . Why?'

'I want to speak to all the people Papa spoke to that morning. I want to understand what was going on in his mind.'

Amit shook his head, as if to discourage her. 'What good will it do now, *didi*?'

'For Papa? Nothing maybe! But for me? A world of good!'

'How can worrying be good for you? Especially, right now?' Amit looked at Radhi for support, but she stayed silent.

'Because it's better than not knowing! Not comprehending! Don't you see, Amit? It's better than just wondering and guessing and hoping!' Sanjana put her glass down carelessly on the side table. Some of the coconut water spilled out, but her eyes did not leave her brother's face.

'Ranjan spoke to Vinod *bhai* today,' Amit informed her quietly. 'He called him because he couldn't get through to Papa's phone. He didn't know about Pa — Papa's death . . . It seems Papa's lost a couple of *crores* in the markets in the last year.'

The colour drained out of Sanjana's face. 'What?'

'I know. Ranjan and I are going to go to his office tomorrow after the funeral to try to understand better.'

'Oh, God. Perhaps that's why—'

'*Didi*, we are all shaken up about it. But don't—'

'None of you knew? Not even Mummy?'

'No. But please don't worry about it. I wouldn't have said anything, if I hadn't found you obsessing about why he did it . . . All's not lost. He had an insurance policy which will — will help us cover most of the debt. So again, don't worry. You just need to take care of yourself right now. OK?'

Sanjana nodded slowly. Amit, seemingly satisfied, left the room.

'How could I have been so blind, Radhi?' Sanjana had a stricken look on her face. 'He cancelled his Alaska cruise, which he'd planned a year ago, saying he was short-staffed and that he couldn't take time off. He let go of his driver, Ashok *kaka*, who'd been with us for over two decades. Then a few months ago, he told me he needed my help writing a classified ad. He wanted to rent out a part of his office, since he worked from home half the time.

'The signs were all there, Radhi! He was in trouble! If only I had paid attention and not been so caught up with my own life!' Sanjana buried her face in her hands, sobbing.

'Sanjana,' Radhi hugged her friend, ' Sanjana . . . you're forgetting something. The pills. How did Kirti Uncle consume those? I doubt he crushed them and put them in his own food! He may have been in trouble, but I'm not convinced he took his own life.'

Sanjana looked up, her face tear-stained. Radhi continued, 'We need to contact the people he spoke to that day.'

Sanjana nodded and wiped her wet cheeks with her *dupaata*. 'Give me the numbers.'

For the next few minutes, Radhi dictated the numbers, which Sanjana took down beside the list of names. Then she took a screenshot of it and sent it to Radhi.

'I'll call them when I get home,' Radhi said.

Sanjana gave her a sad smile. 'Thanks, Radhi. I feel so bad about dragging you into all of this. It's your first week home.'

Radhi smiled back. 'I've been dragging you into my problems all my life! Besides, focusing on this prevents me from dwelling on my own issues, which, as you and I both know, are many. So don't go thanking me.'

Sanjana finished her coconut water. She made to get off the bed. 'I'll just put this glass in the kitchen.'

'Here, let me. You lie down.' Radhi took the glass from Sanjana and stepped out of the room.

In the kitchen, Manjula was standing with her back against the sink, a glass of water in one hand, a pillbox in the other.

'Hello, Aunty.'

'Hello, *beta*, did you want something?'

'Just some water.'

Radhika placed Sanjana's glass in the sink.

As Manjula turned to open the cabinet behind her, Radhi studied the assortment of pink, blue and yellow pills in the older woman's pillbox. Manjula always seemed so strong, mainly because of her personality, but she was sixty-four years old, and this tragedy would inevitably take its toll.

Manjula took out a glass, then just as she was about to shut the cabinet door, she noticed something and opened it again.

'Where did this come from?' She seemed to be speaking more to herself than to Radhi. She removed a glass serving bowl with a thick floral pattern etched into it.

'Kamal, is this new?' she said to the young woman who'd just entered the kitchen.

Kamal took the glass bowl in her hand, turning it to examine it, before handing it back. 'I don't know, *bhabhi.* I haven't seen it before.'

'Seems like Hetal's been online shopping again,' Manjula muttered to herself, as she took the bowl into the living room. Radhi followed her.

Most of the guests had left. Hetal was sitting talking quietly to an older woman, who Radhi thought might be her mother.

'Hetal, do you know anything about this bowl?' Manjula asked, holding it out.

Hetal glanced at the bowl and shook her head. 'No. Why?'

'It was in the kitchen, in the glass cabinet. I was wondering if it was a new purchase.'

Hetal shook her head again, visibly pleased that for once Manjula was wrong.

'Radhika, *beta*,' Manjula turned to Radhi. 'Will you check with Sanjana if it has come from her house?'

Radhi took the bowl to Sanjana.

She brought it back to Manjula a few moments later. 'It isn't hers.'

'Bhawani, just one minute please,' Manjula called to Bhawani, who was passing them on his way to the kitchen. 'Whose is this? Did Sonal *bhabhi* get it? Do you know?'

Bhawani took it in his hand to examine it.

'I think this is that custard bowl.'

'What custard bowl?' Manjula looked confused.

'From that fruit custard that the third-floor *bhabhi* sent that day.'

'Which *bhabhi*? Sutaria or Poddar?'

'Poddar.'

'When was this?'

Bhawani thought for a few seconds and then his face assumed a sombre expression. 'On Wednesday. After all of you left for work. Around 11.30. I asked Kirti *bhai* if he wanted some and he sa—'

'Said "yes".' Manjula completed the sentence softly. 'He loved fruit custard.' She seemed to withdraw into herself.

'Send the bowl back to them after the thirteenth-day ceremony,' she told the cook absently, as she sat down on the sofa. 'And remember to fill it with *ghooghras* or *gud paapdi* or even puris will do. Just don't send it back empty.'

Radhi returned to Sanjana's room, her expression thoughtful as she asked, 'Did Kirti Uncle get along with Mr Poddar?'

Sanjana looked surprised at the question. 'Yes . . . I guess so. I mean they had their differences sometimes as part of the building committee. For instance, Papa didn't agree with Mr Poddar's choice of contractor for the upcoming building renovation. And I know they argued about it recently. But what's that got to do with any of this?'

Radhi told her about the bowl. 'What if the pills were crushed into the custard?'

Sanjana frowned. 'But why? It was a minor disagreement. Hardly a motive for murder! Besides, how could he be sure Papa would eat it? Anyone in the house could've had it, no?'

'I don't know,' Radhi admitted. 'But he's on that call log. *And* the custard came from his house. Both happened on the day that Uncle died . . . That's two good reasons to talk to him.'

CHAPTER 9

'Sanjana?' Manjula entered the room with a slight knock. 'What time does Jayesh's flight land tonight, *beta*?' She walked towards the bed and sat down beside Sanjana. 'I'll ask Ranjan or Amit to go fetch him from the airport.'

Sanjana shook her head. 'No, Mummy. Don't bother them. They have enough going on as it is. I've already asked the driver to go.'

'That's good then.' Manjula lifted her feet up on the bed and leaned wearily against the headrest, her eyes drifting closed.

'Aunty, do you need any help tomorrow? I can come earlier if required.'

'You've been a great help already, *beta*.' Manjula opened her eyes briefly to look at Radhi. 'You're a very good friend to Sanjana.'

'She'd have done the same and more for me, Aunty. But I'm serious, if there are any errands to run, please don't hesitate to ask me.'

Manjula smiled gratefully. 'Well, not tomorrow . . . but on the day of the prayer meeting, I may need some help. I'll let you know.' Her eyes drifted closed again.

The three women were silent, each lost in their own thoughts. Finally, Sanjana murmured, 'Mummy, did you know?'

Manjula opened her eyes and stared uncomprehendingly at Sanjana.

'About Papa's financial problems?' Sanjana prompted. 'The losses?'

'Who told you?' She sat up. 'I told your brothers I didn't want you worried.'

'I need to understand why this happened, Mummy! Please just tell me.'

Manjula hesitated before shaking her head. 'No, I didn't.'

'How come? I mean there must have been some signs, surely? Papa must have said something or behaved differently?'

Manjula sighed. 'Well, he didn't contribute towards my Helping Hands charity event this year. Said all his money was tied up in an investment. I've been organizing this bazaar for seven years now. He knows it's important to me. I was a bit miffed. But we'd had a very sizable contribution from one of the new parents in my school, which really helped. So I didn't push him. It would've just led to another argument.'

'What about when he cancelled the Alaska cruise?'

'He booked that without consulting me in the first place! And do you know who he planned it with? Naina Aunty and Nilesh Uncle . . . when he knew that I don't enjoy their company one bit. And that wasn't all. The dates he chose coincided with my annual bridge tournament. You know the one I play with Asha Aunty and the Ghadiyali sisters?'

Sanjana nodded.

'I was just glad when he decided to cancel it! Didn't ask too many questions. Honestly, I didn't even think about it much.'

There was a soft knock on the door. Ranjan poked his head into the room.

'Mummy, Parul and Lata Aunty are here to see you.'

'Sit with them, please,' Manjula instructed. 'I'll be there in a few minutes.'

She waited for Ranjan to leave, then turning to Sanjana again, said sadly, 'Look, *beta*, I wish more than anything that he hadn't died like this. Even more painful than losing him is the thought of how desperate he must have been. I wish he'd talked to me. I wish I'd been more accessible. Available, both physically and emotionally. But the truth was, we were leading parallel lives.

'He wasn't the "sharing" type and I was too proud to pry. I didn't look too deeply into his motives. I didn't want to. A few months ago, for instance, he didn't pay the EMI on the loan we took when we bought the Khandala farmhouse. He said he'd lent money to someone and was waiting for them to pay him back. He asked me if I could cover it this time. And I did. I didn't ask any questions. I just wanted to avoid confrontation with him. It was just too taxing for both of us. But how I wish now that I had dug deeper.'

Manjula was crying now, her tears falling freely for everything that should have been. This was such a rare display of emotion that Radhi felt uncomfortable witnessing it.

Sanjana hugged the older woman. 'Ssh, Mummy . . . don't cry.'

Feeling she should do something, Radhi rose from her perch on the bed. 'I'll go get some water for Aunty.'

'No . . . no . . . don't bother please. I'm okay.'

Manjula pulled away from Sanjana, wiping her face with the end of her sari's pallu. She got up from the bed and stood in front of her dressing table, looking in the mirror. She took a deep breath and tucked away a few stray strands of hair that had come undone from her bun. She pulled a tissue from the box on the table and began to dab away at the smudged *kajal* under her eyes.

When she looked like herself again, she turned back to Sanjana, reaching down to lay a hand on the younger woman's arm. 'Don't worry about me, okay? You just need to look after yourself right now.' Then with a final pat on Sanjana's arm, she left the room to see to her visitors.

'We should've just told her, Radhi!' Sanjana burst out when the door had closed. 'She is just blaming herself! Poor thing! We can tell her what we suspect, can't we?'

'Not right now, Sanjana. Please.' Radhi was alarmed at the chaos such a declaration could unleash. 'We can't say the word "murder" just yet. We literally have no proof!'

Sanjana sighed unhappily.

Radhi rushed on. 'Let me first call all the phone numbers we've noted. I'll go back home to do that . . . and I'll call you if I learn anything. OK?'

Sanjana nodded, her reluctance obvious.

Radhi got up from the bed. 'I'll see you tomorrow. Rest up.'

* * *

Radhi enjoyed coming home to her apartment that evening. The workers who'd been setting up the furniture had all left. And Lila had taken the evening off to spend some time with her son. After the bustle of the day, the apartment was quiet and restful. Radhi opened her new curtains, cream with a cheerful pattern of green parrots and borage blossoms, and let in the pink light of the evening sun. She'd been craving a cigarette all morning. She riffled around her handbag and produced a pack of Four Squares and her lighter, decorated with a golden phoenix. It was Mackinzey's and was the one thing she hadn't been able to let go of. She lit her cigarette and inhaled deeply.

As the warmth of the smoke spread through her chest, she felt calmer and realized she was hungry. In all the shuffling between the Kadakias' home and her own, she'd missed lunch.

Radhi wandered into the kitchen, hoping Lila had cooked even though she hadn't given her any instructions. The counter was sparkling clean and devoid of a single pot or pan or any sign that any cooking had been done.

'Serves me right.'

She opened the refrigerator, thinking that she'd have a bowl of cereal and milk instead, but was pleasantly surprised to see three glass containers of food, stacked one on top of the other. She pulled them out, laying them on the counter, then rifled through the cupboards and drawers to get a plate and some cutlery. Finally, she served herself some yellow lentil dal, brown rice and a creamy vegetable dish, made from cashew paste and paneer. She microwaved it all, then carried the hot food out to the sofa, where she sat, demolishing her meal in a span of mere minutes, thinking fondly of Lila as she did so. 'God bless her soul!'

Looking about the room, she realized she needed to buy a new TV. She'd have loved to watch an episode of *Monk* with her meal. She enjoyed puzzling out the clever little mysteries alongside the eccentric American detective, played so brilliantly by Tony Shaloub. The old TV had worked but was over two decades old, so Radhi had told Lila to sell it off to a scrap dealer. Lila had asked if she could take it home instead for her son, and it was only then that Radhi realized that Lila didn't own a TV. She resolved to be more mindful in the future and to take over the boy's school- and tuition-related expenses. She would've done more and sooner, but Lila took pride in being self-sufficient and caring for her son single-handedly. Radhi knew that whatever extra help she provided her friend would have to be done gradually and with tact.

She scrolled through the Amazon app on her phone, browsing through TV models, but was overwhelmed by the level of choice. When it came to technology, her understanding was limited and her interest even more so. Usually her modus operandi would have been to pick the most expensive product on offer — her theory being that the more advanced the tech, the more it should cost. Then she thought of Hrishi and, on an impulse, she texted her friend.

What's a good TV to get?

Tell you over chai, tomorrow? he texted back a few minutes later. *4.15 p.m. Blue Beard Café, Worli?*

Yes, she typed back. Radhi smiled at the prospect of meeting her old friend.

Her phone pinged again. It was an email from her agent, George, asking her how she was doing. Radhika felt guilty for having absconded so completely. He'd been a good friend to her and deserved a proper explanation. She hated typing on her phone, so she went to her room and got out her laptop to access email.

She didn't have any answers to the questions he had asked in his previous messages.

How's your writing going?

What are you working on?

Are you interested in editing an anthology of short stories for women writers living in foreign countries?

Have you written anything of late?

Can I please have a look at it?

A paragraph, a page, anything at all?

But Radhi didn't have answers to any of these questions. Or at least none that he might appreciate. But she could definitely answer 'How have you been?' So she did.

In the end, she penned a long email telling George how the move back had been so far. The big welcome-home dinner party, the move to the old apartment and Mr Kadakia's death. She told her agent everything about it, including her suspicions about how Kirti Uncle had died.

> *. . . Honestly, George, such things just don't happen on Temple Hill. So it's all the more unpalatable. It's not like there's zero crime here, but it's rarely the violent kind. Most of the Gujaratis on Temple Hill are Jain, like me. A fairly prosperous and peace-loving people — among India's richest, in fact. You've probably heard of Jainism in the context of Gandhi? The religion that advocates a non-violent way of life? In any case, that's not to say that everyone here's a saint. No, far from it. The Jains are primarily a thriving business community, which means, there's enough money-laundering, tax-evasion, bribery, stock manipulation . . . that sort of thing always going on. But murder? These people shy away from hurting a fly! The entire idea is absurd. And yet, it's the only one that makes sense. But the question is who would do such a thing? And why? . . .*

When she'd sent off the email, she felt strangely buoyant. The mere act of writing anything after such a long time had felt wonderful. Albeit it was an email and yet, stringing together those two thousand words one after the other had felt therapeutic.

Rummaging through her handbag, she brought out a cream diary with golden polka dots. Typically, she'd have used it for new story ideas or snippets of conversations she'd overheard and wanted to use in one of her books. Yet in spite of being lugged around everywhere for a whole year, this diary was completely blank.

At the top of the first page, she wrote: Kirti Kadakia. Below it, she copied the names and numbers from all his calls and thought about what she would say when she called them.

9.50 a.m. — outgoing Sanjana (2 mins)
10.07 a.m. — Hemendra bhai (missed call)
10.08 a.m. — incoming unknown landline (missed call)
10.10 a.m. — outgoing Vinod Shah (13 mins)
10.24 a.m. — outgoing Ranjan (10 mins, 25 secs)
10.43 a.m. — K. Poddar (20 secs)
11.00 a.m. — incoming — same as 10.08 (50 secs)
12.30 p.m. — incoming unknown (27 secs)
1.10 p.m. — incoming Manjula Aunty (32 secs)

She dialled the first number. Hemendra *bhai* picked up after two short rings. His voice was coarse and middle-aged.

'Hello,' Radhi said. 'Is that Hemendra *bhai*? My name is Radhika and I'm calling on behalf of Kirti Kadakia—'

'Where the hell *is* Kadakia?' The voice erupted at the other end. 'On Wednesday, he told me he'll send me my money and now he's absconding! Switched off his bloody phone also! You can't trust anyone these days! You tell him to call me himself, this minute!'

Radhi decided not to say anything about Kirti Uncle's death just yet. Instead she asked, 'I'm sorry, but what money is this?'

The voice at the other end went ballistic. 'What do you mean, what money? Is this some sort of joke? Who are you, again? I'm talking about the fifteen lacs he borrowed from me, of course! He was supposed to send me the interest, two lacs! But what did I receive? Nothing! Zilch! *Thenga*!'

'Hemendra *bhai*,' Radhika said quietly, waiting for him to calm down slightly before she continued. 'Mr Kadakia passed away on Wednesday afternoon. The funeral is tomorrow morning.'

There was a shocked silence. Radhika waited patiently while the other man processed the information.

'He's d-dead?' He sounded stunned.

'Yes. They're taking the body to the crematorium at 7 a.m. tomorrow.'

'And my mon . . .' He trailed off into embarrassed silence.

'What's that?'

'No. Nothing. I'll be there. I have his address.' He ended the call.

Radhi put the phone down contemplatively. So, Kirti Uncle had been in debt. She wondered if Hemendra *bhai* was the only one. Who else might he have borrowed from and could that have anything to do with his death?

She crossed Hemendra *bhai*'s name off her list and dialled the next down, the incoming unknown number.

Again the phone was picked up almost instantly, the voice at the other end familiar.

'Uhm . . . Hemendra *bhai*?' Radhi asked uncertainly.

'Yes, madam.'

'Oh, sorry . . . I didn't realize this was also your number,' Radhi murmured and hung up.

It seemed that when Kirti Uncle had failed to answer his call, Hemendra *bhai* had tried again from a different landline number, in the hope that he'd answer. Radhi wondered whether Mr Kadakia had genuinely missed both the calls or avoided them on purpose. She cancelled the number and called Vinod Shah, the next name in the list. Kirti Uncle's broker already knew about his death, so Radhi had lost the element of surprise. But still, she felt she might be able to learn something by speaking to him.

'Hello, Vinod *bhai*?' Radhi asked when he answered his phone.

'*Ji*,' he confirmed.

'My name is Radhika Zaveri and I'm calling on behalf of Mr Kadakia.'

'What's this regarding?' He already sounded like he was on his guard.

'I'm a friend of Sanjana's, actually. She's been very upset about her father's death and we were wondering if you could tell us anything that might help her understand his actions.'

'Sorry, madam. I'm not at liberty to discuss my clients and their business with strangers. I've already told his son whatever he wanted to know.' Without waiting for an answer, he said, 'Goodbye,' and hung up.

Radhi frowned, then circled his name on the list in front of her. She didn't blame Vinod *bhai* for being reluctant to talk to her. He would probably attend the final rites the next day, but she doubted she'd get a chance to talk to him then. She would just have to find another opportunity.

The next two names were those of Ranjan and Mr Poddar. Radhi wondered if she could simply go down to the third floor and talk to Mr Poddar, instead of calling him. Doing this in person might be a little less awkward.

She checked her watch. 8.30 p.m. She decided to try her luck.

CHAPTER 10

Radhika was surprised to see the Poddars' main door. It looked old and rundown, its once-beige veneer now discoloured to a dirty grey, the paint on the wall around it cracking and peeling off. The golden coating on the steel bars of the grilled safety window had chipped off, exposing rusted metal. The letter "H" was missing from the "KAUSHAL PODDAR" of the nameplate. You could see its faint outline still on the door.

Radhi wondered at this state of affairs. Once upon a time, the Poddars had been known to have the best cars in the building. When Ford launched the stylishly long Escort, the Poddars were the first to get it, and all the boys in the building had asked to be taken for a ride. The Poddars were one of the two Marwari families in the otherwise all-Gujarati building. The Aggarwals were the other. Both used to have thriving steel factories and were often in competition with each other. But while the Aggarwals had got into export and established a robust business in Africa, the Poddars, it seemed, hadn't fared so well.

Radhi rang the doorbell. She could hear the sound of the gameshow *Kaun Banega Crorepati* playing on the TV in the living room. The door was opened by a young maid.

'Is Kaushal Uncle here?' Radhi enquired.

'Who is it, Tarika?' Mrs Poddar's familiar voice carried out to them from the living room.

'Radhika Zaveri,' Radhi told the maid, helpfully adding, 'From the seventh floor.'

The girl disappeared for a few moments and then Mrs Poddar came to the door, peering out short-sightedly, an uncertain smile on her face.

'Oh, it *is* you,' she exclaimed, when she saw Radhika. 'Come in. Come in . . . haven't seen you in years!'

'How are you, Aunty?' Radhi removed her slip-ons at the door before entering the Poddar home.

'All well, dear, with God's grace.'

Even though it wasn't late, Mrs Poddar was already in a nightie. A modest, loose garment with a blue paisley pattern and a large, frilly collar buttoned right up to the neck. A small, neat woman with meticulously dyed black hair, she had an ever-ready smile.

'Is Uncle home?'

'He's gone for a haircut but should be back any minute now. Can I help?' Her expression was curious, as she led Radhi down a short passage into the living room.

The room was neat and orderly but a stark contrast to how Radhi remembered it. The velvet four-seater sofa, which had once been a bright crimson colour, was now threadbare, its seats worn down to a dull maroon. The TV was an old 90s model. There was a hole in the false ceiling where the chandelier used to hang. And there was a big patch of wall by the window that had been damaged through leakage, where ugly bubbles had formed on the peeling plaster.

Mrs Poddar smiled self-consciously. 'A little different than how you remember it, I suppose.'

Radhi was embarrassed. She hadn't meant to stare. 'I was just thinking about how much fun we used to have at Nehal's birthday parties.' The Poddars' daughter was a couple of years older than Radhi and Sanjana. Her birthday party, each year, had been so lavish that any kid who missed out felt they'd missed the event of the year.

'Yes, those were nice, weren't they?' Mrs Poddar seemed pleased that Radhi had remembered. 'We loved having all you children over. Now, of course, people just book a hall and let a professional MC handle everything. But in those days, for you children, all the food was homemade. I used to call the *maharaj* from Savour,' she said, referring to the chef of the most popular vegetarian restaurant in town, 'and have him make all the items on the menu. But all you kids were just interested in two things. The cheese nachos and—'

'The chocolate fudge brownie with vanilla ice cream,' Radhi finished for her, grinning.

Mrs Poddar laughed delightedly but then a shadow fell across her face.

'Now, things are different. Nehal lives in Australia with her husband and children. They visit once every two or three years, but other than that it's just Uncle and me. I've told him so many times that we should sell this apartment and move to a smaller place. What use are four bedrooms to us now? It is difficult to maintain this place. And we don't have the kind of staff we once had . . . we don't need to . . . Tarika here is enough to cook and clean for us.' She glanced at the young woman who'd just brought a glass of water on a tray.

'Of course.'

'But look at me rambling on about myself . . . how have you been and what is it that you wanted to see Uncle about?'

Radhi was just about to explain the reason for her visit when the doorbell rang. A few seconds later, Mr Poddar walked into the living room, a plastic bag of bananas in his hand.

Radhi got up, greeting him with a small smile. 'How are you, Uncle?'

He smiled back with the polite expression of people who know they're looking at a familiar face but can't place it.

'*Aare*, this is Radhika. You forget? Sameer Zaveri's daughter from the seventh floor,' said Mrs Poddar.

Mr Poddar's face immediately cleared. He smiled at Radhi in recognition, but he was still awkward. He had known her as a young girl and now she was a grown woman. For a few brief seconds he seemed unsure of how to behave towards her. In an off-white *kurta* and pyjama, which might have been white at one point, he seemed to have shrunk with age, a mere shadow of the man with the big booming laugh that Radhi remembered. His hair was oiled and dyed a shade of soot black. He seemed to have done the job himself, because the dye had dripped over his hairline and stained the edges of his forehead.

'Of course, sit, sit! It's been what, a decade? How have you been?'

'What'll you have, Radhika? Tea? Coffee? Something cold?' Mrs Poddar interrupted before Radhi could answer.

'Nothing, Aunty, I've just eaten dinner. Please don't bother.'

'What bother-*shother*. It's nothing. I'm sending you some pink rose milk.' She bustled away to the kitchen.

Radhi turned her attention to Mr Poddar. 'I've been well, Uncle. Can't complain. Sorry to drop in like this, at this hour, but—'

'Please, this is not your America,' interrupted Mr Poddar. 'In India, it is exactly what neighbours do. They drop in, unannounced. You seem to have forgotten. You youngsters go abroad to study and become so formal. I tell Nehal also to be careful about how she is raising her kids. All this "thank-you" and "excuse-me" is all very well, as long as it doesn't interfere with the closeness of relationships. You know?'

Radhi smiled in agreement and hurried to continue before they got distracted again. 'Uncle, as you might know, you were one of the last people Kirti Uncle spoke to before he . . . passed away.'

The smile on Mr Poddar's face faltered when he heard Mr Kadakia's name. 'Oh . . . I didn't realize.'

'Sanjana has been very upset, as you can imagine. She is just trying to understand his frame of mind that morning. And we were wondering what it was you spoke about?'

'Hmm . . . let's see, let's see . . .' He removed a large handkerchief from the pocket of his *kurta* and began to wipe his forehead.

'*Tarika*! Could you switch on the AC here!' he called out.

'The AC hasn't worked in two months!' Mrs Poddar called back from the kitchen.

'Then ask her to open the windows in here, please!'

Tarika came out of the kitchen bearing a tray with two glasses of rose milk with black basil seeds floating in them. She offered a glass to Radhi who accepted it with a smile.

Radhi waited until she had opened the windows of the living room and gone back to the kitchen, before continuing. 'He didn't call too many people that day. How did he sound to you? Normal? Worried?'

Mr Poddar's eyes widened a little. 'Call? . . . Yes, it was just a regular call . . . about Sea Mist Society business mainly. The Bhatias on the first floor have applied for an extra parking spot and so have the Parekhs on the same floor. The Bhatias applied first, but they already have two spots while the Parekhs have only one. So we were wondering who we should allot it to . . .

'What else? . . . Oh yes, the annual general body meeting is coming up next month, so we made a list of items to be discussed that day. You see all the Society members need to be informed beforehand, about the meeting's agenda. It must be here somewhere.' He rifled through a file on the table in front of him. 'Aah, here.' Removing a paper, he handed it over to Radhika, who gave it a quick once over before handing it back.

'So that was it?'

'Yes . . . he sounded completely normal. In fact, we even discussed Modi's last speech in the Parliament and how we both thought the BJP would definitely get re-elected.' Mr Poddar fell silent, thinking back to his last interaction with the dead man.

Radhi took a sip of the rose-flavoured milk. It had three times the sugar it needed. But not finishing it was out of the question. She took two large gulps and swallowed.

Mr Poddar shook his head. 'Who'd have thought he'd kill himself soon after.'

'And the custard? He must've thanked you for it?'

Mr Poddar looked at Radhi blankly.

'Didn't Aunty send custard to the Kadakias that morning?' asked Radhi.

'Of course!' he said, as if suddenly remembering. 'Oh yes! He loved it.'

Radhi smiled. 'Okay, thank you, Uncle, for taking the time to talk to me. It will mean a lot to the family.'

He smiled freely for the first time. 'Again this thank you-*shank you*? What did I say? These formalities are not for our people. I'm just glad I was able to be of help.'

Radhi rose to her feet, her mind working furiously — she'd just realized something important. She said her goodbyes to Mr Poddar quickly and promised Mrs Poddar that she would drop by again soon.

Back on the seventh floor, she hurried to the sofa and opened her polka-dot diary to the page with the list of the people Mr Kadakia had spoken to on the day of his death. What she saw there confirmed her suspicions. She called Sanjana, intending to tell her what she'd learned, but didn't get an answer. It would have to wait until tomorrow.

Radhi picked up the diary again. There was still one more unknown number on her list. She tried calling it, but it went unanswered. Checking her watch, she saw it was 9 p.m. She circled the number and decided to try it again the following day. Then turning to a fresh page, she began to write an account of her visit to the Poddars' home. She described in detail her conversations with Mr and Mrs Poddar, ending her writing with the big question that she'd returned home with.

It was all so strange and troubling.

CHAPTER 11

Mr Poddar was in bed watching the late-night show with Kapil Sharma and laughing in sync with the laughter track. Beside him, Mrs Poddar's lips moved quickly and silently as she read from a thick little book of religious scripture, which she'd promised her God she'd read one-hundred and eight times in exchange for a little help with their problems. She'd read it twenty-six times so far but already the words had had a powerful effect. She glanced at her husband, slapping his thigh in response to something hilarious the comedian had just said, and smiled.

He noticed her looking at him. 'What?'

'Nothing. It is good to see you so relaxed for a change. God has finally started listening to my prayers again.'

'Come now, you can't possibly give your God credit for this.'

'*Aare*, who else? I admit you've been rather clever. But you're just His agent, you know that, right?'

Mr Poddar switched off the television and turned to face his wife. 'Is that right? So the next time you make carrot halwa at home, you had better not hover around the table waiting for compliments. I will be saying my thanks directly to God.'

'Never mind. Please forget I said anything. You can be so literal sometimes!' Mrs Poddar shut her book and placed it on the side table with an irritated thump. Then realizing that it was a book of God, she lifted it and touched it to her forehead thrice, murmuring an apology.

'That's convenient. But you know what religion has essentially done? Absolved people of responsibility. Everything can't be blamed on God. My business, when it failed, happened because of my own foolishness. I should have stuck to manufacturing and not tried to enter local retail — a market I knew nothing about. Everyone advised me against it, but I didn't listen. That can't possibly be God's fault, no?'

'Oh God! You and your philosophising!'

'See again you're bringing God into it!' Mr Poddar chuckled. Then seeing his wife's infuriated expression, he added, 'OK, listen, listen. I want you to plan a nice dinner party soon. Like one of our old ones. You can invite whoever you like from the building. Say next month, once this whole Kadakia business is forgotten. Would you like that?'

Mrs Poddar opened her mouth to say something and then shut it again. But her husband knew what she was feeling. He knew what his own failures had cost his wife. He hadn't realized it at first. Initially, when his business failed, he had believed they could spend the rest of their lives on their savings. They had this house, their daughter was married and well settled, and they didn't have any other responsibilities. They had downsized their staff to two full-timers, then to one full-timer, sold two of three cars and one of two garages, and decided to live well but simply. How foolish they'd been! He'd forgotten that this was Temple Hill. Here, living simply came with a cost of its own.

It hadn't been immediate or even very apparent in the beginning. At first, he told his wife she was imagining it. The slights. When the Bhatias on the first floor didn't invite them to their grandson's head-shaving ceremony, he'd told his wife they probably wanted it to be a small, intimate affair. When the Kajarias in the B Wing sent them a regular box of sweets instead of their usual over-the-top Diwali hamper, he told her it was a good thing for their diabetes. They had to give away more than half the hamper to the servants anyway. But slowly, the dinner invitations had dwindled, and the watchman had stopped jumping up to open the door of their car, and eventually they had realized what a terrible thing it was to live on Temple Hill but not have the means to support a life on it.

'What do you say?' he asked Mrs Poddar again. 'You can hire the chef from that new Italian food restaurant your friends were talking about. And you can even make a few changes to the living room furniture. How about it?'

Mrs Poddar nodded happily, her eyes shining with tears. Smiling, Mr Poddar pressed her hand and shut off the television and the lights.

In the darkness, he reached out for his bottle of sleeping pills. But a moment later, he put the bottle back again. These pills had literally saved his life. Even his wife didn't realize just how much he'd relied on them. He decided to save the few he had left for a night he actually needed them. Tonight he felt a lightness he hadn't experienced in years. His luck was going to turn again. He could feel it in his bones.

* * *

Radhi was in bed toying with her bottle of sleeping pills, trying to decide if she should take one tonight. They'd last her only for a few nights more.

She knew she'd have to go off her sedatives at some point. But she wasn't ready. No sleeping pills meant she'd wake up in the middle of the night and the anxiety, which she kept at bay during her waking hours, would spring on her like some depraved predator. In the dark, its assault would be fierce, ruthless and accurate. Every thought, doubt or worry that lay submerged in her subconscious would float up to the surface, surrounding her, closing in on her like a dreadful vortex of fears. Her chest tight, filled with dread, she would no longer be able to lie down. She would either pace in the apartment or curl up with a book on the living room sofa and there, hopefully, if she were lucky, she'd be able to fall asleep again.

No, she needed her sedatives. She doubted Dr Bihari would give her any more. She'd either have to find a new physician or take an appointment with the therapist Dr Bihari had recommended.

* * *

The next day, Radhi was down in the building lobby by 6.45 a.m. Relatives and friends of the Kadakias had already started arriving. Mr Kadakia's body had been laid out on a bier in the centre of the lobby, covered to the neck with a white sheet and a grey shawl. There was a smear of sandalwood paste on his forehead and a garland of sandalwood flowers around his neck. The Jains didn't use natural flowers during funerals. They believed that flowers were living beings with souls of their own, and it was their duty to spare every life form to the fullest extent possible. A large swastika of white rice had been made on a low table placed next to the body. The four arms of the swastika symbolized the four states of existence: *deva* (demi-gods), *manusy*a (humans), *naraki* (hell-beings) and *tiryanca* (animals, plants and microorganisms.) The Jains believed that a person's karma, their actions in their current life, determined what state of existence they would be granted in their next birth.

Upon the swastika, there was a whole coconut and a lamp filled to the brim with oil, which would be kept burning until the body was cremated. There was also a cluster of incense sticks, which burned gently in one corner, purifying the environment with the fragrance of plumerias. Mr Kadakia's eyes had been shut and a white flower had been put inside his half-open mouth. The lobby was filled with women clad in white, except Manjula, who, as the widow, was the only one allowed to wear colour that day. The men, also all in white, were standing in the compound outside the lobby. They would accompany the body to the crematorium and stay there till the body had been completely burned to ashes. After which, they'd go to their respective homes, where they'd be required to take a cleansing bath before they could touch anything else in the house.

Sanjana was standing next to Manjula's chair at the front of the lobby. Radhi slowly began to make her way towards her. Most of the building's residents were present, and Radhi recognized and acknowledged several women as she passed them. Mrs Poddar and Mrs Maniar were standing together alongside Mrs Bhatia and her daughter-in-law from the first floor. Mrs Maniar gave Radhi a broad smile, which given the sombre occasion, Radhi acknowledged only with an awkward nod.

Sonal was standing next to Hetal, their heads bent together, talking softly. Nobody was crying much. Sanjana's tears seemed to have all been spent. She now just looked tired.

Mrs Kadakia sat calm and composed, her gaze fixed at a point above her husband's head. It wasn't surprising that she wasn't crying. On her, any open display of grief would have unsettled people.

'Hi,' Radhi greeted Sanjana softly. She got a small, sad smile in return.

Radhi glanced over to where the men stood and found Mr Poddar looking at her contemplatively. When their eyes met, he immediately rearranged his features into a smile, before turning away. Radhi looked to where Amit and Ranjan were standing, along with other close members of the family. Amit had his arms folded across his chest and seemed to be listening to the pundit explaining the significance of the rituals that would follow. As Mr Kadakia's eldest son, he would be the one to light the pyre. Ranjan was talking seriously and at length with one of the visitors.

'Who is that?' Radhi asked Sanjana.

Sanjana following her gaze. 'Vinod *bhai*.'

Mr Kadakia's broker was a short, tubby man. A tuft of white hair bordered his otherwise bald scalp.

'I want to speak with him . . . He didn't say much on the phone last evening.'

'You spoke to everyone, then?' Sanjana seemed surprised.

'Most of them.'

'And?'

Just then someone announced that it was time for the final rites. One after the other, all of Mr Kadakia's family members, immediate and extended, took three circles around his body, each chanting the powerful Jain Navkar Mantra as they put a garland of sandalwood flowers on him to bid him goodbye.

Finally, the male members of his family stepped forward. Both his sons took the front two ends of the stretcher on which he lay, while Jayesh and another relative picked up the two ends at the back. Then invoking the name of God, the four men picked up the stretcher and began to walk towards the gate of the building, while all the other men followed them. The procession would walk only for a few minutes, after which the body would be transferred to the ambulance waiting outside the building. Everyone else would go to their own cars, reaching the crematorium in time to receive the body when it got there.

Once the men had left, the women began to disperse. Close relatives and friends would go home for their baths and come back to the Kadakia house to have a meal with them.

As the women began to leave, Radhi told Sanjana softly, 'Stay a minute.'

'Sanjana?' Manjula murmured. 'Are you going home for a bath?'

'Yes, Mummy. I'll come by in half an hour.'

Manjula nodded. She patted Radhi's arm as she passed, and Radhi gave her a small smile.

When the two young women were alone, save the security guard fiddling with his phone at the other end of the lobby, Radhi turned to Sanjana and recounted Mr Poddar's conversation with her father.

'So Papa seemed completely normal, then?'

'We don't know that for sure . . . but what we do know is that Mr Poddar was lying.'

Sanjana seemed startled by Radhi's comment.

'They couldn't possibly have spoken about the parking issue, the agenda for the committee meeting, the general elections *and* Modi's speech. Not when their call lasted just twenty seconds.'

Sanjana's eyes widened as Radhi continued, 'Besides, when I asked him, he said Kirti Uncle thanked him for the custard. Which is also impossible since the custard came almost an hour *after* the call.'

'That is so strange,' Sanjana mused. 'Why in the world would he lie?'

'That's what I've been wondering.'

The friends parted after agreeing to meet back at the Kadakias' home in an hour. Sanjana went to her wing, but Radhika didn't go straight home. She'd been meaning to check the security guard's register for the day of Mr Kadakia's death.

The guard was a young fellow with barely any facial hair. When Radhi approached him, he got up and stood to attention smartly.

'May I?' Radhi pointed to the register with a smile.

The guard blushed fiercely and slid the register towards her. Radhi picked it up and quickly turned to Wednesday.

The book logged all visitors to the building and the time they entered and left. This included guests, servants and drivers, as well as other assorted vendors like the milkman, the vegetable seller, the coconut wallah, the dhobi, the old woman who delivered fresh pooja flowers to the Society each day, and the various couriers who fed and nurtured the online shopping addicts in practically every apartment. What it did not have was a record of the goings and comings of all the residents, nor the live-in domestic staff, who had their own ID cards and did not need to use the register.

While understandable, from Radhi's point of view, it was not very helpful. There were no out-of-the-ordinary guests to the Kadakia home that day. One entry, however, did catch her eye. She was surprised that she hadn't thought of it before. She made a mental note to follow up on it.

'What's your name?' she asked the young guard as she slid the register back.

'Prashant, madam.'

'Your handwriting is very neat.'

'Thank you, madam.' He blushed furiously again.

'Were you on duty all of this week?'

The guard nodded.

'Every day?'

'Yes'

'You were at your desk from—?'

'9 a.m. to 7 p.m . . . Except when I went to the bathroom.'

'What about a tea break? Lunch?'

'I have both at my desk.'

'So you probably saw everyone who came this week?'

'Yes. Unless they entered from the terrace entrance.'

'The terrace?' Radhika was surprised. 'I thought that was always kept locked.'

'They opened up the connecting terrace between both the buildings on this Tuesday because the lifts were getting serviced — if the A Wing lift is being serviced, residents can use the B Wing lift, go up to the top floor and enter A Wing from the terrace. And vice versa.'

'So the terrace is open right now?'

'No, they locked it again yesterday. Usually they close it off on the same day. But Doshi Sir on the top floor was getting some waterproofing work done on the terrace before the rains, so it was kept open till now.'

'Does anyone from security sit at the terrace entrance?' Radhi guessed the answer even before the young man replied.

'There is no need to, madam. Either they enter the building from here, where I make the entries, or from the B Wing entrance, in which case Shukla*ji* makes the entries. There is no other way to reach the terrace.'

The guard was looking at her curiously, probably wondering what she was after. Radhi realized that if she asked any more questions, she'd need some sort of cover or else the guard might find it strange.

'Thank you, Prashant. You've been most helpful.'

'No problem, madam.' The young guard looked visibly gratified, his chest puffing out in an effort to stand up even straighter.

The open terrace entrance had opened up a whole new set of possibilities for Radhi. She decided to go over to Sanjana's side of the building to check the visitors' register there.

When she reached the B Wing, Radhika smiled at the old security guard manning the entrance.

'Chaacha, could I see your register please?'

Unlike the younger security guard, the older man had been at this job for decades. He didn't bother hiding his curiosity. 'What happened, baby? What do you need to see? You can just ask me. It'll be easier.'

'I had ordered a parcel which I haven't received, but the courier company insists it has been delivered. I am wondering if there has been some mix-up,' Radhi improvised. 'Do you record all visitors to the building?'

'Yes, of course.' He handed her the register.

Radhi turned away, pretending that she needed more light to see clearly, then turned the page to Wednesday. She had to be careful not to pique the curiosity of the guards. The last thing she wanted was word to get around that she was asking questions about the day Kirti Uncle had died.

The names and entries were written in Hindi, and Radhi went over them one by one, until she reached 12.30 p.m. when she stopped short.

There, unmistakably, in a shaky yet legible hand was a name that had no business being there in the middle of the day.

Ranjan Kadakia.

Radhi struggled to contain her shock. What was Ranjan doing back at Sea Mist in the middle of the day? And why in the B Wing? Was it possible that it was some other Ranjan altogether? She was dying to ask the guard, but he was looking at her inquisitively. She had to stick to her story about the missing parcel or risk unnecessary gossip. Quickly she finished scanning the rest of the page. And the page after that. But did not find what she was looking for. There was no entry for when Ranjan had left the building. She knew that he had come home around 4 p.m., when his mother had called him. So where had he been until then? Her mind was buzzing with questions. She contemplated going to Sanjana's house but decided against it. She was still in her funeral clothes and needed to have a bath. And think.

CHAPTER 12

'Nice.' Radhi took a bite of Lila's *makai-poha*, a flattened rice and corn dish seasoned liberally with lemon.

Lila beamed.

Radhi had finished her bath and was eating her breakfast, before heading to the Kadakias' house. Eating regular meals had done wonders for the recurring burning in her stomach. She was feeling better than she had in days.

'*Didi*, the cartons are coming today, no?' Lila asked Radhi.

'Yes.' Her books.

'Can I open them and start arranging the books on the shelves?'

Radhi knew that Lila was getting bored. Now that they were settled in, there was hardly any work to do. But she wanted to arrange her books herself.

'How about you make me some *khandvi* instead? I haven't had any for years! Here, I am forwarding the recipe to you. It's a YouTube video, in Hindi . . . There . . . did you get it?'

Lila nodded as she checked her phone.

Khandvi was a traditional Gujarati side dish made with chickpea flour, yogurt and lots of skill. It required technique, experience and patience.

Lila looked happy. This seemed challenging.

* * *

When Radhi arrived at the Kadakias' apartment, the door was slightly ajar, so she walked in without ringing the bell. The living room was empty. Sanjana hadn't arrived yet, and everyone seemed to be off in their respective rooms. She walked towards the kitchen. She had a question for Bhawani and Kamal.

Bhawani was on his knees in the kitchen, hastily going through the contents of a small cupboard below the counter. Plastic bags, a couple of worn-out non-stick pans with the black coating missing, some paper plates, foil containers and plastic cutlery, were all lying strewn on the floor. His head was stuck so deep inside the cupboard that he didn't hear Radhi approach.

She stood observing his frantic movements for a few seconds, before calling softly, so as to not startle him, 'Bhawani?'

It didn't help. His reaction was immediate and unfortunate. He bumped his head hard on the cupboard's ceiling, then backed out gingerly, getting to his feet. He turned around scowling. When he saw who it was, his scowl deepened.

'Sorry, I didn't mean to surprise you.'

Bhawani just stood there, glaring at Radhi.

She continued, 'I just wanted to know if either you or Kamal opened the door to the vegetable seller on Wednesday?'

'Vegetable seller?' he repeated, surprised. 'Might've . . . I can't be sure.'

'Can you please try to remember?'

Bhawani paused to think for a moment. He seemed to be assessing the situation. Radhi could almost see the moment he made up his mind. Since the question was not about him, he figured he had nothing to lose by being helpful.

'No. He didn't come while I was here, or Kamal. She would've bought some carrots, since we were out of them.'

Radhi was pleased by his answer. 'Thank you, Bhawani. Just one more thing. The fruit custard. Did Kirti Uncle eat all of it, or was there any left?'

Bhawani's guard came up instantly. This was going in a different direction. 'He ate everything. Why?'

'No reason. Did you serve it to him with lunch or after that?'

'Before lunch.' His eyes narrowed, as if he were trying to understand what these questions were leading up to, as if afraid that it might be some sort of a trap.

'Manju *bhabhi* had prepared *aamras* for Kirti *bhai* which was to be served with lunch. So I gave him the custard earlier . . . but I don't know when he ate it . . . He sent me to the bank soon afterwards.'

'And when you came back—?'

'Look here, *didi*,' Bhawani interrupted, 'what's the meaning of all these questions? You are a friend of Sanjana *didi*, so I'm being respectful. But I don't like being grilled like this, time and again.'

Radhi decided to change tack. There was a famous saying in Gujarati which said that if you couldn't get the ghee out with a straight finger, you'd do well to bend the finger.

'Why are you so reluctant to answer questions, Bhawani? I bet if I ask Kamal the same things, she'll answer without hesitation. Sanjana told me that the family trusts you implicitly. But to an outsider like me, it seems like you have something to hide.'

Radhi was astonished to see how afraid Bhawani looked. She had expected him to either cooperate grudgingly or to be even more outraged. His fear was palpable.

'Did you need anything, Radhika?' a voice floated out from behind her.

Radhika started, turning to see who was there. Manjula stood at the door to the kitchen, her whole demeanour stiff with displeasure. Radhi had no idea how long she had been standing there or how much she'd heard.

'Uhm . . . no, Aunty . . . I was just trying to get a clearer picture about . . . the . . . that day—'

'Why?'

'It's just that Sanjana and I were talking . . . and the . . . whole thing is really bothering her—'

'And what is all this?' Manjula asked Bhawani, looking over Radhi's shoulder, noticing for the first time the contents of the small cupboard strewn on the floor.

Bhawani had completely forgotten what he'd been doing before Radhi's arrival.

'Uh . . . I was looking for the plastic spoons, we'll need them for lunch when everyone comes right now, no?'

He was clearly lying. There had been a huge bundle of plastic cutlery lying on the floor when Radhi had found Bhawani with his head stuck deep into the cupboard. But this was not the time to bring that up.

Manjula turned her attention back to Radhi. 'Look, *beta*.' She sighed, her voice thawing. 'As Sanjana's friend, you need to help her move past this. She's going to have a baby in less than four months. She needs to get into the right frame of mind . . . She can't be brooding about this.'

'Yes, Aunty . . . of course . . . you're right.'

Manjula patted Radhi's arm. Together, they walked back to the living room.

'What is Sanjana worried about anyway?'

Before Radhi could answer, Sonal entered, phone in hand.

'It's done . . . They're on their way back.' She was referring to Ranjan and Amit and the men who'd accompanied them to the cremation ground.

Manjula nodded. 'I'll tell Bhawani to get started.' And then addressing Radhi, she added, 'You'll remember what I said, okay?'

'Yes, Aunty.'

Radhi was relieved that she wasn't about to be grilled.

She waited until Manjula went back to the kitchen, then she said to Sonal, 'Hey, will you tell Sanjana that I'll be back in ten minutes? I just need to run home for something.'

* * *

Back home, Radhi asked Lila to pull up a chair, but Lila squatted on the floor. In spite of Radhi's numerous attempts to make her feel comfortable, Lila still didn't sit on any of the furniture. So, rolling her eyes, Radhi sat on the floor beside the woman. She'd had a mild epiphany. She was going to tap into the great servant's grapevine and enlist Lila's help to ask all the questions that she could not.

The servants' grapevine on Temple Hill was a force to reckon with. And not just because of its sheer numbers. Though between all the nannies, cooks, cleaners, guards, drivers and the live-in maids and man-Fridays, each building lodged a small army, it was the way that this army was invisibly entrenched in the lives of the employers that made it so powerful. The grapevine knew everything about everyone.

Who had a wedding in the family and when.

Who had out-of-station guests and from where.

Who ate chicken when the in-laws were travelling.

Who bought things from Crawford Market and passed them off as posh.

Who was having marital problems and why.

Who hid their alcohol stash inside the bedroom drawers.

Who was on a diet, and whether it was working.

Who was going on holiday and for how long.

Many helpers had worked with the same family for years, and their knowledge of their employers' affairs was as intimate as it was all-encompassing. But the trouble for Radhi was, they wouldn't talk to her. Not freely. The divide between them was too wide and too deeply ingrained. And their loyalty to each other often surpassed their commitment to their employers. She didn't blame them. They had to look out for each other.

'OK — *khandvi* cancelled. I have a different job for you. Three actually. First, do you think you could find out a little bit about Bhawani? Where he was employed before this? Who his friends are? What his reputation is like? Anything at all.'

Although Lila seemed surprised at the request, she nodded silently.

'Next, talk to the girl who works at the Poddars' house on the third floor. She is youngish, wears tight kurtas and applies lots of talc powder on her face . . . I think her name is Tarika—'

'I know who she is, *didi*,' Lila interrupted. 'But what do you need to know?'

'Any conversations she might've overheard . . . anything odd she might've noticed . . .'

Lila looked like she had many questions herself but, to her credit, she continued to hold her tongue. Radhi made a decision. In a few short sentences she told Lila what she suspected and why. Lila looked shocked.

'How come you're not going to the police, *didi*?'

'We will. Once we know enough.'

Lila nodded, then very matter-of-factly, 'I'll talk to Tarika . . . and don't worry, *didi*, she won't realize that I'm trying to find out things . . . It will be like our regular chatter.'

Radhi gave her a grim smile.

'There's one other thing, I need you to do . . .'

* * *

Back at the Kadakia home, the living room was filled with people in white. Radhika spotted Sanjana talking to a few cousins in a corner and decided not to disturb her. She walked towards the kitchen, hoping to find Bhawani again. She wanted to finish her conversation with him. She found Sonal instead, cutting up tomatoes on a chopping board.

'Oh hi.' Sonal greeted her with a startled smile. 'Did you need something?'

'I was actually looking for Bhawani.'

'Oh he's gone to pick up the food. We've only made the daal and rice at home. The rest of the meal, two sabzis, parathas, etc. will be coming from outside. There's this lady who specializes in traditional Gujarati food tiffins. We've tried her stuff before. It's fresh and tastes like home food.'

'That makes sense,' Radhi replied easily. 'This way all of you are free to spend some time with all the visitors.'

'Yeah, that's what Mummy said.' Sonal began busying herself with the tomatoes again.

Radhi observed the woman for a moment. 'Do you need any help with that?'

Sonal looked up with a smile. 'Not really, I'm just making this salad to keep myself busy. I, uh . . . I don't know too many people out there. Not well, anyway. I prefer being in here.'

Radhi smiled but didn't say anything. She knew that Sonal had been married for more than seven or eight years, long enough to have gotten to know the Kadakias' family and friends.

Sonal hurried on, blushing. 'Don't get me wrong. Everyone's perfectly nice and everything. It's just that I'm not from Temple Hill and they never forget it. It's hard to form genuine connections when everybody keeps you at arms' length.'

Sonal moved on to peeling cucumbers, while Radhi helped herself to a glass of water. Radhi knew that Temple Hill was not the most inclusive and warmest of places, but she'd never really witnessed its cliquishness herself. 'I didn't realize it was like that.'

'You know how it is, right? You guys all go way back. Whether you like each other or not, there's a lot of shared history. When you gossip, there's context. With your jokes, there's backstory. When you guys compare your favourite places that serve baklava, I need to google baklava! Honestly? I'm far too busy with my children and work to really care if I don't get invited to one of their bingo lunches. But yeah, social gatherings like these can be a bit of a drag.'

Even as Sonal said that, Radhi could tell that it wasn't the truth. A betraying bitterness had crept into the woman's voice — and whether she realized it or not, Radhi knew that being accepted on Temple Hill did matter to Sonal. It mattered very much.

She felt sorry for her, so she changed the subject. 'Where's work? Are you also in Fintech like Amit?'

'Not exactly. I work for XKC. It's an insurance company. We're based out of Andheri.'

'Gosh, that's a long commute every day! And the traffic, is it still as terrible?'

'Worse. Takes me more than an hour to get home every day! Luckily on the day that Papa passed away, I was in the area for meetings. Otherwise I'd never have been able to reach here in time when Amit called.'

'Radhi?' Sanjana's voice floated out to them, before she materialized at the door. 'I thought I saw you. Will you come with me?'

Radhi bid goodbye to Sonal, and together the two friends made their way to Manjula's room, where they stood at the open window.

'Listen, do you know where Ranjan was on Wednesday afternoon?' Radhi asked, as soon as the two of them were alone.

'Yes, with a patient. Why?' Sanjana seemed surprised.

'I saw a Ranjan Kadakia on the register of your building, that same afternoon. I was wondering if it was our Ranjan.'

'Yes, it must have been . . . He had an appointment with Mr Ganatra in my building. He's had a hip fracture from his fall in the bathroom. Ranjan has been making home visits for him these last couple of months.'

'And what about after his session? Did he go home? Or back to his clinic?'

'I think he said he went to the Gymkhana for a workout and then to the clinic . . . but why so many questions about Ranjan?'

Radhi paused, before answering, 'I didn't say anything earlier because I didn't want to worry you . . . but did you know that Ranjan had a massive fight with your dad, the day before he died? I checked with Hetal about it. She insists it was just an argument, nothing major. But I'm not sure I believe her. And now that I know Ranjan was in the building that afternoon . . . can we find out what the fight was about?'

'Radhi, please don't even go in that direction!' Sanjana sounded horrified. 'That's my brother we are talking about! Papa and Ranjan argued all the time! It's likely to have sounded like a big fight even though it may not have been because they were both loud and hot-headed. But what you're suspecting . . .' Sanjana shuddered. 'No. Never.'

Murder was an ugly word. And on leafy Temple Hill, with its little designer galleries and clued-up vegetable sellers who sold kale, bok choy and other imports, which the rest of Mumbai only saw on *Master Chef*, it was discordant. Unheard of. If Sanjana dared to say it aloud, it would unleash unmitigated chaos into the life of every single person in her family. Radhi doubted if her friend was prepared for it. Was anyone?

'Look, Sanju,' Radhi said gently, reverting to the name she'd used for her friend as kids, 'we don't need to ask these questions. The police have done their job and now, regardless of what we discover, Uncle is not coming back. You, on the other hand, have a baby on the way, and this brooding is not doing either of you any good. The deeper we dig into Kirti Uncle's relationships with his family, friends, neighbours and colleagues, the more doubts are likely to arise and the more uncomfortable things are going to get. So my question is, do you really want to go down this road? And more importantly, is it wise?'

Sanjana was quiet for some time. 'I do. I have to. For myself and my unborn child. How can I trust myself as a mother, if I fail as a daughter?' Her eyes filled up with tears but her voice remained strong.

Radhi searched her friend's face for any signs of weakness, but there were none. Sanjana seemed determined to get to the truth regardless of how unpalatable it was.

'OK,' Radhi said, finally. 'Then help me with these questions . . . One, how does one get access to such a large quantity of sedatives? Two, where was Bhawani employed before he came to work for your family? And finally, how long was Ranjan's appointment with Mr Ganatra? Why is there no entry of him leaving the building post his session? Is it possible that he used the terrace to go to the A Wing?'

'Ranjan's sessions usually last for about forty minutes. So he will probably have left by 2.15 p.m. or so. I can check with him if you like,' Sanjana offered. 'But please don't go by those entries. That old Shukla*ji* falls asleep most afternoons.' She was referring to the security guard in her building. 'I've seen him dozing often. But I didn't want to complain. Poor fellow would just lose his job.'

'So you are saying that Ranjan could've left and Shukla might not have even realized?'

'Oh, yes. It's entirely possible.'

Radhi and Sanjana gazed at the choppy grey waters of the sea. Dark clouds had begun to gather in the sky. It was going to rain soon.

'You know, it's the saddest thing,' Sanjana commented, after a while. 'Mummy and Ranjan were both in the building at the time this was happening.'

'Oh, I didn't realize Manju Aunty was here as well?'

'Yes. She had left work early to attend the *satsang* in the party hall on the ground floor. It happens every Wednesday or Thursday afternoon.'

'Oh!' Radhi was surprised. Manjula had never struck her as the religious type. An occasional temple visit or a pooja, maybe. But attending large religious gatherings every week required a different kind of mindset, not to mention commitment.

'Yes, it's a fairly recent development. I was surprised that she could find the time to spare.'

Radhi filed this new information away to chew over later. Suddenly, everybody's behaviour seemed suspicious to her. Manjula at a *satsang* was out of character. But then faith could be like that, couldn't it? Radhi herself didn't have any experience of it, but she knew it could come at any age, often at a time in life when you were most likely to need it. Maybe this was the universe's way of prepping Manjula for the trials that lay ahead.

Both the women fell silent. As young girls they'd stood at this same window watching boats. How simple life had been then, even if it hadn't always seemed so.

'Do you know if it's a boy or a girl?'

At the mention of her baby, the shadow on Sanjana's face lifted a little. 'I'm not supposed to, but my sonologist is an old friend.' Her hand involuntarily touched her belly as if cherishing her secret.

Radhi smiled. 'Have you thought of a name?'

Sanjana nodded, then smiled sadly. 'Papa suggested it.'

CHAPTER 13

'What's your name?' Radhika asked the man in front of her.

She was back in her own apartment, having spent a couple of hours with Sanjana until she got a call from Lila telling her that the person Radhi most wanted to meet was waiting for her at home.

'Santosh,' the vegetable seller confirmed. He was middle-aged, with a broad smile and surprisingly big, white teeth.

While looking at the register earlier that morning, Radhi had noticed that the vegetable seller had come to the building around noon on the Wednesday Mr Kadakia died. If neither Kamal nor Bhawani had opened the door to him, Mr Kadakia might have. Which meant Santosh was probably the last person to see Mr Kadakia alive.

'You come to the building daily, Santosh?'

'Yes, madam, except on Sundays.'

'What about this Wednesday? Did you go to the Kadakias on the fifth floor at your usual time?'

Santosh thought for a second, then nodded confidently. 'Yes, madam, why? What happened?'

Radhi ignored the question. 'Who opened the door?'

'Nobody. I stood there for a good ten minutes because I could hear loud voices coming from inside. I thought somebody might open the door, but nobody did.'

Radhi's heart beat faster. She tried to contain her excitement. 'Do you know who was talking? Did you recognize the voices? What were they saying?'

'One was definitely the older Mr Kadakia, the one who passed away. And the other . . . was also familiar, a man's voice . . . but I can't place it.' He frowned, trying to recollect it.

'Did you hear what they were talking about? Do you understand Gujarati?'

'Not much but, madam, they were speaking in Hindi . . . They were talking about money and Mr Kadakia was very angry.'

Radhi stared at Santosh in surprise. *Hindi! What a stroke of luck this was!*

'Santosh, if you hear that person's voice again, do you think you would recognize it?'

'I'm not sure, I could try.'

Radhi smiled at the man. 'No worries . . . You've been most helpful, Santosh.' She dug out a 500-rupee note from her purse, pressing it into his hand. 'Just keep this to yourself, okay?'

'Yes, madam. Thank you,' he said happily.

'We may need your help again.'

'Any time, madam.'

Lila showed Santosh out, then closing the door, announced, 'Wow, *didi*, this is becoming like a proper Bollywood film!'

Radhi was about to respond when the doorbell rang. Lila opened the door and ushered Santosh back in.

'Yes, Santosh?'

'Madam, I may or may not recognize the other man's voice, but I could definitely recognize his chappals.'

Of course! The visitor would've had to remove his footwear at the door!

Radhi grinned at the man and gave him another 500-rupee note. 'Remember. Not a word to anyone.'

Santosh nodded happily as Lila showed him out of the apartment.

When Lila brought out Radhi's lunch, Radhi hadn't realized how hungry she was until she'd taken several bites of the hot, millet roti with the bell-pepper-and-peanut sabzi and finished a whole bowl of the creamy, black-lentil daal. Lila went back into the kitchen and came back carrying a tray with more daal, a bowl of brown rice topped with a spoon of ghee, a roasted *papad* and a jar of homemade pickle made of vinegar-soaked carrots and mustard powder. For herself, she brought out a cup of strong ginger tea. As Radhi ate, she filled Lila in on some of the other details of the situation.

Then, finally, she gave Lila one more job to do.

* * *

'Ramzan *bhai*, please stop at Worli Naka when you get there. I want to see if I can find something for my friend's daughter.'

Radhi was on her way to meet Hrishi. It was about 3.30 p.m. but the sky had already turned the colour of slate.

'*Ji*,' the older man asked, 'anything in particular?'

'If we find a bakery, I can take some cupcakes . . . or maybe some fruits. Peaches and plums should be in season right now.'

She'd forgotten how old Hrishi's daughter was, or for that matter her name. Her memory was so selective. On the one hand, it could hold vast amounts of pointless trivia, and on the other, it was completely inadequate when it came to information that could ease social interaction.

'Radio?' asked Ramzan *bhai*.

'Sure,' Radhi replied absentmindedly.

On the radio, an RJ who called himself the Love Guru announced that the next song would be from Shekhar Kapur's *Mr India*, a classic about an endearing young man who ran an orphanage and fought the forces of evil with the help of a watch that could make him invisible.

Before a startled Radhi could ask Ramzan *bhai* to change the station, Kishor Kumar's inimitable baritone filled the car and Radhi was paralyzed. The words stuck in her throat, as a flood of memories washed over her in heartless, thrashing waves. It was a soulful song about how victory and defeat, joy and grief, were as inevitable as night and day, and how such was the way of life.

It was the same song that had been playing on the car stereo on the day her parents died. Her father had been humming along, and Radhi had been sitting contentedly in the back seat, cradling her shiny, new trophy and munching on peppery *makhanas*.

Her mother always packed food for a trip. Regardless of where they were going and for how long they'd be out, she'd keep power-packed little treats and snacks in her handbag to be distributed steadily. Dates stuffed with almonds and cashews, homemade *chikkis*, or brittles made with peanuts and golden jaggery, dark-chocolate Lindt truffles, which she never failed to pick up at the airport during her many travels, wholewheat *theplas* made with fresh fenugreek leaves and coriander, spread with *chundo*, a sweet mango pickle, and made into rolls.

The list of things you could expect to come out from her mother's cream Chanel handbag was long and often surprising. These snacks were for herself as much as for the kids. Managing a home, an office and two children, not to mention all the various commitments in their vast social circle, meant that she was always busy, always running, multitasking long before multitasking was even a thing.

Radhi's last memory of her mother had her gazing out of the window, munching on roasted chickpeas spiced with her favourite *chaat* masala. Every few minutes, she'd pop a few into Radhi's father's mouth. He'd protest he wasn't hungry, but she'd feed him anyway. How perfect they'd been for each other. Now they were no more, and Radhi would never forgive herself for it.

'*Didi*? *Didi*?'

Radhika came back to the present with a jolt, then realized her face was wet. Ramzan *bhai* had switched off the music and was looking at her, concerned.

'Are you OK, *didi*? Would you like me to pull over or turn back?'

'No.' Her voice came out small and cracked.

'No,' she repeated, this time stronger. 'I'll be fine.'

He glanced away, unconvinced, as she wiped away her tears.

Radhi got out her compact, then looking at herself in the mirror. She wiped her face carefully with a tissue and redid her *kajal*.

When they reached Worli Naka, Ramzan *bhai* slowed the car. Radhika looked out of the window to see if she could spot a bakery. There were two rows of fruit and vegetable stalls on either side of the road, but all the stalls were covered with cloth and tied with string.

'Why is everything shut? Is there a religious holiday today?'

Ramzan *bhai* looked around him. 'Not that I know of, *didi*.'

Radhika was wondering what to do when she spotted an open stationery shop.

'Here, let's stop here.'

Ramazan *bhai* pulled over, and Radhi ran into the shop. She would get art supplies for Hrishi's daughter. Either she was old enough to use them now or they could save them for later.

Quickly, enjoying herself a little, she bought a set of Camlin soft pastels, a pack of glitter pens, a quilling set, a dozen stencils, some zigzag scissors, a box of fluorescent poster colours, canvas boards and paint brushes of various sizes.

She paid for all her purchases and was back in the car within ten minutes. In another ten, they had reached the café. Hrishi was already seated at a table, working on his laptop. His shirtsleeves were rolled up, and his long fingers were flying over the keyboard trying to keep up with the speed of his thoughts. He had beautiful hands. In college, once, when they'd come close to being more than friends, she'd felt the hard callouses on his palms that came from years of playing basketball and had imagined them on her body.

As she watched him, Radhi felt something long-forgotten stir inside her. A thought strayed into her head. She pushed it away immediately, horrified at herself. Hrishi was a married man. A father, no less. There was no possibility of the two of them now.

Yet, once upon a time their names had sounded perfect together. Hrishi–Radhi. Radhi–Hrishi. Their friends had teased them for a whole year. And they'd secretly relished it. But they'd both been shy. Unwilling to make a move or do anything that would jeopardize the friendship so precious to both of them. Then, one night, he'd kissed her.

They'd both been studying late in the college library. It had been raining, and they'd got wet. It had been just like the movies except she didn't look very Sridevi-like. Her hair had been plastered flat on her head and her eyeliner had run. Giggling, she'd got into the cab they were sharing, quickly rolling up the windows to keep out the rain. She'd been about to remark on how it was the perfect weather to grab a spicy *pav bhaaji* from Sukh Sagar, when she stopped. He'd been looking at her with such an intense longing that the sheer force of it propelled her towards him. They'd kissed. It had been staggering.

She could remember it now. How her heart had hammered deafeningly inside her chest like some coked-up drummer of a heavy-metal band, and how the thousand slumbering butterflies in her stomach had risen, frenzied, euphoric. The kiss had ended as abruptly as it had begun. They'd reached her building, and she'd jumped out blindly from the taxi, without even a goodbye.

As Radhi approached Hrishi's table, she saw that he had a notebook lying open on his lap. From time to time, he would glance at it and then back at the computer. There was a large cup of coffee beside him. He picked it up to drink from it, then realized it was empty. He was just signalling the waiter when he saw her.

'Hi!' He beamed, jumping up to give her a hug. He smelled of cigarettes, coffee and cinnamon, exactly as he'd done in college.

Radhi was wearing a flowing, ankle-length crushed skirt with a blue batik print, paired with a snug, white tank top and dangling, silver-elephant earrings. She'd made an effort to dress up. After eons, she'd finally felt like it. Her therapist would consider this progress. She smiled as she took a seat opposite him. 'Big story?' She raised her eyebrows at his laptop.

Hrishi frowned, as he put his computer away. 'Not big, just ugly.'

Hrishi was a senior editor at one of the leading newspapers in the country. Once they'd ordered their coffees, he told Radhi about the story he was working on. A few weeks ago, a nun had filed a rape case against the Bishop of Jalandhar, Frank Thomas. One day ago, however, the priest who was a key witness in the case, a Father Jacob, had been found dead in his room on the church campus at Dasuya in Punjab. Father Jacob's family alleged foul play, but the police who inspected the spot said everything appeared normal, and the death seemed to be of natural causes.

Radhi hazarded a guess about how Hrishi felt. 'You don't agree with the police?'

'No,' admitted Hrishi. 'But we're so short-staffed, I don't think I can send someone out there to poke around.' He shook his head as if clearing his mind. 'Enough about my work! Let's talk about you. Why are you back?'

Radhi groaned. 'Must we really? It's not that interesting.'

Hrishi continued to watch her expectantly.

Radhi sighed. 'There's a longer version of this, which I'll tell you someday over a nice dinner. But for now, the answer is I was done with the US. There was nothing there to hold me back.'

Hrishi raised his eyebrows. 'What about your career? Your friends? What about . . . Mackinzey?'

'The career has been in the doldrums for a couple of years now. Moving countries might actually help my writing. And friends will keep. I've some here as well, don't I?' Radhi grinned at her old friend.

He smiled back.

'And there is no Mackinzey. So that's that.'

Something in Radhi's eyes must have deterred Hrishi from probing further, for he remained uncharacteristically silent, although he seemed to be studying her face for clues.

'Oh, before I forget.' Radhi reached down, bringing up the bag of art supplies from under the table. 'This is for, uh . . . your . . . your little one.'

Hrishi grinned as he took the bag from her. 'Thanks, you really didn't have to. Her name is Anoushka, by the way.'

Radhika smiled sheepishly. 'Well, I hope she likes art. The other options were cupcakes and peaches, but somehow, most of the shops at Worli Naka were shut today.'

'They're shut in the afternoons. From two to four,' said Hrishi. 'You may find them open on your way home.'

'Oh!' Radhika frowned as something occurred to her.

'What is it?' Hrishi asked.

Radhi shook her head. 'Nothing.'

The waiter came with their coffees. Hrishi had also ordered cream puffs and some open sandwiches.

Radhi picked one with avocado, carrots and spicy mayonnaise.

'So . . . how is Neha? How is married life?' she asked him, between bites.

'She's fine. It is fine.' He looked as if he wanted to say more.

Radhi waited, chewing away, and after a few seconds, Hrishi continued. 'Marriage is tough. It takes a lot of . . . work. But you already know that, I suppose.'

Knowing he was referring to her divorce, Radhi replied honestly, 'I don't know if we worked on it, though. We were much too young. There was a lot of passion and spontaneity and not enough restraint. Too often during a fight, we did things and said things . . . nasty things, just to get a reaction from each other. We didn't really work to save our marriage. In fact, just the opposite. We spent our energies on thinking up ingenious ways to cause each other pain.'

Radhi smiled. 'Look at me rambling on about something that happened a decade ago. Don't worry about me.

Aadil and I are actually good friends. In fact, on much better terms now than while we were married.'

'We aren't friends, Neha and me. We might've been at one point. But not right now. We are trying though. Counselling and everything. She wants this to work as much as I do. And we both love Anoushka.'

In the end, Radhi and Hrishi spent close to three hours at the café. They spoke about everything — office politics, new Netflix shows, recent holidays, mutual acquaintances from college, Radhi's great big writer's block, the book that Hrishi hoped to write someday. At one point, Hrishi got his phone out and showed Radhi pictures of Anoushka, who was a carbon copy of her father.

At seven, Hrishi cursed and jumped up, hurriedly calling for the cheque. 'I'm sorry. I didn't realize the time. Neha is expecting me back home by 7.30 today. It's Friday. Both sets of grandparents come home today and we eat dinner together.'

Radhi smiled at him. 'Of course.'

Hrishi grinned back at her. 'I told ya it was a lot of work.'

They parted, with Radhi promising Hrishi that the next time they met she'd tell him more about her time in the US.

'Over a nice dinner.'

'Over a nice dinner,' she agreed.

* * *

It wasn't until Radhi was back in the car that she remembered what had struck her as strange.

When her car neared Worli Naka she kept her eyes on the road outside. Just as Hrishi had said, all the shops and stalls were now open, and the market was bustling.

As Radhi observed the late shoppers haggling for better prices, making the most of the last light of the sun, she thought about the Kadakia family, one of them in particular. And wondered why they had felt the need to lie.

CHAPTER 14

Lila handed Radhi a glass of water. 'Sit.'

Radhi had just come home from meeting Hrishi. In the living room, there were more than a dozen cardboard boxes piled on top of each other, in two neat rows. Radhi felt a flutter of excitement at the sight of her books.

Lila followed her gaze, guessing that Radhi wanted to unpack her books right away. 'Later, *didi*.'

'So,' she announced, when she was sure she had Radhi's full attention. 'It turns out that our Bhawani Lal is in the market for a new job.'

Lila had spent the afternoon loitering in the lobby of their building. She'd chatted up the other maids who were supposed to be running errands but were more than happy to linger a few minutes, gossiping and sharing the stuffed betel nut *paan* that Lila had ingeniously thought to offer them. From one of these conversations, she had learned that Bhawani was deeply unhappy with the Kadakias. Mr Kadakia had refused to lend him the one lac, fifty thousand rupees he needed for his daughter's wedding, offering instead a modest sum of twenty-five thousand, which had enraged Bhawani.

'This is how he rewards almost a decade of service? Abandon a man when he needs help the most! Are *our* daughters' weddings not as important as theirs? What am I going to do with twenty-five thousand? Where do I go for the rest of the money? Rob a bank? I'll show that heartless son of a b**** to not treat people like this!' — is what he'd been heard telling anyone who would listen.

'When was all this?'

'A week before the old man died,' Lila replied.

'And now he is looking for a new job?'

'Yes, quite desperately from the sound of it.'

'Why desperately?'

'He told one of the drivers, in confidence of course, that he was even willing to take a pay cut, as long as he could get a job with a decent family. Which as you and I know is bullshit. No matter how decent the family is, nobody will voluntarily take a pay cut, unless they're really desperate.'

'Hmm.' Radhika understood why the cash-strapped Mr Kadakia must've had to refuse Bhawani, but she could also appreciate why Bhawani, who didn't have an inkling of Mr Kadakia's financial troubles, was upset. He must have felt like this was a betrayal in his time of need. The question was, exactly how upset was he?

'Thank you, Lila. You've been brilliant. And what about Tarika? Any luck?'

Lila shook her head. 'She didn't come down all afternoon. I'll try again tomorrow.'

Radhi nodded and was about to get up, when Lila added, '*Didi*, there's one more thing. You know the girl who works with the Kadakias?'

'Yes, Kamal.'

'I saw her crying profusely. She was sitting on the steps, near the landing between the third and fourth floor. She immediately stopped when she saw me climbing up. "My granny passed away," she said, without me even asking her, and then without waiting for my answer, she jumped up, wiped her eyes and ran up the stairs to the fifth floor.'

'Oh . . . do you think—'

'No . . .' Lila interrupted, reading Radhi's thoughts. 'I don't think she was telling the truth.'

Both women fell quiet.

Then Radhi asked, 'Why were you climbing the stairs anyway? Was the lift not working?'

Lila grinned sheepishly, 'It's good *excershize, didi*. A single woman has to watch her figure, no?'

Radhi laughed. 'Yes, of course.'

* * *

Bhawani dawdled in the kitchen that evening. Usually, he'd finish serving dinner to the family and hurry down to the garage for his nightly card game of teen patti with the other servants and drivers. He'd pack his dinner in a plastic lunch box and take it down with him, eating it much later, when he was alone, accompanied by a glass of his favourite toddy. Washing the dishes, cleaning the kitchen counters and then putting everything away in its proper place were all part of Kamal's job. Today, however, he ate his dinner with Kamal, sitting cross-legged on the kitchen floor.

'Why don't I clear up today? You look tired. Go on, take a break.'

Kamal looked at him suspiciously. She'd been here five years and this was the first time he'd offered to help. Something wasn't right. But she was tired of asking. He'd only feed her lies. She shrugged her shoulders and went off to the servant room.

Bhawani began the washing up, his ear trained to the sounds coming from the living room. He waited until the television was switched off and, one by one, the family members retired to their rooms for the night. When the lights were all out and he was sure he was alone, he tiptoed out of the kitchen.

Kamal, who'd been keeping an ear out for the sound of running water and clinking dishes, came out of the servant room as soon as the noises stopped. She hurried to the entrance of the kitchen and peered out to see what Bhawani was up to. She came back puzzled, a worried frown on her young face.

* * *

Radhi stared at her laptop. It was about 11 p.m. and she was sitting on her bed, trying to write. She'd given Lila the rest of the evening off, and spent a few happy hours listening to Prateek Kuhad's latest single on loop while setting up her books in her new bookcase. There had been thirty-four boxes and about 950 books in all. With a dry duster, she had lovingly wiped down each book and shelved it according to genre. When she stepped back, she was amazed to see the staggering number of mysteries she'd collected. That had always been her favourite genre, but now seeing all her books together, she wondered about her love of solving puzzles. Was that why she was so intrigued by what had happened to Kirti Uncle?

The company of books had had a therapeutic effect on Radhi. Feeling lighter than she had in days, she'd decided to write. It had been one hour, and so far she had a page number and a title — 'The Indian Writer in New York'. It was something George suggested before she left. He wanted Radhi to chronicle her experiences as a writer living in the city, in the context of being a foreigner. How New York had influenced her writing. If it had changed her writing voice, sensibilities and the subject matter she wrote about. Whether she'd involuntarily made her homeland sound exotic to live up to the average American's idea of India. If in any way her writing had differed from her peers' simply because of where she came from.

George wanted her to write a few personal essays and stories before attempting a novel again. It was a good idea, and there was plenty she had to say about how being Indian and being a New Yorker were such an integral part of her, and how both these identities tended to play off each other in interesting ways, not only in her writing but in how she negotiated the world. But she couldn't write. She wondered how she'd ever managed to pen the three bestsellers she had.

Radhika sighed and shut the file. It was becoming more and more easy to give up. Once upon a time she'd have berated herself for procrastinating, but not anymore. She didn't have a pressing deadline that she didn't dare miss and, more importantly, there was no Mackinzey to show a finished piece of writing to. He'd not only been unfailingly honest, but her conscience, too. When she didn't write, Radhi'd felt guilty on his account. Now there was no guilt. Not the terrible, motivating kind that propels you to take action, anyway.

Closing down Word, Radhi checked her mailbox. There was an email from George.

Radhi! Thank God you're not lying in a ditch somewhere. Or worse, married off to some rich-as-fuck diamond merchant. I can't tell you how happy I was to hear from you! Sorry your friend is having such a shit time. But I was super worried. You're never to do this to me again. Never. You understand?

By the way, is it terrible that I think all of this is just a teeny-weeny bit exciting? I mean, how often do you move countries and land smack in the middle of a murder mystery? OK, I can see that this is in bad taste, so I'm going to stop now. But on a serious note, why won't you guys go to the police? Also, do you have the faintest idea who could've done it?

XOXOOO

George

p.s. I <u>am</u> sorry for the poor dead sod.

p.p.s. India may not have been such a bad idea after all.

p.p.p.s. (is this even a thing?) You know, you're finally beginning to sound like yourself again!

Radhi grinned. George could be such a drama queen. He'd been vehemently opposed to the idea of her moving back.

'Who in their right mind leaves New York? And this is *me* saying that! A Londoner! My country will probably try me for treason, but for artists it doesn't get better than this! Have you not been sleeping again? Do you need someone to prescribe you your pills? Is that it? Because I have a guy. What? No! He is a doctor. Do you have such a low opinion of me? Anyway, have you really thought about all of this properly? What about your career? This gorgeous Upper East Side apartment with its mad views? What about this life you've built for yourself? You're going to move to India and spend the rest of your life attending weddings, and we'll never hear from you again! If you are finding it hard to write here, imagine how difficult it is going to be among all that chaos!'

He'd pestered Radhi for weeks, cajoling, begging and even trying to scare her with the grimmest of forecasts, before finally getting on-board with the idea.

She typed her response.

George, you're terrible! Can't believe I miss you already! Sorry again for absconding. But I'm here now and bang in the middle of this terrible situation. We did think about going to the police, but what would we say? He couldn't have killed himself because you can't have so many pills with such little water? Honestly, that's hardly proof of foul play. I've read enough Agatha Christies to know that the police will want motive, opportunity, suspects, that sort of thing. Currently, we have nothing. Just a whole lot of questions. And the more we ask, the more they seem to crop up. For instance, I was thinking that whoever laced Kirti Uncle's food or drink with the sedatives would've had to enter his study while he was unconscious to tie the plastic bag around his face. Essentially, it was the plastic bag that caused the suffocation. If this wasn't a suicide like we suspect, then the murderer (God, what a dark and ugly word!) had to have done it. Which means that not only did they need to have easy access to the house but they also had to have known the exact time that he consumed the sedatives and was bound to be unconscious. Which should narrow it down but doesn't really. Because this is a joint family. Five other adults live in the same house, all of whom had some inkling of his routine, as well as their own sets of keys. Not to mention the servants. One of whom was in the servant room at the time this was happening, while the other had access to the keys and could've easily come back in. The Kadakias keep a spare set of their own home keys hanging by the main door. So not only the servants, but literally any of the half-a-dozen people who show up regularly at their doorstep, like the dhobi (that's the fellow who takes in the ironing) or the milkman, could help themselves to them. Why would they do it, though? Zero ideas.

What we do know is that one of the servants had a major row with him a few days before he was murdered. Also, so did his own son! (Yes, he wasn't an easy person to get along with.) Both of whom, by the way, were on the premises of the building at the time of the murder. Besides, at least two of the six people he spoke to in his final hours are lying about something. Again, no idea why.

And finally, the one thing that would be stupid to ignore — Kirti Uncle was in massive debt. I don't know yet how all of this ties up, but I'm going to find out. Sorry to offload all of this on you, but it did help me think. ☺

Besides, you did ask. ☺

XOXO

Radhika was still mulling about these questions when her phone vibrated. She'd hidden it under her pillow like she always did when she was trying to write, so as to not get distracted.

It was a message from Hrishi.

You haven't changed at all. I had a good time today. Glad we caught up.

Radhi stared at the text. She could think of so many things to say. But all she sent him was a smile. He was having a hard enough time with his marriage. The last thing she wanted was to make matters worse.

CHAPTER 15

'147B, Ratna Mansion,' Radhi muttered to herself, as she checked Sanjana's message once again to confirm the address. It was raining fiercely again. Radhi struggled to hold her umbrella upright as the wind raged, as if in competition with the rain to decide, once and for all, which was the more powerful. She berated herself for what seemed the hundredth time since she'd started out from home. 'What a terrible day to do this.'

She was making her way through a narrow by-lane in Kalbadevi, one of Mumbai's most crowded commercial districts. There were stalls and shops on either side of the pavement, each covered with blue tarpaulin that amplified the sound of the falling raindrops, making them sound thunderous. Her sister's Jaguar was too large for a street like this, so she'd asked Ramzan *bhai* to wait on the main road with the car and, despite his protests, had braved the waterlogged street on foot.

She only had herself to blame. Lila had tried to warn her. '*Didi*, it's going to rain cats, dogs and donkeys. Better you don't step out today.'

But it had been dry, albeit cloudy, when she left home. And she'd got up feeling it was important to meet Vinod *bhai*.

Kirti Uncle's broker may or may not have had anything to do with his fate, but money was almost certainly at the root of this death.

Radhi stopped outside a three-storey, crumbling, grey building. Ratna Mansion wasn't a mansion at all, but it was what Radhi was looking for.

She entered the building, hoping to find a watchman or even a liftman so that she could ask them which floor to go to. Sanjana's message didn't have the floor number, and Radhi didn't want to call and bother her.

There was an empty stool at the gate, but the security guard was nowhere in sight. As for a liftman — there was no lift.

Radhi looked around and found a small board hanging on the wall, with floor and office numbers painted in faded maroon paint alongside the names of the owners. She couldn't find any offices in the name of Vinod Shah, but there was a Shah Stocks & Securities on the second floor, which seemed like a good bet.

She took the stairs, careful not to touch the dirty banister, repulsed by the betel-nut juice stains splattered on the grimy wall beside her. On the second floor, however, she stopped, surprised. A pristine white office, with large glass doors and a new ceramic nameplate announced that she had come to the right place. Underneath the company name, in smaller letters, was the name Vinod Shah. And underneath that was a sign requesting visitors to remove their footwear.

Unlike the stairwell, the floor looked clean and swept, so Radhi took off her white sneakers, put her dripping Burberry umbrella into a plastic bin, and stepped inside, her arrival announced with a jingle of multicoloured wooden parrots attached to brass bells. The peon at the front desk looked up and seemed surprised. Either he wasn't used to visitors or rather, it occurred to Radhi, as she looked around the small, all-male office, he wasn't used to lady visitors.

'Vinod *bhai*?' Radhi hoped the man was in. She hadn't called ahead to inform him that she was coming. If their last phone conversation was anything to go by, he was certainly not going to wave her in for a chat and a cup of tea.

'And you are?' The peon spoke to her in Hindi.

Radhi pulled a notepad and pen towards her and scribbled her name on it. Along with '*Mr Kirti Kadakia*' in brackets.

The peon went off to a closed cabin at the far end of the square office. While she waited, Radhi looked about her.

There were eight employees, each with his eyes glued to the computer in front of him. Some were also on the phone, scribbling away furiously in identical little notebooks and sipping on tea, a masterful display of multitasking. Almost all of them had several empty cups on their desks. One man was eating what looked like a cheese sandwich from a little plate with a puddle of impossibly red ketchup, while another was munching from a large, round Tupperware box, full of homemade popcorn. Neither was paying the least attention to the food in their hands. The only time they looked up was to check the two large TV screens mounted on the wall above them. Both were on mute, with one set to ET NOW and the other to CNBC, with its trademark ticker tape scrolling incessantly at the bottom.

The cabin door opened and a young man in his early thirties came out. He walked purposefully towards Radhi, the peon following.

'Ma'am,' he greeted her, even before he had reached her. 'These are trading hours. Papa can't meet anyone right now. Can you tell me what this is about? I can give him a message.'

'I wanted to talk to him about Mr Kirti Kadakia. He died earlier this week.'

'Yes, but what about him? Papa has already spoken to his son. And handed over all the related papers, etc. The police were also here. They've spoken to Papa as well.'

Radhi had been expecting this. She knew it would be difficult to reach Vinod *bhai*, so she'd come prepared. 'In exchange for a little cooperation, I'm willing to make a significant investment with your father.'

The young man clearly didn't believe her and looked irritated. 'Ma'am, this is really not how we do business here.

Please call us and we can set up a mutually convenient time to meet.' He moved towards the door. 'Now if you don't mind, these are our trading hours—'

'Forty lacs,' Radhi announced crisply. 'I have my cheque book right here. *If* your father will talk to me and answer all my questions. You should at least check with him, before you turn down my money.'

The sum stopped the man short. He looked at her again with suspicious, narrowed eyes. 'Could you give me your full name again?'

'Radhika Zaveri. Maybe you've heard of Zaveri Jewellers? Why don't you google me?'

'Please wait, one minute.' Then obviously afraid that Radhika might actually be the real deal, he admonished the peon. 'Offer Madam a chair, at least! And get her something to drink,' he instructed, before hurrying back to his father's cabin.

Radhi had just declined the peon's offer of chai as well as Fanta, when the young man came back, this time with a slightly warmer demeanour.

'Please come.'

He led the way down the corridor and showed her into a spacious office, all done up in cheap but durable white laminate. It had two desks. His father sat at one of them.

'I'll take care of that other thing,' the younger man told his father, before shutting the door.

Radhi had seen Vinod *bhai* before, on the day of the funeral. But up close, she was struck by the loose folds of skin beneath his eyes and the rings of flesh around his neck. He was looking at her curiously, obviously puzzled by her offer. She could imagine him looking at it from all angles, trying to gauge why she was really there.

He got up just a little bit, his large derrière rising slightly in a sort of courteous chair squat, and gestured to the chair opposite him. 'Please, sit.'

Radhi smiled. 'Thank you for agreeing to meet me.'

'You've made quite the offer, madam. I would be a fool to refuse. Tell me, how can I help you?'

'Kirti Kadakia. I understand he lost a lot of money in the last year. Can you tell me how?'

Vinod *bhai* looked at her, wondering if he should ask her why she wanted to know and whether she would tell him the truth, if he did. On the phone that day she'd said that she was a friend of Kadakia's daughter. But that didn't explain why she was here. In the end he decided, it didn't matter. How Kadakia lost the money was hardly a state secret. For forty lacs, Vinod *bhai* would've shown her the skeletons in his *own* closet.

'Kirti *bhai* was a seasoned investor. But there are so many variables in this business that experience alone may not always get you through. Natural disasters, political events, economic crisis, the death of a film star, there are all sorts of micro and macro influencers which you can't even predict, let alone control.'

'Is that what happened to Uncle, bad timing with a stock he bought?'

'Well . . . yes and no. Kirti *bhai* liked to play big. He had a gambler's temperament with a teenager's appetite for risk. He wasn't afraid to take chances. In fact, more than skill or knowledge, it was this natural tendency to operate on gut that helped him succeed all these years . . . until the day it didn't.'

Vinod *bhai* paused at the perfunctory knock at the door. A peon entered, carrying two cups of steaming ginger tea and a plate of assorted biscuits, arranged in a half moon.

Vinod *bhai* waited for the peon to leave before talking again. 'Does that help you? Or would you like to go into specifics? I've taken his son through most of this anyway. You could've just asked him, you know.'

'Some detail would be great.' Radhi delved into her bag, bringing out a pen and her cream-coloured diary with the golden polka dots. 'And I prefer to hear it from you.'

Vinod *bhai* looked at her curiously but didn't comment. He pulled out a large ledger from a drawer in his desk and opened it. Then, licking his middle finger, he began to turn the pages.

'Everything is computerized in our office, but personally, I'm not very fond of computers. For my own clients, I note down the trades in my ledger before my son, the one you met earlier, keys them in.'

He stopped at a page, taking a rather noisy sip of his tea as he studied it. 'There . . . In January last year, Kirti *bhai* asked me to pick up some 20,000 shares of a tech company called BlueGlue at 220. He said he'd got a tip from someone that the price would go up to 300 at least. In February, the price hit 270. But instead of selling part of the stock and covering his cost like I advised him to, Kirti *bhai* bought 20,000 more. "I did a little research, Vinod. This company's solid, has healthy numbers," he told me.'

Vinod *bhai* drank his tea, waiting for Radhi to finish making a note in her diary before continuing.

'Later that same month, however, the price fell by almost twenty-five per cent to 200. But Kirti *bhai* decided to stick with it. He'd found out that the promoter, Ajay Mishra, was selling some of his other assets, like his share in a tech park in Bangalore, to raise funds. Word was that Mishra had made a massive profit with that sale. Kirti *bhai* bought another 5,000 shares at this stage to try and average out the cost.

'I didn't know then that for this particular transaction, he'd actually borrowed money from the market. I would've stopped him if I'd had even an inkling. At least, I think I would have.'

Vinod *bhai* looked out of the window, his eyes focused on some distant point. Radhika wondered if he were thinking about the man he'd worked for, according to Sanjana, for more than thirty-five years.

He took another sip of his tea. 'Then after two weeks of absolutely no activity, the price dropped to 170.'

Radhi looked up from her diary, one brow raised.

Vinod *bhai* read her expression. 'Yes. It *was* very alarming. There was a rumour in the market then, which later turned out to be true, that Mishra had borrowed heavily from a politician who was pressurizing him to pay up. Unable to cover the debt by selling his other assets, Mishra had started selling his own stock of BlueGlue, which led to the steep price drop.'

'Did Kirti Uncle sell then?'

'Yes, but just the 5,000 he bought at 200. If he'd sold everything, he'd have made a loss of almost *eighty lacs*. It wasn't a decision he could take overnight. And then the next morning, that decision was taken for him. There was a newsflash that Mishra had committed suicide, was found hanging from the fan in his living room, the reports said. That was it. The price of the company plummeted to 110. You can imagine the rest.'

Radhi closed her diary and leaned back on her chair, thoughtfully. Both of them were quiet, as if observing a moment of silence for the departed man.

'This one trade proved to be his undoing.' Vinod *bhai* shook his head sadly. 'Like I said, with our business, experience is only one part of the puzzle. Luck is the other.'

'How did he get into such debt?'

Vinod *bhai* frowned. 'Well, I don't know everything about his finances. I just handle his stock investments. But from what I've understood, he had borrowed money from the market at very high rates of interest, with the expectation that when this trade made money, he could pay them back and still make a sizeable profit. When the trade went belly up, he had to borrow money from other sources to pay interest to the original lenders. And that drew him into a vicious cycle.'

'But surely he must've had other assets that could've helped pay for this?' asked Radhi.

'Well, there was the Nariman Point office and the Temple Hill home, from what I know. But I don't think he wanted to sell property yet. You see, he'd made another large investment in a pharma company, which he was confident would pay off sooner or later. And when that happened, he would be able to pay off his debtors in full. He'd still have suffered a loss, of course, but he wouldn't be in debt. In fact, until the day he died, he was hopeful that the pharma tip would come through.'

'Is that what you spoke about in your last call?'

'In a way, yes.' He frowned. 'The government has just reduced import duty on a couple of chemicals that are widely used in the pharmaceutical industry. And the entire sector was up because of that news, that day. That's what he'd called to tell me.'

'How did he sound?'

Vinod *bhai* tipped his head to one side, thinking back to that last phone conversation. 'Well, I'd say he sounded like himself. Not depressed, if that's what you're wondering. A tad upbeat in fact, because of the positive news. I certainly didn't suspect that he would take his own life soon after—'

Vinod *bhai*'s attention was suddenly caught by the ticker tape on his TV.

'Madam, sorry, but can you wait? I need to make a quick phone call to my client.'

Radhi rose, her hand outstretched. 'That's fine. I got what I came for. Thank you. Please have your son call me. I'll put him in touch with my business manager. They can discuss the investments you suggest for me.'

Vinod *bhai* got to his feet, fully this time, and awkwardly took Radhi's hand, clearly not used to shaking hands with a woman. 'Looking forward to working together, madam.' He gave her his card. 'Please call me on my personal line, anytime you need to.'

* * *

'Hi, can you talk?' Sanjana asked when Radhi picked up the phone.

'Hey, what's up?'

Radhi dipped her left foot in a tub of frothy, warm water and extended the other leg towards the beautician. She was at the salon, getting a pedicure, in time for her dinner at Madhavi's that night.

'So I'd gone to the gynaecologist for my monthly check-up and I realized that Dr Parikh's clinic is in the same building. He is our family physician. Actually, *was*. Now he's just Papa's doctor. Has been for the last thirty-five years that I know of. Anyway, I asked him if Papa was on sedatives of any kind. Or if he had complained of having trouble sleeping. Or if he'd ever suspected that he was suffering from some kind of depression. And he said never. He consulted his file, just to double-check and said that the last time Papa visited him was almost six months ago, when he had a virus.'

'So either the pills were not his or—' Radhi grimaced in an effort to stay still, feeling ticklish as the beautician scrubbed her foot — 'he didn't get them through Dr Parikh . . . How difficult is it to get the pills in India?'

'Well, for a lay person, I'd say it might be hard, but if you're connected to a doctor or even a medical professional or say a pharmacy, it wouldn't be too difficult.'

'Hmm . . . that doesn't really narrow it down, no, Sanju?'

'Yes.'

'Do me a favour and text me the name of the pills found on Uncle, would you?'

'Sure . . . Did you get to meet Vinod *bhai*?'

'Yes.' Radhi quickly filled Sanjana in on her meeting with the broker.

'I also called him on my way back to ask him if he knew who had given Uncle the initial tip. He couldn't remember the name but said that it was a neighbour, somebody from our building.'

'Oh! I wonder who that could be.'

Radhi had an idea, but she needed to confirm that theory. There was no point in saying anything to her friend right now. They hung up, with Radhi reconfirming the time for the prayer meeting the next day.

A middle-aged woman with freshly washed hair took the seat next to Radhi with a friendly nod.

Radhi watched as the hairstylist put on a pair of latex gloves and mixed a hair protein oil with a deep conditioner to prepare a thick, white cream. The sight of the latex gloves triggered another memory, and with it, another thought.

Suddenly, it seemed to her that she had all these ideas, but no real explanation for what had happened and why. She retrieved the golden-polka-dot journal from her bag and jotted down some notes.

'How about something for *your* hair?'

Radhi looked up to see one of the stylists smiling at her in the mirror. She stared at herself. Really looked. She hadn't paid any attention to the way she looked after Mackinzey. She'd gone through the motions, keeping up her salon visits, so she looked well groomed, but she hadn't taken any *joy* in her appearance in a long while. Her face wasn't traditionally beautiful — she had her mother's sharp nose and her father's broad forehead — but it was striking. Combined with her large, kohl-rimmed eyes, it was a face that asked to be noticed. Now, finally, for the first time in many months, Radhi paid it some attention.

CHAPTER 16

How was it that nothing had changed? Radhi marvelled, as she looked around the vast, lush expanse of the park.

Stretched out lazily by the Arabian Sea, snug within a circle of swaying palms, Cotton Green Park or CGP, as the regulars referred to it, was where the residents of Temple Hill descended for their daily dose of fresh air and news. Ever since she moved back, Radhi had been yearning to go for a walk in CGP. Lean since childhood, Radhi had never seen the inside of a gym or taken an aerobics class, but she'd always found walking therapeutic.

Once upon a time, she couldn't have completed a circuit of the park without bumping into someone she knew. Aunts, uncles, friends, family friends, classmates, neighbours, teachers — there was always someone to wave at, someone who would insist on stopping for a chat so that she was forced to pause the music on her Walkman, remove her earphones and say hello. Even now, Radhi knew that if she looked closely, familiar faces would emerge, and she would be enveloped in a gush of 'Oh my God! How long has it been? You look the same! What are you doing here?', pressed into answering questions that a decade-long absence warranted. So, she kept the hood of her windcheater up and her eyes averted, focusing instead on drinking in great big gulps of the salty sea air and listening to Shubha Mudgal's earthy voice urging her lover to learn the language of stolen glances.

Around her, middle-aged women, in *salwar-kurtas* and sneakers, walked briskly in expertly synchronized lines of three and four, not missing a single step as they attempted to reconstruct a Hungarian goulash without onion and garlic or tried to estimate how much a daughter's recent wedding must have cost their friends. In corners, where single benches had been placed, small clusters of retired uncles discussed the glaring flaws of the ruling party or the vagaries of the stock market for the millionth time, just happy to be out of the house and away from their wives, who were equally happy to have their homes and televisions to themselves, even for just a couple of hours.

On the far right of the park, a stout white building housed a gym on one floor, and a large, airy, sunlit yoga studio on the ground floor. On the other side, right beside the sea, a gently inclined slope led to a path paved with stones and lined with benches, partly sheltered by a cover of shrubs. Here, lovers met after sunset, for a little discreet necking, but never more than that, for on close-knit Temple Hill, there was always the possibility of being observed by someone who knew someone who knew your dad.

As Radhi walked up the slope, her eyes were drawn to a lone woman sitting on a bench, staring pensively at the sea. There was something familiar about her. As she came closer, Radhi realized it was Hetal. A part of her wanted to continue walking — she was enjoying the familiar sights and sounds of the park too much to stop. And yet, the stubborn part of her, the one that could tirelessly obsess over a knot until it unravelled and revealed itself, urged her not to waste the opportunity of finding Hetal alone in a possibly unguarded moment.

Radhi approached the bench and was about to call out to Hetal when she realized that the woman was using her earphones to talk on the phone.

'Yes,' Hetal was saying, 'I'd like to go ahead as planned.'

She waited to hear what the other person was saying. 'No, no, in fact the timing is perfect.' After saying goodbye, she removed her earphones.

Radhi cleared her throat, 'Uhm . . . Hetal?'

Hetal looked up immediately, startled. She tensed. Then, making a visible effort to shake herself out of it, she smiled at Radhi, who watched in amazement at the transformation of her face. Gone was the thoughtful, almost melancholy expression, replaced almost instantly by the animated appearance that Radhi had come to associate with Sanjana's sister-in-law.

'Wow, I love your new haircut! I would never dare to go that short!' Hetal cried, shifting to one end of the bench to make space for Radhi.

'I should be walking,' she continued. 'My dietician told me I needed to walk for at least an hour a day. Brisk walking. In the beginning it really helped and I did manage to lose some weight. But for a few weeks now it has plateaued. I'm losing the motivation, you know?'

Radhi smiled sympathetically. 'Why not try something different? Like a yoga class. The body gets used to the same kind of exercise.'

Hetal frowned. 'How I hate skinny people like you. I bet you've never had to watch your weight a single day in your life . . . Anyway, I think you're right, I should join a class . . . but now, in any case, it's going to be a challenge. You heard about Bhawani, right?'

When Radhi shook her head, Hetal explained. 'He wants to leave. Has asked my mother-in-law to clear his dues by day after. With him gone, the bulk of the cooking responsibilities will fall on Sonal and me. Where's the time to exercise then?'

Radhi was surprised at this news. 'What happened? Why so suddenly?'

'Oh we have my husband to thank for that! Bhawani and he had a massive argument this morning. He accused Bhawani of stealing from us. No proof, no nothing. Just went straight out and asked him if he'd taken two lacs from my father-in-law on the day he died. Seriously, the man has no tact.'

'What did Bhawani say?'

'Oh, he went ballistic! He said we didn't know how to treat our helpers. That we were the worst employers he'd ever known. He said he cooked for our kids like he cooked for his own. But that we didn't value any of it, et cetera, et cetera.'

Hetal made a face. 'Honestly? I don't blame the man. I don't like him much, but I get why he feels the way he does. You should see the way my parents take care of their staff. Exactly like family members. They have free run of the kitchen. They cook for themselves and eat what they like. Here, my mother-in-law dictates what they eat. And how much. Their rice is different. Not the superior brand of basmati we eat. Even the number of cups of tea they have is restricted to two in a day. I'm sure they have more when we're all at work. There's no one to check. But those are the rules.'

Radhi had been quiet, taking in what Hetal was saying. 'Why did Ranjan think that Bhawani had stolen from Uncle?'

'Well, on the day he died, Papa asked Bhawani to go to the bank. When Ranjan was looking through his papers yesterday, it seemed he'd asked for a withdrawal of two lacs from his account. But now we don't know what Papa did with that money.' Hetal frowned. 'He died just a few hours after Bhawani came back with it. So where did it go? Ranjan's already searched the study. And Bhawani denies any knowledge of it. So where is it?'

* * *

When Radhika reached home from the park, Lila opened the door excitedly.

'I have news, *didi*.'

Radhi removed her muddy sneakers at the door. 'What's happened?'

'Our man Bhawani is leaving.'

'Yes, Hetal just told me. Apparently, he had a big fight with Ranjan this morning.'

Lila handed Radhi a glass of cool water. 'Yes, *didi*, but that's not the news!' Her eyes were dancing. When she was sure she had Radhi's full attention, she continued, 'So it turns out that Bhawani has had his bags packed for the last couple of days. He'd enquired for train tickets to his village the day the old man died, and managed to get one yesterday.'

Radhi's eyes widened. 'So he was going to leave regardless of his fight with Ranjan?'

Lila nodded, looking satisfied with the reaction her news had generated.

'How do you know this?'

Lila blushed. 'One of the drivers below, he's a bit . . . sweet on me . . . tries talking to me whenever I go downstairs. He told me. He plays cards with Bhawani and was one of the people Bhawani asked for help with the train ticket.'

'My! Aren't you a smooth operator?'

Lila giggled. 'I don't know what that means, *didi*, but it sounds wicked!'

Radhi laughed, then continued more soberly, 'That man . . . I've always felt there was something off about him and now this. What if he actually did murder Kirti Uncle? He certainly had the opportunity. He could easily have mixed something in the food and then come back later using the spare keys. But was he really angry enough to do that?'

Lila nodded solemnly. 'One of the servants told me that his daughter's wedding got called off because he couldn't arrange the money. And that his wife was so angry with him that she took both his daughters to her father's home.'

'Really?'

'Honestly, *didi*, I can't be sure . . . You know how people are? They love to gossip. That's why I didn't mention it earlier.'

Radhi was quiet for a moment, then she shook her head as if trying to clear her thoughts. 'I just know in my gut that he's hiding something. But what? If we don't find out soon, he'll take off and we'll never know. Do you think talking to Kamal might help? Let me ask Sanjana to send her here on some pretext—'

'Let me do it, *didi*. She's more likely to talk to me.'

'That's true . . . Okay, good luck.' Radhi checked her watch. 'I need to get ready now. My sister specifically asked me to be on time.'

Lila grinned. 'Say hello to Palak*ben* from me.'

'Oh I will.' Radhi smiled back.

* * *

Bhawani sat alone in the garage drinking his toddy. In a plastic tiffin beside him was his dinner. There was a black lentil daal thickened with a generous dollop of fresh cream, soft rotis made of cornflour, and a spicy mango pickle. But he had no interest in food. He was excited and nervous. He'd taken a huge risk, and finally it seemed things were going his way.

He'd skipped his nightly card game. He didn't want to deal with his friends' questions about why he was going and when he'd be back. And he didn't want to say or do anything that would jinx his good fortune. All he wanted to do now was go to his village, sleep under the arjuna tree in his courtyard till noon every day and eat the hot chilli fritters that his wife would serve him straight from the wok.

At first, he'd thought all was lost and he'd despaired. And when that bitch Radhika had started asking questions, he'd panicked. But then he had looked at the situation differently and another idea had struck him. He knew what he was going to do wasn't a good thing, but they deserved it. There was no end to how shoddily they treated their servants. Why just today that buffoon Ranjan had asked the watchman to check Bhawani's bags and search the garage. Had the fool really thought he wouldn't find out?

Ranjan Kadakia was as much a mule as his father had been.

* * *

Radhi stood outside Madhavi's house at exactly the designated hour.

Madhavi had called her the previous night and reminded her again to 'please be good'. Which meant Radhi wasn't to aggravate Madhavi's mother-in-law — if she could help it.

The problem was that everything about the sour Mrs Bansal got on Radhi's nerves. She was pompous, full of an inflated sense of her own importance and rigid in her outdated, often outrageous views. All of which, Radhi would've ignored had it not been for how critical she was of Madhavi. That Radhi couldn't bear, and she hoped, for everyone's sake, that this evening Mrs Bansal would reserve her sanctimonious little pearls of wisdom for Radhi alone.

To start things off on the right note, Radhi carried a small gift for the old woman, a gilt-edged Bhagavad Gita, which even Mrs Bansal could not find anything wrong with. Surely? And Radhi had covered up. She was wearing a black silk jumpsuit, so that Mrs Bansal couldn't complain to Madhavi about how her sister needed to realize she wasn't in a Western country anymore.

The jumpsuit, however, was far from modest. It fit Radhi snugly and accentuated her curves, not to mention making her look even taller than her already striking five foot eight. It had a big red bow at the back, and she had matched her lipstick to it. It contrasted spectacularly to the bronze of her skin. Her new bobbed hair framed her face perfectly and drew attention to her long, slender neck. Radhi knew she looked sexy despite not showing any skin — and that would rile the old tyrant. Especially, because she wouldn't be able to find any fault.

'Oh my!' Madhavi exclaimed when she opened the door. 'Just look at you . . . that haircut! I love it!'

Radhi grinned and hugged her sister. 'Thanks, *di.* So, what's going on?'

'Well, Nishant and Prachi have stepped out for a coffee, so that they can "get to know one another".' Madhavi mimed quotation marks in the air. 'Once they're back, we'll have dinner.'

Radhi followed Madhavi into the living room, where Roma Bansal, Madhavi's mother-in-law, along with their two aunts, Vrinda *fia* and Ila *kaki*, were enjoying tall glasses of *jaljeera*, a spicy, water-based drink famous for its appetite-whetting properties. With them was an elegant woman with silver hair, dressed in a golden raw-silk sari.

Vrinda *fia*'s eyes lit up with pleasure when she saw her niece, but it was Ila *kaki* who called out to her in her most simpering-sweet voice. 'Oh you're just in time, Radhika! We were just talking about the many benefits of a timely marriage, and Roma *ben* was wondering whether you plan to settle down now.'

'The girl's just come, Ila. Let her sit a moment,' Vrinda chided. Ila didn't look the least bit discouraged.

'Hello, Roma Aunty.'

Radhi greeted Mrs Bansal first, before saying her hellos to the other women.

'This is for you.' She handed over the Gita to Madhavi's mother-in-law.

'Thank you, Radhika.' Roma put the gift away without so much as glancing at it. 'Come sit by me and answer your *kaki*'s—'

'Radhi, this is Parul Aunty, Nishant's mum, and a very dear friend of Mummy*ji*,' Madhavi said, smiling at the woman in the golden sari.

Mrs Bansal nodded. 'Aah, yes, Parul and I go a long way back. We met at a fundraiser for widows in Jodhpur, where we bid for the same antique clock. I'm not going to tell you who finally won the bid because I hate boasting, but since then we've attended scores of events together and have become great friends!'

Parul smiled politely at Radhi as Palak*ben* bustled into the room to offer Radhi a chilled *jaljeera* — and an even frostier smile. Once Radhi had seated herself, Mrs Bansal zeroed in on Radhi again. 'So tell me, what are your plans now?'

'She's trying to figure it out, Mummy*ji*.' Madhavi was trying hard to help Radhi again, but this time Mrs Bansal would not be deterred.

'Shh, let the girl speak, Madhavi.'

'No big plans, Aunty. I just wanted to live closer to my sister and the family, and work on my next book.'

Mrs Bansal wrinkled her nose distastefully. 'All that is very well, but what about marriage? I know it'll probably be hard because of, well, your age . . . *and that other thing*.' Radhi knew she meant her divorce. 'But with all of our connections, I am sure we can find you someone suitable. And luckily, you're rich. So, that will help.'

While Radhi was livid at the older woman's presumptuousness, for the sake of her sister, she bit her tongue, instead answering her with a broad, fake smile. 'It's good to know that I have options, Aunty. And that I have all of you here so invested in my future. Let me just settle in a bit and I will be sure to come to you to find me a good boy.'

Mrs Bansal, who hadn't expected such uncharacteristic agreeableness from Radhi, was at a loss as to what to say. But Ila *kaki* wouldn't let the matter rest.

'I have made it very clear to my Prachi, find a good boy, settle down and have children. Everything has a proper age and time. Nowadays people try to get pregnant in their early forties through IVF and God knows what else. It's such a travesty of nature.'

'I agree, *kaki*.' Radhi's eyes twinkled as she looked at the woman. 'Do you know in the US people actually inject their own fat into their wrinkles to try and look younger? Can you imagine that? If only they'd let nature take its own course.'

Ila *kaki*, who had flown to the US for a Botox treatment and a lip plumping procedure just the previous year, flushed red with embarrassment. Luckily for her, she was spared a response by the ringing of the doorbell. A moment later, Prachi and Nishant walked in.

Nishant was tall, with a full, well-groomed beard and serious black eyes. He was impeccably dressed. Radhi's cousin, Prachi, had a pretty face and her own successful line of formal wear, but she was sly like her mother. Radhi had never been close to her.

Prachi made a beeline for her mother, while Nishant stood unsure of where to seat himself among the women.

Madhavi gestured for him to take a seat between Vrinda and Radhi, introducing him as he sat. 'Nishant, this is my sister, Radhika . . . Radhi, this is Nishant. He was also in New York for many years. Keep him company, will you? I'll get dinner organized.'

Radhi smiled at him.

'New York, huh? What a small world. What were you doing there?' He had just the hint of an American accent in his voice.

'Oh, just a bit of writing. Some articles, books that sort of thing. What about you?'

'Come now, Radhi, you can do better than that!' Vrinda *fia* had heard Radhi's lukewarm introduction and felt the need to intervene. 'Our Radhi is an award-winning author.'

Radhi blushed, embarrassed. '*Fia*, please. Nishant is the guest of honour here. Let's focus on what *he* does.'

He smiled. 'Oh, I am just a boring old architect. Nothing even remotely as interesting as what you do. What kind of books do you write? Would I have heard of something?'

'Well,' Radhi murmured reluctantly, 'there was *Happy Now?*, an exploration of marriage and its many frailties. Then there was *A Vain Moon*, and then more recently *Chalk & Cheese*.'

'*Chalk & Cheese*, now that one sounds familiar. Wasn't there a movie by that name?'

Radhi nodded. 'Yes, it got adapted.'

'I remember seeing it! It was a satirical portrayal of an upper-class Gujarati family through the eyes of a servant girl, wasn't it? Oh! It was hilarious. Very sharp and insightful!'

Radhi smiled with pleasure. 'Yes, the filmmakers did a great job of taking it to the screen.'

'*Phissh*!' Vrinda looked cross. 'Really, Radhi! I understand you don't like attention, but this is a bit much even for you.' She turned to Nishant. '*Chalk & Cheese* won the prestigious JCB prize of Literature that year. Not to mention, it was on the *New York Times* bestselling list for a whole month!'

'Sorry, Nishant, my aunt is just proud of me. Please ignore her. And, *fia*,' Radhi raised one brow, 'may I remind you of why Nishant is here.'

'Aah, yes.' Vrinda glanced over to the other side of the living room where Prachi sat surrounded by Mrs Bansal, Ila *kaki* and Parul.

'So, Nishant, do you only build buildings or also people's hopes?' Vrinda tilted her head towards Prachi and laughed at her own joke.

Now it was Nishant's turn to blush.

'Jeez, *fia*, that was terrible!' Radhi laughed.

'When you get to my age, you can get away with being terrible,' her aunt replied. Then more smoothly, 'Nishant, what kind of buildings do you design?'

'Well, mainly hotels and resorts. My speciality is restoring heritage properties.'

'Now, that sounds nice!' Vrinda said. "I do love spaces that have some history — it sort of roots them in time and place, doesn't it? Do you enjoy it?"

'It *is* rewarding,' Nishant agreed. 'There's joy in taking something that's ancient and beautiful and adding a bit of yourself to it. In knowing that you're the reason it will be enjoyed for generations to come.'

Radhi smiled at the man's answer. It was thoughtful, but more than that there was a refreshing sincerity to it, which was rare for a drawing room conversation on Temple Hill. On impulse, she told him, 'I have a small property in Udaipur. A *haveli*. Must be a hundred years old or so old. It came to me as part of my divorce settlement,' she added, when Nishant raised his eyebrows. 'Anyway, it's just been locked up for the last decade or so. I would love your opinion of it.'

'Oh, I'd love to check it out,' Nishant replied instantly.

'What are you three talking about?' Mrs Bansal's voice floated across the room at the same time that Palak*ben* and two servants entered the room carrying soups and platters of starters and dips.

'Come here, young man. Sit beside me. I have a few questions I want to ask you.'

Radhi smiled at Nishant, who blushed again as he got up to join the old woman.

CHAPTER 17

Radhi stood outside the Lord Vasupujya Swamiji Temple aching to go in and yet sure that she wouldn't. Dedicated to the twelfth Jain Tirthankara, this was the smallest and, in Radhi's opinion, the most beautiful of all the temples on Temple Hill. Made of the finest white marble, with four intricately carved pillars that described Vasupujya Swami's journey to *moksha,* the release from the cycle of rebirth, this had been her mother's favourite temple. When Radhi was little, accompanying her to the temple was the highlight of her day. One, because with Madhavi away at school, it was her time alone with her mother. And two, because of the delicious hunks of rock sugar that people left there as offerings, which Radhi craftily pocketed to enjoy later, alone in her room. Of course, this was all back when she and God were still on talking terms.

'It's done, madam.' One of the musicians interrupted her thoughts, bringing her back to the present with a start.

Manjula had requested that Radhi reach the temple complex early to coordinate with the musicians who were performing at the prayer meeting that morning. In the far right of the temple complex was a large, newly constructed hall, with a stage and seating for up to two hundred people. This was where the prayer meeting would take place. Radhi had been waiting for the musicians to finish setting up and successfully complete their soundchecks.

Radhi looked at her watch. There was still almost an hour before the event would start. She left Lila on a bench inside the complex, with a few special instructions, and made her way outside. The temple was situated inside a wide lane at the base of Temple Hill. Radhi walked out to the main road, crossing over to what had been a video library the last time she was here but was now a coffee shop called White.

Inside, she was surprised to find Ranjan, sitting by a windowless wall, hunched over his phone, an untouched cup of tea on the table in front of him. From the steam rising out of the teacup, it looked like it had only just arrived.

Radhi had often played with Ranjan as a kid, though not always out of choice. He had insisted on accompanying Sanjana on all their playdates, which wouldn't have been so bad were he a better loser. She couldn't count how many Monopoly games he'd spoiled by getting up midway and storming off. Once, in a fit of anger, he'd even toppled the entire board over. But that wasn't all of it. He was also an unscrupulous cheat, whispering to his partner during Pictionary, peeking during hide-and-seek, manipulating the dice to throw a six each time while playing Ludo — there was no end to his tricks. Sanjana never had much patience for his antics, and they would often end in yelling matches between the siblings, which sometimes turned physical, if Amit or a grown-up didn't intervene. As he grew older, however, Ranjan developed friends and interests of his own and, much to Sanjana's and Radhi's relief, began to leave them alone.

Radhi didn't know the grown-up Ranjan. How much had he changed? She hadn't really had the chance to talk with him since she'd got back.

She walked towards his table. 'Hi.'

'Oh, hi!' Ranjan looked startled, almost embarrassed to have been caught idling away here.

Radhi slipped into the chair opposite him. 'Waiting for the prayer meeting to start?'

'Waiting for it to end actually.' Ranjan put his phone away, then picked up his cup, taking a sip of his tea. 'Sorry, that was probably not the correct thing to say. But I just can't wait for things to go back to normal . . . Can I get you some tea?'

When Radhi nodded, Ranjan signalled to the waiter.

'Thanks for taking care of the musicians by the way. I told Mummy I could do it but she wanted me home with the family. But I can't bear to be home these days. Losing a parent, and you know this better than me,' he looked at Radhi meaningfully, 'it's hard enough. But everything that's followed Papa's death has actually been worse. The whispers, the questions, the curiosity, as if somehow it is our fault. As if we failed him as a family!'

Ranjan fell silent when the waiter came to serve Radhi her tea, staring, instead, moodily into his teacup. Radhi waited for him to continue.

'I'm worried about Mummy. She has stopped sleeping completely. And the children? Poor things. They sense that things are not right but aren't asking much, afraid that a wrong question might upset the grown-ups.' Ranjan took a long sip of his tea.

'Were you very close with your dad?'

Ranjan snorted bitterly. 'Ha! No! That would be overstating it . . . We didn't see eye to eye on a lot of things.' He frowned. 'Papa was too rigid. Did what he wanted to and believed what he wanted to, even in the face of proof to the contrary. It was like dealing with a headstrong toddler. He literally threw tantrums if he didn't get his way.'

'Still.' Radhi's tone was gentle, mindful that she was crossing a line, but seeing no other option. 'That last fight must rankle now, it can't be an easy thing to live with.'

Ranjan stared at her intently, suddenly alert. Perhaps wondering how she knew about the fight. His expression hardened. He took another sip of his tea before answering.

'Yeah, it was bitter. But honestly? I don't regret it. I'd been asking him to consider selling our apartment for a while now. It's a big place, three bedrooms, one study, one servant room, even a prayer room, but our kids don't have a room of their own. My eldest is eight now. How long can we continue sleeping together?

'I would've moved out, but I can't afford to buy an apartment on Temple Hill. We'd have to move to the suburbs, which honestly both Hetal and I didn't want to do. My clinic, Hetal's studio, the kids' school, our friends, our entire lives are in and around Temple Hill. We didn't want to uproot all of that. So, I suggested that we sell this apartment, divide the money between Amit and me, then each of us could add our own money to it and buy our own places. Sounds reasonable, right?'

Radhi frowned. 'But what about Kirti Uncle and Manju Aunty? Where would they stay?'

'With me, of course! I'd already told him that. We'd easily be able to afford a large flat with three bedrooms once we'd added our own money to it.'

'But Kirti Uncle didn't like the idea?'

'Hated it. Wouldn't hear of it. In this apartment, we all live by his rules, his and Mummy's. I think he felt that if they moved in with us, the dynamics would change. That they wouldn't be in charge anymore. That day when I brought it up again, he reacted very negatively. Told me I needed to stop grovelling and make my own way in the world just like he had. Told me I needed to stop being such a mama's boy and be a "man".' Ranjan made air quotes with his fingers. 'So, to answer your question, does the fight bother me? Just in that it turned out to be needless—'

Ranjan's phone rang. He checked the name flashing on the screen before answering it.

'Yes, Mummy . . . Yes, close by . . . Okay, I'll be there in a minute.' He ended the call, signalled to the waiter for the cheque. 'It's starting. Will you come now or in a little while?'

'A little while,' Radhi replied. 'I'll just finish my tea.'

As she watched Ranjan leave, she thought about what he'd told her. He'd been upfront about his last interaction with his father, in fact, more forthright than she'd expected. So, why was she left with the feeling that he hadn't told her everything?

* * *

The soft strains of a devotional song floated out to Radhika as she entered the temple complex. It spoke of how the entire life span of man was but a fraction of a moment in the great passage of time. The prayer meeting was well underway, the hall a great sea of whites and off-whites. On the left, the men sat in crisp cotton shirts or *kurtas*, while on the right, the women wore Lucknowi *salwaars*, flared cutwork palazzos and organza saris, dazzling in their diamonds and pearls. On Temple Hill, a prayer meeting was as much a social occasion as a wedding. It was common for attendees to show up in their longest cars and largest solitaires. Though the mood was sombre and there wasn't much conversation, it was still an opportunity to see and be seen.

Right at the front, below the stage where the musicians were performing, there were two rows of chairs facing the audience reserved for the Kadakia family. On the left, Mrs Kadakia headed one row, followed by Sanjana, her sisters-in-law Hetal and Sonal, and a couple of other female members from their extended family. While on the other side, Amit, as the eldest son, sat at the beginning of the row, followed by Ranjan, Jayesh and a few other uncles and close cousins. From their vantage point, the Kadakias could clearly see when someone entered the room and acknowledge them when they came forward to pay their respects.

When Radhi looked around, she saw a lot of familiar faces. Neighbours, acquaintances, friends from school and college and even a few of their old teachers, who'd probably come because of Manjula Kadakia's powerful position on a number of school boards. Radhi saw Mrs Maniar sitting a few rows ahead, busy whispering to Mrs Poddar and Mrs Gandhi. Mr Poddar was at the other end of the room, sitting right at the front in the first row, along with Mr Parekh from Sea Mist's first floor. At the back of the room, Bhawani was sulking in one corner with Kamal and the Kadakias' old driver, Ashok*ji*.

Mrs Kadakia seemed to have aged a few years in the last days, Radhika thought. Her eyes were sunken, the circles around them dark and deep, and yet her gaze was alert, her back straight.

This was a woman who only seemed to grow stronger in grief.

* * *

Manjula Kadakia looked out on to the roomful of people who'd shown up to offer their condolences for her husband's death. What a circus these prayer meetings could be. How did it matter if other people were sorry for your loss? Even if it were genuine, how did their fleeting presence relieve your constant suffering? What did their empty words do for the cloying emptiness that you felt within? When she died, she didn't want a prayer meeting to be held. She would leave strict instructions for the family. If she'd had her way, she wouldn't have had this one either. She knew Amit and Ranjan wouldn't have minded that much, but Sanjana would've protested. She was her father's daughter — mulish, if she thought she was right. And Manjula didn't have the energy to fight her. Not now. All the bitter arguments, the spiteful slights and the cold clashes with her late husband had taken the fight out of her. At least for the time being. Right now, she just wanted to be left alone. To mourn. To rest. To remember.

* * *

Hetal looked out on to the roomful of people who'd shown up to offer condolences for her father-in-law's death. All the chairs were occupied and the people who were entering now had to stand. Some had positioned themselves at the back of the room, while still others were leaning against the side walls. She could see her yoga friends seated in the middle row and a cluster of mums from her children's school at the back, by the door. Hetal was glad they'd come at a time when the hall was packed to capacity. The size of the crowd spoke to the Kadakias' standing in their community. It was proof of their social currency. Hetal knew her friends were taking it all in, so she sat up straighter. Perception management was everything. It seemed to her that everyone had a certain image of her. Her friends, her mother-in-law, her husband . . . especially her husband. But now that was about to change. People would have to recalibrate their idea of her. It wouldn't be easy. No, she'd seen how negatively her father-in-law had reacted when he'd found out. He'd sputtered, incredulously, then furiously. He hadn't known what to do with the information. She had begged him not to say anything, but he'd refused to cooperate. Stubborn to the very end.

* * *

Amit looked out on to the roomful of people who'd come to mourn his father and felt a great surge of pride. This. This was real. This was what mattered. How you were mourned was proof of the life you had led. It wasn't important now how he had felt about his father these last few days. Even Gods had character flaws. His father was only human. And humans make mistakes all the time. It didn't matter what Sonal said. She didn't know him the way Amit did.

* * *

Mr Poddar looked around at the roomful of people who'd shown up to offer condolences to the Kadakia family. This. This was what money did. It got you friends who called you back. Colleagues who wanted to stay in touch. And relatives who were comfortable being related to you. Money got you a packed prayer meeting. Mr Poddar wondered how many people would attend his prayer meeting when he died. He had long lost touch with people he'd called friends in a previous life. He had a small extended family, but most of them were in Rajasthan. He doubted if many of them would travel to Mumbai for his funeral. They weren't very close. Luckily, on his wife's side there were a lot of them, all in and around Temple Hill. Even if only the first cousins showed up, there'd still be fifty of them. A good, respectable number. There were also his neighbours at Sea Mist. He'd known each family for more than four decades now. He was certain that most of them would come. Not out of love — he was optimistic, not delusional — but out of propriety. Because it was the right thing to do. And on Temple Hill, righteousness was prized. Then there were his daughter's in-laws. His daughter, God bless her soul, had married well. They were a small family, but they had a large social circle. This was what the lack of money did, it made you worry about who would show up when you died. Money was why he had done what he did. He had tried to explain it to Kadakia. But how rigid he had been. How unreasonable. How glad he was to be rid of him.

* * *

Sonal looked out on to the room full of people who'd shown up to offer them condolences and was instantly reminded of her wedding reception. That was the last time she'd had to receive so many people. The memory of it made her cringe. How uncomfortable she'd been. How terrified that something would go wrong, that her parents or her relatives would say or do something to embarrass the Kadakias. She'd known that the Temple Hill crowd was sizing her up. They were nice enough when they walked up on the stage to wish them well, but she knew they were taking it all in, her clothes, her jewellery, even her accent! They'd analyse everything as soon as they were off the stage. But Sonal had an even greater fear. What if they didn't? What if they found her so unremarkable that they promptly forgot all about her? Sonal had made herself utterly miserable that day. She knew how hard Amit had worked to convince his parents to agree to an "inappropriate" marriage. It was probably the only time Amit had quarrelled with his father. Apart from that one other time.

* * *

Bhawani looked around at the roomful of people who'd shown up to offer condolences to the Kadakia family. He wondered how many of them really knew the old man. Like *really*. Wasn't the true test of a man's character how he treated those who were inferior to him? What did that say about the miserly Kadakia, then? Kadakia who'd looked the other way when his daughter's wedding fell through because Bhawani hadn't managed to come up with the dowry money. His daughter had cried for days after that. His brothers had mocked him. What was the point of working in the big city, they said, if he couldn't manage a simple wedding dowry? It had hardly been simple. The groom's family had asked for gold worth five lacs! Maybe they thought that because he worked in Mumbai, he shat gold bricks. But it would all be OK now. By this time, the day after tomorrow, he'd be sleeping with his head in his wife's lap and Kadakia's death would be like a sour dream. Yes, it would all be okay, he thought, looking at Kamal sniffling beside him, if only this foolish girl would keep her trap shut.

* * *

Ranjan looked out on to the roomful of people who'd shown up to offer condolences for his father's death and supressed the overwhelming urge to run away. Here were all these people expressing their sorrow while he, Ranjan Kadakia, still had to shed a single tear. Wasn't it meant to be easier to be charitable towards someone after they'd died? So how was it that he was finding it so impossible to grieve the man who'd sired him? How had it come to this? If the theory of karma played out like it was meant to, what would be Ranjan's fate? He shuddered to think of the consequences of his actions. His last conversation with his father played over in his mind on a loop. And the thing that his father had asked of him at the end? How cruel, how cold Ranjan had been. Not for the first time, he wondered how unforgivable it was what he had done.

* * *

'A big thank you to each and every one of you on behalf of the Kadakia family,' the lead singer of the musicians announced as they reached the end of what seemed to be the final song of the day. 'The family is grateful to you for having taken the time to attend this prayer meeting, as they say farewell to a beloved husband, father, father-in-law and grandfather, Shri Kirti Kadakia. Before we wind up, would anyone from his family and friends like to say a few words about Mr Kadakia?'

An expectant silence descended on the audience as they waited to see who would come forward to speak. It seemed to Radhi that the Kadakias had not anticipated this. Amit, painfully shy as always, looked down at his feet. Ranjan squirmed uncomfortably in his seat. Hetal and Sonal looked at each other and then at their mother-in-law for some cue, but Mrs Kadakia continued to stare out on to the audience, her expression unreadable.

The silence was just about to become awkward when there was a simultaneous sound of scraping chairs. Radhi saw that the old Mr Ganatra had risen with the help of his son and a walking stick. At the same time, at the front of the room, Sanjana had got up as well. She didn't seem to have registered Mr Ganatra.

Radhi, who knew her friend's face as well as her own, felt her stomach lurch. Sanjana had a strange, almost reckless expression on her face. She watched, nervously, as Sanjana climbed the few steps up to the stage, without a backward glance at her brothers or anyone else in the family.

CHAPTER 18

'Let me start out by saying that I know that my father wasn't an easy man to get along with,' Sanjana began lightly. That drew a few laughs from the audience.

'He was certainly not an easy-going father. He was strict, impatient, and when he was angry, he raised his voice and yelled at us. And yet, he was wonderful in the most surprising ways.

'He would suddenly take the day off to teach the three of us kite flying. Or take us all for a drive in the rains that would end all the way in Lonavala. Or he'd announce on a school night, much to my mother's exasperation, that we were all going out to have *faloodas*, post-dinner. He was always involved in our lives, present at dinner time. Not with one eye on the TV, watching the news while eating, but really present in the moment, asking us about our day in school, offering advice and suggestions.

'I remember one time there was an older boy in our school who was bullying Amit. Asking for his lunch money and threatening him with dire consequences if he told the teachers or his parents. When I finally got it out of him, I told Papa, but Papa did absolutely nothing. He waited for Amit to gather the courage and come and tell him himself. Almost a week later, when Amit finally did, he went with him to school. But instead of talking to the teacher or telling off the other child, he stood unseen in the corridor, and asked Amit to look the boy in the eye and flat out refuse to give him the money. "I won't fight your battles for you," he told Amit, "but I have your back." Amit got beaten up that day and for a couple of days after that as well. But he never gave the boy the money again. He'd seen the worst the boy could do and he was no longer afraid.'

Sanjana had been smiling as she said this, but now her expression changed. 'My father was a fighter, in every sense of the word. The world may think he committed suicide, but I can't believe it. I refuse to.' With these final words, Sanjana handed the mic back to the singer and made her way down from the stage.

Radhi's heart was beating hard in her chest. Sanjana shouldn't have said anything. They would have had a far better chance of arriving at the truth without putting people on their guard.

She scanned the faces of the Kadakias beneath the stage to see the impact of Sanjana's words on her family. Mrs Kadakia looked stricken, as if someone had slapped her. Beside her, Hetal was furious, although her eyes were trained on the phone in her lap. Sonal seemed distinctly uncomfortable. She caught Radhi's eye and shook her head, obviously troubled by the speech. Amit was talking softly, yet urgently, with Jayesh. While beside them, Ranjan looked sick, like he was about to vomit.

Luckily for the Kadakias, most of the audience had not registered the family's acute discomfort, nor the gravity of what Sanjana had effectively said. Most seemed to have taken it as an emotional outburst from a grieving, and hormonal, pregnant woman. They were listening to the lead singer instead, who had the mic again, and who was talking about how different people left for God's abode in different ways.

Radhi scanned the front row for Mr Poddar, but he was nowhere to be seen. She looked around the hall, but he seemed to have disappeared.

At the back of the room, she noticed Bhawani standing with Kamal, his face as white as a sheet.

* * *

'Done?' Radhi asked Lila, as soon as she entered home that afternoon.

Lila nodded triumphantly.

'Where are they?'

Lila went to the shoe cabinet and came back with a plastic bag, which she shook out on the floor. A pair of old and worn-out, brown leather Kolhapuri chappals fell out.

'And you're sure they are the right ones?'

'Yes, *didi*,' said Lila.

'Good. Let's call up the vegetable vendor now. What was his name? Santosh, right?'

'Already done, *didi*. I called him as soon as I got back. He'll be here any moment now.'

Radhi smiled. 'Perfect. You really have a knack for this kind of work, you know?'

'Honestly, *didi*? So do you!'

Radhi couldn't hide her satisfaction. This had been a good idea. At the prayer meeting, everyone who entered the temple complex had to enter barefoot. She'd asked Lila to wait on a bench by the gate, where everyone would remove their shoes. It was the perfect opportunity to pick up the footwear of the person who she suspected had come to meet Mr Kadakia on the day he died. Of course, people owned more than one kind of shoe, but it was worth a shot. Santosh hopefully would be able to confirm her theory.

The doorbell sounded.

Lila shrugged. 'Must be Santosh.' She turned to the door.

'Wait,' Radhi instructed. 'Put these back in the bag and don't remove them until I ask you to.'

While Lila did as instructed, Radhi answered the door. Instead of Santosh, it was Sanjana.

'Sorry to barge in like this.' Sanjana walked past Radhi and made her way to the sofa, seating herself slowly, wearily.

'I just couldn't bear to be at my parents' place right now. Everyone's a little upset with me. Mummy's giving me the cold shoulder. Ranjan's sulking. Even Hetal, of all people, is angry with me! I think they're being mindful of the fact that I'm pregnant and trying not to upset me further. But I can tell that they want to give me a piece of their mind.

'The only person who sympathized a bit was Amit. He told me that even he finds it difficult to accept Papa's suicide. He was asking me what I meant and why I said what I said. And if I knew something . . . Don't worry!' she said quickly, seeing Radhi's alarmed face. 'I didn't tell him about your theory. I attributed it to my woman's intuition, that I just felt it in my gut that something wasn't right. Nothing more.

'Listen, don't you worry about him. You know how he is. He's not going to question anything or ruffle any feathers. I finally just told Jayesh that I needed to lie down.'

Sanjana looked flushed and sweaty. Radhi switched on the air conditioner while Lila offered her a glass of chilled water. She took it gratefully and finished it in one quick gulp.

'I'm famished.' She looked at Lila hopefully. 'Is there anything to—?'

'Of course, *didi*.' Lila bustled away to the kitchen.

When they were alone, Sanjana apologized to Radhi. After the prayer meeting the Kadakias had been surrounded by family, friends and well-wishers and the two women hadn't had a chance to talk to each other.

'I don't know what came over me. I just couldn't sit there while all those people who'd known Papa for so many years thought the worst of him! Thought him weak or cowardly! I've probably ruined our chances of finding out the truth, but I just had to say something, you know?' She looked imploringly at Radhi.

'You haven't ruined anything. At first, I thought it was a rash thing to do, but what if it helps us? What if it makes the murderer nervous enough to say something or do something?'

Lila returned with two steaming bowls of a coconut-flavoured, vegetable stew, a large bowl of white, long-grain basmati rice, and a platter of cucumber, carrot, beetroot and tomato slices, arranged in perfect concentric circles.

The two women ate in silence for a few minutes. Radhi hadn't realized how hungry she was until she took her first bite.

Lila, who'd been looking out of the window, announced that Santosh had entered the building. Sanjana looked puzzled, and Radhi quickly told her friend what they were up to.

* * *

Sanjana and Radhi were waiting for someone to answer the door. They were tense. On Temple Hill, relationships were important, forged over decades, through a continual give and take of favours and food. Words chosen wisely, compromises expected and adjustments routine — the history between families far more important than the connections between individuals. Sanjana and Radhi were about to make a serious accusation. If they turned out to be wrong, they would irreparably fracture a long relationship. But they'd discussed it at length. This had to be done. The only other option was to go to the police. But they couldn't do that, not yet, not before giving Mr Poddar a chance to explain himself.

When Santosh had arrived earlier that day, Radhi had asked him to describe the shoes he'd seen. Only when he said the words 'brown', 'old' and 'Kolhapuri' had she removed the chappals from the plastic bag.

'Yes, these,' he'd stated confidently, confirming that the chappals were similar to the ones he'd seen outside the Kadakia home on the day that Mr Kadakia had died.

It all came down to language, Radhi thought. Santosh had mentioned that the conversation he'd overheard between Kirti Uncle and his visitor was in Hindi. If it had been anyone from the family, or even Vinod *bhai*, the conversation would've been in Gujarati. Which is why she'd thought of Mr Poddar. He was Marwari and spoke in Hindi.

Tarika opened the door, her hair dishevelled and her eyes heavy with sleep. She told them that the Poddars were both taking their afternoon nap. She started to close the door, clearly wanting to go back to her own siesta.

'Please wake them up,' Sanjana stated firmly. 'We'll wait.'

Something in Sanjana's voice seemed to alert Tarika to the fact that this was no ordinary house call. She opened the safety door to let them in, then hurried away to wake her mistress. A few minutes later she was back, followed by a curious Mr and Mrs Poddar.

'What's happened?' Mrs Poddar asked immediately. 'Is everything all right?'

'We just need to talk to Uncle for a minute,' Sanjana replied, and left it there.

Mrs Poddar took the hint. 'I'll organize tea.' She called Tarika, who was lurking at the back of the room, and the two women went off to the kitchen.

When they were alone, Mr Poddar smiled nervously at Radhi and Sanjana. 'So, girls, what's this all about then?'

Sanjana fixed him with a grim gaze, while Radhi spoke up. 'Why did you lie about the phone call, Uncle?'

'What phone call? When? What are you talking about?' asked the elderly man, with more confusion than the question warranted.

'You didn't speak to Kirti Uncle about parking allotment or Modi's speech or the elections — or any of that other stuff you told me about.'

'Says who?' Mr Poddar's tone was aggressive.

'The call was too short. It lasted just twenty seconds,' Radhi replied evenly.

'Must've been the day prior to that then.' Mr Poddar's voice was rising. 'We spoke often enough. I can't be expected to remember exactly what was said when!'

Radhi had anticipated this response.

'We've checked Mr Kadakia's call log for that whole week. There was no call with you.'

Mr Poddar was sweating profusely now. 'I'm telling you we spoke about all of this! How does it matter when? You're just raising my BP for no reason. What do you want to do? Give an old man a stroke?'

Radhi was quiet for a few seconds, letting him sweat it out.

'You're right, Uncle. You did have this conversation, but it wasn't on the phone. You went to meet Kirti Uncle at his home on the day he died. And you had a massive fight with him. What was it about?'

All the colour seemed to drain from Mr Poddar's face. 'Who's feeding you these lies?' he sputtered nervously.

'The same person who told us that your fight was about money.'

Mr Poddar gulped. He started to say something, then fell quiet.

Mrs Poddar, who'd most likely heard every word from the kitchen, came hurrying into the room now.

'What's going on? You leave him alone! Can't you see he is not well? If something happens to him, you will be responsible.'

But no matter the result, Radhi felt that they'd come too far and said too much, to stop now.

She turned her attention to Mrs Poddar.

'Aunty, why did you send the fruit custard to Mr Kadakia's house that morning?'

That stopped the woman in her tracks. She stared at them, then glanced at her husband, her mouth opening and closing wordlessly.

'Wha — what's that got to do with anything?' she asked finally, in a small, choked voice.

Mr Poddar took his wife's hand, pulling her down to sit beside him.

Radhi studied them. 'Did he hand over money to you that day? Two lacs?'

'Were you the one to give him that tip which led to his losses?' Sanjana asked the elderly man. 'Is that what the fight was about?'

Mr Poddar remained quiet, various emotions crossing his face, as if he were making his mind up about something important.

'You are not going to let this rest, are you?'

Sanjana didn't respond.

Mr Poddar shook his head wearily. He sighed. 'You girls . . . you girls, you've got it all wrong.'

CHAPTER 19

Radhi was lying on the sofa in her living room, a cigarette in one hand and her polka-dot diary in the other. The palm-shaped bronze ashtray on the centre table was filled with cigarette butts. It was about 3 p.m. She'd returned to the apartment from Mr Poddar's house an hour ago and had been lying in the same spot ever since, chain smoking, drinking multiple cups of tea, which Lila filled frequently, and staring at the ceiling. She wondered if Mr Poddar had told them the truth, wondered if anyone at all in this whole sordid affair was being completely honest. She took another drag of her cigarette and looked down at her notes. She was on the page where she'd listed Kirti Kadakia's call log, with scribbled comments beside each name.

Ranjan's call with Mr Kadakia had lasted for ten minutes. He'd told them that his father had phoned him because he couldn't find his chequebook. This conversation could not have taken up ten whole minutes. Maybe they had talked of something else as well. But what? What was Ranjan not telling them? She underlined Ranjan's name, going over the line several times, while she tried to think of what she was missing. Her eyes fell on the unidentified number that she'd tried calling before but had gone unanswered. She picked up her phone and dialled the number again. This time it was picked up in two short rings.

'Dr Dastoor's clinic. How may I help you?' a woman's voice asked at the other end.

Radhi sat up straight, improvising fast. 'Uhm . . . my father received a call from this number on the . . . third of June. Can you please tell me what this was about?'

'Ma'am, we were probably calling him about a dental appointment. Hold on, let me check. The third, did you say?'

'Yes, please.'

The voice went silent for a few minutes, and Radhi could hear the rustle of pages being turned and the sounds of a busy clinic in the background.

'What did you say your name was?' the voice asked after a few seconds.

'Sanjana,' Radhi repeated. 'Sanjana Kadakia. You called my father Kirti Kadakia? He has passed away since.'

'Oh, I am so sorry to hear that! I'll be sure to tell Dr Dastoor. Please accept my condolences,' the voice at the other end gushed. 'Yes, I see his name. He had an appointment with us on the 3rd at 5 p.m. We confirmed with him that morning. But he didn't show up. Of course, now I can understand why.'

'Are you sure he confirmed he would come?' asked Radhi, aware that it was a strange question to ask.

'Yes, we have a system of writing "C" against every name we confirm. Why?'

'No reason.' Radhi hung up after thanking the woman for her time.

Her heart was beating fast. At 12.30 p.m. on the day he allegedly committed suicide, Mr Kadakia had told his dentist that he'd be there at 5 p.m. If there ever was a doubt in Radhi's mind that Mr Kadakia had been murdered, it now vanished. But she had a distinct feeling in her gut that she was running out of time. That the longer she took to find the answers, the harder it would be. The trail would run cold. Bhawani was going away tomorrow. She didn't know whether he had murdered Mr Kadakia, but she was sure he was hiding something. And when he left for his village the next day that information would leave with him.

* * *

Radhi's phone vibrated as she got in the lift. A message from an unknown number.

> *Hey Radhika, this is Nishant. It was good chatting with you the other night. I was actually hoping to take you out for dinner sometime. Would that be okay? I know its awkward, seeing that they tried to set me up with your cousin. But I don't mind awkward. If you don't.* ☺

Radhi smiled. Nishant seemed nice, and it had been some time since she went out on a proper date. But her sister's mother-in-law would be furious. And Ila *kaki* would create a scene. Neither of which would have deterred Radhi on its own, but it would put her sister in a tough spot. Madhavi wouldn't hear the end of it. With a slight and surprising pang of regret, she decided she'd have to find a gentle way of saying no. She put her phone back in her bag.

She was in the elevator of the B Wing at Sea Mist and it had just reached its destination. Radhi got out at the Ganatras' floor.

* * *

'It's good to see you after so long, Radhika.' Mr Ganatra smiled warmly at her from his oversized armchair. 'When Shukla called me on the intercom to say that Sameer Zaveri's daughter wanted to come and see me, I thought it was Madhavi. She comes by on Diwali every year with her little ones you know . . . but you . . . I haven't seen you in a decade!'

Radhi returned the man's smile. 'I just moved back from the US, Uncle. Thought I'd come by and say hello.'

'I'm glad you did! No place like home, is there?'

Mr Ganatra had aged well in the years since Radhi last saw him. His thick mop of dark hair was now completely grey, but other than that it was completely intact. There was no receding hairline or thinning bald spot.

Radhi had been meaning to speak to him for a few days now. Ranjan had said he was at a physio session with Mr Ganatra at the time that Mr Kadakia died. Besides, Mr Ganatra and Mr Kadakia were old friends.

'So, tell me, do you still steal sugar cubes from temples?' The man's eyes twinkled.

Radhi laughed. She was just about to answer when an attractive young woman, with big doe-like eyes, entered the living room.

'Aah, Kanika, there you are.' Ganatra looked fondly at the woman. 'Come say hello to Radhika. She lives in the A Wing. Her father and I were very good friends. Radhi, this is Sumit's wife,' referring to his youngest son. 'She is an interior designer.'

'Used to be,' Kanika corrected, with a small, sad smile. 'In Hyderabad, where I lived before marriage. In Mumbai, I'm just a housewife.'

Radhi smiled but didn't say anything, unsure of how to respond to someone so clearly unhappy with her lot in life.

'Papa, your medicines.' Kanika handed Ganatra a tiny bowl containing two pills, along with a glass of water.

'Thank you, child.'

'I'll organize some snacks.' Kanika left the room with a friendly nod at Radhika.

'I feel bad for her,' Mr Ganatra said, after his daughter-in-law had gone. 'Sumit is just so busy with his new job. Comes home after midnight most days and works most weekends. It gets very lonely for her. She has no family in the city, nor friends.'

'What about work? Has it been difficult to find interior-designing projects?'

Mr Ganatra nodded. 'Yes, work would be ideal. In fact, Ranjan did bring her something. . . . you know Ranjan, right?'

Radhi nodded.

'He comes home for my physio. And they've gotten friendly. His friends wanted their daughters' room done up and he recommended Kanika to them. That went very well. Kept her happy and busy for a while. But she's feeling lost again. Anyway, I'm glad she has met you. Now that you'll be in the building, maybe you can introduce her to other young people?'

This was the kind of opening Radhi had been hoping for.

'Of course, Uncle. Has she met Sanjana, Ranjan's sister? If not, I'll introduce them . . . That's once things are a bit settled with the Kadakias again.'

At the mention of the Kadakia name a cloud passed over Mr Ganatra's face. 'Yes, that is a sad affair.'

Radhi waited, hoping he would say something more, but he remained silent, lost in thought.

'You and Kirti Uncle were good friends, no?'

'Yes. We'd become quite friendly over the years. Kirti *bhai* and I, along with Mr Poddar, were on the building committee together. We'd often meet at each other's houses to discuss the society's affairs. Garage allocations, housekeeping issues, that sort of thing. And then once the work was done, we'd stick around to have tea and chat a bit. Kirti *bhai* and I got along exceptionally well. We'd even go on morning walks together, until this happened, of course.' He looked at his wheelchair.

Radhi waited in vain for him to continue. 'I heard he made a huge loss on the stock market.'

Mr Ganatra nodded sadly. 'It was very unfortunate.'

Radhi waited again, and this time he did speak.

'You know . . . I feel even more terrible about it, because it was I who gave him the initial tip. Sumit's bank was helping this company raise funds and he was confident that its stock was going to go through the roof. We, of course, couldn't buy it because of the direct conflict of interest, but I mentioned it to Kadakia. We were in the habit of passing on tips to each other. He decided to invest.'

'But the price didn't go up as planned?' Radhi asked, even though she knew how the events had panned out.

'No, it did! Initially, it went up just like we had thought it would. He bought more at that stage. But then the price dropped. Sumit said the promoter had just sold some assets and had made a killing on the sale, so he said to hang on to the stock. This was still a good buy. But I didn't think so. I sometimes have a strange intuition about these things. I told Kirti *bhai* to sell then. But he didn't listen. He went and bought even more. And then the price dropped again. I got very worried about him at this point. He was really deep into it by then. I told Ranjan about it. He was obviously very concerned and promised to talk to his father. I don't know if he ever did. But very soon after that, the promoter committed suicide and it was all over.'

Mr Ganatra sighed sadly. He seemed like he was about to say more, when Kanika re-entered the room, followed by a maid carrying a large tray. She put it squarely in front of Radhi.

There were two tall glasses of coconut water, along with two large platters piled high with crunchy, deep-fried, fenugreek flatbreads, diamond-shaped gram flour *dhoklas*, steamed and generously seasoned with sesame and mustard seeds, vegetable sandwiches thickly smeared with fresh mint chutney and *rasgullas*, dimpled, white cottage-cheese balls soaked in a saffron-based sugar syrup.

'Oh dear,' Radhi protested. 'This is too much food!'

'Not at all.' Kanika smiled back, as she handed Radhi and her father-in-law small, cerulean-blue ceramic plates, taking one herself.

As Radhi helped herself to a couple of soft *dhoklas*, she chewed over in her mind the two important things she'd just learned. One was that Mr Ganatra was the neighbour Vinod *bhai* had referred to. And the other was a piece of information so completely unexpected, that it threw up at least a dozen more urgent questions than Radhi had started with.

'These *dhoklas* are delic—'

A distant but loud thud followed by a woman's piercing scream made Radhi break off.

Startled, the two young women looked at each other. Almost in sync, they put their plates down, rose from their seats and hurried wordlessly to the window.

'What is it? What's happened?' Mr Ganatra tried to manoeuvre his way across the living room with his wheelchair.

From the ninth floor in the B Wing where Mr Ganatra lived, it was difficult to see what had happened clearly. Except that there was a fast spreading, ruby-red pool of blood on the ground, and a person was sprawled in the middle of it.

CHAPTER 20

'What's happened?'

'Slipped from the fifth floor!'

'No, sixth!'

'How?'

'Move aside, I can't see!'

'Has someone called an ambulance?'

'Oh my God, I'm going to be sick!'

'Who is he?'

'Is he really dead?'

Snatches of frantic, disconnected comments and conversations in Hindi, English, Gujarati and Marathi made their way to Radhi and Kanika as they approached the crowd of residents, servants and security guards gathered around the body in one large, horrified circle. All equal for once in their life, transfixed, powerless and afraid in the presence of that great leveller — death.

Radhi noticed Ranjan and Amit standing at one edge of the circle, and she led the way towards them.

'Bhawani,' Ranjan murmured gravely, when he saw them.

Shocked, Radhi searched the man's face for more, but there was a curious lack of emotion there. As if he was present physically but too preoccupied to respond properly to another death. She looked at Amit. His face was pale, beads of perspiration shimmering above his upper lip.

'Don't go in there.' He nodded to the crowd around the body. 'It's, it's . . .' He shook his head, clearly disturbed, unable to find the words to describe the scene.

But Radhi had to see for herself. Dreading what she'd find, yet unable to walk away, she made her way to the front, followed by Kanika.

Bhawani was lying at the centre of the circle, his face turned towards the sky, his body lifeless, twisted at an unnatural angle, like an old, abused doll. A dark, crimson puddle had spread around his head, the blood fast seeping into the ground, a stain that would probably remain for months, a dreadful reminder of the capriciousness of life.

Radhi had seen two other unnatural deaths before this. Her own mother's bloodied and mangled body flashed in front of her eyes and her chest constricted. She found herself unable to speak or even to draw breath. The shock of that day, the unrealness of that moment, the utter misery and the abject hopelessness of the following months, all came crashing down on her in a single, sickening jolt.

Beside Radhi, Kanika gasped, a strangled 'Oh!' and dropped her phone to the ground. She swooned, grabbing hold of Ranjan's arm to stop herself from falling to the ground. Ranjan swiftly put an arm around her, while Radhi, struggling to come back to the present, picked up the mobile phone. Its screen was shattered irreparably. Together, they walked Kanika towards a nearby chair.

'Sorry,' Kanika apologized after a few minutes. She was still a sickly shade of yellow but had recovered enough to talk. 'That was awful! Is he really dead? . . . What happened?'

'He was up on the sixth floor, washing the drawing room windows for the Solankis. He seems to have slipped and fallen.' Ranjan shook his head. 'What a way to go . . . almost feel sorry for the poor bastard.'

They heard the siren of an approaching ambulance.

Kanika paused to listen, before replying, 'I've always found this window washing so dangerous! There are no ropes, no safety clasps, no nothing! I'm surprised it's even legal! In Hyderabad, we have window-cleaning machines for high-rises. Here, they just straddle the railing for support and nothing else! This was a disaster waiting to happen!'

Amit joined them. 'I suppose the police will be back, and wanting to talk to us again.'

Ranjan frowned. 'Us? Why us?'

'Well, we *are* his employers,' Amit reasoned. 'They'll have some questions, I'm sure. If nothing else they'll need the contact details for his family . . . His poor wife will have to be told.'

Radhi looked up at the window Bhawani had fallen from. At every floor, there were heads sticking out in ones and twos. People who'd come to their windows to check what the commotion was about stood riveted, horror-struck by the sight below.

As Radhi's eyes travelled upward, she saw the Poddars whispering to each other. She observed the old couple for a few minutes before continuing to look further up. At the fifth floor, she found herself staring at Hetal and stopped. Maybe it was a trick of the sunlight, in any case it was too far to be sure, but Radhi had the strangest feeling that instead of looking at Bhawani, Hetal had been staring at her.

* * *

'What did the doctor say?' Radhi asked as soon as she entered Sanjana's room.

Her friend had experienced sharp, period-like cramps and had just come back from an emergency check-up with her gynaecologist.

'Forget the doctor. What's been going on here? Jayesh told me about Bhawani! My head has been spinning since then! Did anyone actually see it happen?'

Radhi shook her head. 'Nobody was home. Mr Solanki was at work and Mrs Solanki had the day off but she was out. She said she let him in that afternoon and left for her Rotaract meeting with instructions that he was to shut all windows and switch off all lights and fans before leaving the house.'

Sanjana nodded. 'Yeah, he's been cleaning their windows for years, he knew the drill. So how did it happen? It wasn't even raining. How did he just slip? I saw that police chalk outline and that horrible red stain where he must've hit the ground. It was awful!'

Radhi had been thinking the same thing. She wondered what the police had found out. The team had been crawling all over the building, taking statements from the residents, the security guards and the servants.

'I saw Inspector Shinde on my way here, talking to the Solankis. Do you think we should speak to him?'

'About what? Didn't we say we'd wait until we had some kind of proof?' Sanjana asked.

'Yes . . . but now there's been another death and I'm afraid we are going too slow. We could do with a little help.'

Sanjana's eyes widened. 'Wait. You think these two deaths are connected?'

When Radhi didn't answer, Sanjana looked horrified. 'Dear God, Radhi . . .' She fell silent, thinking about the implications of what Radhi had just said. 'Let me request he come up.' She picked up her phone and starting typing.

A minute later, the phone pinged. Sanjana checked her messages. 'He's coming,' she said to Radhi wryly. 'One of the few perks of being pregnant, people find it hard to say no to you.'

'Meanwhile, will you please tell me what the doctor said?'

'Well, he *said* many things, but to give you the gist — I'm to avoid being on my feet as much as possible. And I am to avoid stress. They're worried that if I'm not careful, the baby will be premature.' Sanjana's expression was grim.

Radhi shot her friend a look of concern. This was really not the time for Sanjana to be involved in investigating one murder, let alone two. What if this turned out to be a wild goose chase? And more terrifyingly, what if it didn't? They had to think of the baby. What if something actually happened to it? Would Sanjana ever be able to forgive herself? Before Radhi could pursue this further with her friend, the doorbell rang, and the maid showed the inspector into the living room.

Inspector Shinde was out of shape. He was perspiring profusely. He had large sweat stains under his armpits, a drenched back and a soaked handkerchief with which he was unsuccessfully trying to mop his wet face and neck. He'd spent the last hour in the sun supervising the site of the accident and talking to the people who had been first on the scene. Awkwardly, the man looked around Sanjana's silk- and velvet-upholstered furniture for an appropriate place to seat himself. He finally chose a settee without a back, where he would do the least harm.

Sanjana whispered a few quick instructions to her maid, who switched on the air conditioner in the room, much to the inspector's relief.

'So, madam, what was it you wanted to talk to me about?' He looked first at Sanjana, then at Radhi.

'What do you make of this death, Inspector? Was it actually an accident?' Radhi asked directly.

Shinde raised his eyebrows, obviously surprised. 'What makes you ask this question, madam? Do you know something, I don't?'

'Don't two unnatural deaths in the same building, in the span of the same week, strike you as strange?'

'It *is* quite a coincidence,' admitted the inspector, 'but honestly, in my line of work we see far stranger things.'

The maid came back into the living room with a tray carrying tall glasses of chilled *kokam* sherbet and a plate of sweetcorn fritters with dollops of fresh coriander chutney and ketchup on the side. The inspector accepted the sherbet gratefully and took a long thirsty gulp of the drink before eyeing the food.

'In any case, this is still early stages. The team is still making its inquiries. What we've understood is that even though he was a full-time employee of the Kadakias, he often washed windows and did other odd jobs for residents of the building in his free time. Am I right?'

He looked at Sanjana as he picked up the plate of fritters. She nodded.

'Did you know that he was leaving? That this was his second last day at work?' asked Radhi.

'Yes, we heard. The Kadakias told us, and so did some of the other servants we spoke to.'

'Don't you find *that* strange? The timing of it?' Radhi pressed.

'Look, ma'am,' Shinde said between bites, 'we don't have the luxury of finding things strange. We work with facts and numbers and science. Now in this case, the coroner will examine the body to confirm the cause of death. We will ensure that he wasn't drugged or hit before he fell. We will speak to his employers and friends to see if there was any animosity with anyone. We will dust the windows for fingerprints. It will all be very thorough. You see, we follow a chain of evidence, finding hard proof to arrive at the most logical conclusion. There's no scope for anything else.'

'What about instinct, Inspector? What about imagination?'

The inspector paused mid-bite, a spot of ketchup glistening in his moustache. He frowned at Radhi. 'Imagination?'

Radhi nodded, 'The great big "What if?"'

The inspector looked at Sanjana to see if she was following what her friend was saying. Sanjana smiled back at him. He took another bite of his fritter, then stared uncomprehendingly at Radhi.

'Don't you have to ask yourself, what if this wasn't an accident?' Radhi explained. 'What if he wasn't alone today? What if someone pushed him? Or he jumped of his own accord? What if he was scared of something? Or someone? Or if he was depressed? I hear that his wife left him because his daughter's wedding fell through. What if this isn't just some rumour? What if the first death wasn't a suicide? If the two deaths are connected in some way?'

When he still looked confused, she added, 'My point, Inspector, is that surely you must examine a situation from every angle imaginable? To see not just what is, but the myriad possible reasons for why it might be so. Surely there are some questions you ask purely on instinct?'

Radhi took a deep breath when she finished. Her passionate little speech had surprised even her. She looked at the inspector, wondering if she'd got through to him.

But the man was shaking his head vigorously. Having finished his last fritter and washed it down with the remaining *kokam* sherbet, he was now trying to speak and supress an urge to burp at the same time.

'*This. This* is the problem with all these Netflix shows! This is why I've forbidden my team from watching all those police procedurals! They've made solving crime so glamorous. What did the victim do twenty-four hours before dying? Why was there no soap in the soap dispenser? Why was the bowl of soup unfinished? They make everything sound so mysterious. But crime is not always this exciting, madam. Chances are the victim didn't finish the soup because he didn't like how it tasted! I am sorry to disappoint you, but I've been doing this for twenty years. Sometimes, things are simply as they appear.'

Radhi watched him thoughtfully. He was wiping his greasy hand on his trousers, having failed to notice the tissue box on the table in front of him. He heaved himself up and brushed the crumbs from his clothes on to the floor.

'Madam, please don't get into all this.' He addressed Sanjana. 'You need to take care of yourself right now.' Then turning to both women, 'This is still the preliminary stages of the investigation. If we learn anything new, I will personally keep you informed.' He bowed slightly and showed himself out.

In the silence that followed, Sanjana fixed Radhi with a grave look.

'So now you know what your problem is,' she said.

Radhi looked at her friend blankly.

'Clearly, you watch far too much TV.'

'Clearly,' Radhi agreed. They burst out laughing.

A few moments later, the two friends sobered up. After their conversation with the inspector, they'd realized that if they were to arrive at the truth, it would have to be on their own.

* * *

Radhi was in bed with a glass of red wine and a book when she received an email from George. She'd taken to writing to him every other day. The act of writing cleared her head and gave her a sense of release, so essential to sorting her thoughts.

Radhi! My love! How's my favourite Nancy Drew doing? Many apologies for the late reply. I'm at a Kundalini yoga retreat in the Hamptons and they've taken away our phones! Can you imagine? Today, they gave us half an hour with the computers at the business centre. 30 mins to reply to 87 emails! Takes me longer to jack off! Anyway, so I'll keep this super quick. I was thinking about your last mail. The one where you said that Mr Kadakia confirmed his appointment with the dentist? That's really not that strange you know. People who're going to commit suicide often go about their normal routines — returning calls, attending meetings, watering their plants, paying their bills — right up to the moment they top themselves! It's almost as if the routine is a crutch to hang on to until they finally have the opportunity or the balls to do the deed. Anyway, this is just something for you to keep in mind. More later. Gotta go now. We're activating the latent energy at the base of our spines today. Is it me or does that sound a little kinky? Anyway, wish me luck!'

XOXO

G

Radhi poured herself another glass of wine before replying to his mail.

There was another death today. Bhawani — the Kadakias' cook. An accident on the face of it. But let's for a moment say it wasn't. The question I'm asking myself is, who would gain from killing a cook? With Mr Kadakia there was money involved. A hefty insurance policy, a prestigious apartment, his debts — any of that could've been the motive. But what about Bhawani? Who would gain? Or what if I'm looking at this completely wrong? What if Bhawani killed Mr Kadakia? — God knows, he was angry enough — and then good old karma got Bhawani? Or someone else did?

* * *

'Shhh . . . enough now, enough . . . Here, have some water.' Lila handed the glass gently to the crying young woman in front of her.

This small act of kindness brought on a fresh onset of tears. Radhi watched as Lila tried pacifying the woman, clucking endearments in Marathi, as if to a small child.

'Where did you find her?' she asked Lila.

'On the stairs between the third and the fourth floor,' said Lila.

Radhi studied the young woman's dishevelled appearance, the red-eyed despair, the hysterical sobbing and knew then that she was looking at love.

'How long were you and Bhawani together?' she asked Kamal softly.

The woman gasped, staring at Radhi, her mouth open, tears forgotten. Radhi looked back at her kindly, well aware of the follies of youth and their unanticipated consequences.

Suddenly, Kamal started to cry again, louder than before, but this time, Radhika thought, in relief.

Radhi waited for her to grow quiet. Finally, she blew her nose and wiped her face with the pallu of her sari, before accepting the cup of fortifying ginger tea that Lila had made her.

'It's been more than a year.' Her voice was so quiet, Radhi almost missed it.

'You knew he was married and had two grown children, right?'

Kamal didn't answer the question. 'It gets really lonely sometimes for us, *didi*. I don't have any family here. I visit my village for a week during the Ganpati festival and another week during Holi. Other than that there's no real human connection. Bhawani had his faults but he . . . he could be really nice if he wanted to be. He used to tell me I had the gait of a dancer and that he loved watching me walk away. He would go to the temple and come back with flowers for my hair. He would say, "Half the flowers I gave my God, and the other half I brought for my Goddess."'

Kamal's eyes had started to water again. 'I know he was just a sweet-talker, but for that short time in the day that we were together, I didn't feel like a maid. I felt seen.'

Loneliness it seemed was another equalizer, Radhi thought.

'May I ask you something, Kamal?' asked Radhi seriously.

Kamal stopped sniffling and gave Radhi a small nod.

'What was Bhawani hiding?' At any other time, Kamal would probably not have answered this question, but right now, in her grief, her guard was down, Radhi suspected.

Kamal suddenly looked scared. 'I don — don't know what you mean,' she stammered, her eyes flitting from Lila to Radhi and back to Lila, making a silent plea for help.

'If there's something you know, you should tell *didi*,' Lila warned sternly. 'This is not the time to hide it. She'll make sure you don't get into trouble.'

Kamal was quiet for a few moments as if weighing her options. 'He'd been in a foul mood ever since Kirti *bhai* refused him money for his daughter's wedding. "I'll teach them a lesson," he would say. He said he was going to quit but I didn't take him seriously. I thought he wouldn't leave me and go. On that afternoon, the day that Kirti *bhai* died, we were together." She blushed fiercely as she said this.

'We heard a noise and we got worried. We thought that Kirti *bhai* had come out of his study. Bhawani went out to check what it was and he was away for a good ten minutes. When he came back, he was behaving very strangely. I asked him what took him so long, but he wouldn't answer. Soon after, he left. Then I found out Kirti *bhai* had died and I was terrified that Bhawani had something to do with it. I pleaded with him, fought with him, even threatened him that I would tell everyone that he was in the house that afternoon, but he didn't pay me any attention. He knew I was too much in love with him to get him in trouble.'

Kamal hung her head in shame, perhaps wishing she'd said something sooner.

'Why did he suddenly decide to leave without a job?'

'I don't know.' Kamal shook her head. 'He was very angry at Ranjan *bhai* . . . but there was something else . . .' She fell quiet. 'There was a sort of nervous energy about him . . . I can't explain it . . . He was skulking around the apartment. Snooping about the study, even though we'd been told not to go in. One night, I even saw him enter Manju *bhabhi*'s room. It was as if he was scared of something and yet excited.'

Radhi was quiet for a few minutes as she studied the troubled young woman in front of her. Kamal was twirling the end of her sari's pallu, around and around her finger, then uncurling it and twisting it back again. Radhi wondered why she was still so nervous. Was she worrying about the consequences of what she'd just admitted? Or was there something else?

Finally, Radhi asked, 'Was there anything about the day Kirti *bhai* died that was unusual? Anything you remember now that you didn't think of before?'

It was so typical, thought Kamal bitterly. Wasn't Bhawani also dead? Hadn't his death been as horrible and as sudden as the old man's? But instead of asking about him, this, *didi*, was still hung up on Kirti *bhai*'s suicide. Clearly, some lives were more valuable than others.

She shook her head, 'Nothing, really.'

'Any conversations, arguments, anything different than before?' Radhi pressed. She wanted to ask if anyone had behaved differently, but she didn't dare. Already Kamal was looking at her curiously, wondering what she was getting at. The maid might be young and uneducated, but she was no fool. She might realize what Radhi suspected, and if that happened then before noon the entire servant network of Sea Mist would be talking about Mr Kadakia's murder.

Kamal appeared to give it thought. 'The family was always arguing, *didi*, Ranjan *bhai* with Hetal *bhabhi*, Hetal *bhabhi* with Manju b*habhi*, Manju *bhabhi* with Kirti *bhai*. If they were together in the same room, they would bicker. Only Amit *bhai* and Sonal *bhabhi* seemed away from all of it. Too busy with their work. They don't get involved in the family drama.'

'Were you there when Ranjan fought with Kirti *bhai*?'

Kamal frowned, shook her head. 'When was this? I don't know about it.'

Radhi instantly regretted asking and hoped that Kamal was too preoccupied with her own troubles to read too much into her questions.

'I was there when Hetal *bhabhi* and Kirti *bhai* fought though,' Kamal blurted out, unexpectedly.

Radhi tried to hide her surprise. 'When was this?'

Kamal thought about it for a second. 'I guess it was on the day that Kirti *bhai* died. Sorry, I didn't mention it before. I had completely forgotten about it! Like I told you, arguments were very common . . . but not between Kirti *bhai* and Hetal *bhabhi*. *They* hardly even interacted. So I was a little surprised when I heard their raised voices coming from the study.'

'What was it about, do you know?'

Kamal shrugged dismissively. 'God only knows. I don't understand Gujarati much. I think she was just in one of her moods that day. Yelled at me about that missing glass and then picked a fight with her father-in-law. Bhawani always said, she was the most unpredictable of the lot.'

At the thought of Bhawani, Kamal fell silent, her eyes again filling with tears. After some time, she said, 'I need to go now. They'll be wondering where I am. You — you won't tell, right?'

Radhi looked at her reassuringly. 'Don't worry.'

She hoped Kamal wouldn't say anything to anyone else about her own questions either. She could have told her not to, but that would probably have the opposite effect. One can't buy loyalty and good housekeeping at Rs. 15,000 a month.

She thanked the young woman. Once Lila had shown Kamal out, she bustled off to the kitchen and, a few minutes later, came out carrying two cups of tea and a plate of spicy parathas stuffed with cauliflower, potatoes and mint leaves. She placed the tea and the butter-smothered parathas in front of Radhi, then, seating herself on the window ledge with her own cup, asked, 'What are you thinking, *didi*?'

Radhi, who'd been staring out the window at the family of five egrets perched on the old banyan tree in their compound, gave Lila a small smile. 'I'm thinking that I should go talk to Hetal. But it's not going to be easy. For all her talkativeness, she has a lot of walls up. She's a very guarded person. I don't know if she'll answer my questions.'

'Why not take Sanjana *didi*, along?'

'Yes, I'll have to.'

'What did you think of what Kamal just told you?'

'I thought she was telling the truth, but not the whole truth.'

'Meaning?'

So, Radhi told Lila what she suspected Kamal was hiding.

CHAPTER 21

Hetal's studio was on the ground floor of a small, heritage building at the bottom of Teertha, Temple Hill's third hill. Radhi had decided to drop by without calling in advance. She wanted an element of surprise. Something to throw Hetal slightly off-kilter. Hetal was busy with a client when Radhi got there, which worked out well, since Sanjana, who was still stuck in traffic, would take a few minutes to arrive. Radhi didn't want to start the conversation without her. Hetal's assistant showed Radhi into a small waiting area with a large glass window, through which she could see the entire studio and Hetal at work. The space was done up in subtle shades of beige, brown and gold, and Radhi was surprised to see how tasteful it was. Somehow, Hetal hadn't given her the impression of being an understated person.

On one of the walls in the waiting area there were six gilded frames, each had a blown-up picture of a piece of jewellery. Underneath each picture was an elaborate "H" embossed in gold, along with the name of the piece, the date on which it had been designed and a little story about how it had been inspired.

A diamond choker, with a stunning emerald centrepiece edged with tear-shaped pearls, caught Radhi's eye. Below it,

Hetal spoke about how she'd grown up watching her mother wear a gorgeous diamond bracelet with emerald accents, but how she'd never quite had the perfect neckpiece to match it.

'Each time Mummy wore that bracelet, I would be bothered by the diamonds or the pearls she'd chosen to match it. Nothing she owned was quite right. So when I began designing jewellery, this was one of the first pieces I conceived.'

Through the large glass window, Radhi observed Hetal's studio. On three sides, it had wall-to-ceiling glass showcases, each with a mannequin neck displaying white-gold jewellery studded with diamonds, sapphires, emeralds and rubies. Hetal's designs were bold, signature pieces. Flamboyant without being loud. It seemed to Radhi that the insecurities she displayed in real life did not translate into her work. She designed with a confident, sure hand and her pieces were unapologetic, not only about their size but about how expensive they were. Hetal looked up and saw Radhi watching her. She gave her a small, surprised wave before turning her attention back to her client.

Radhi had just sat on the sofa and picked up one of the glossy bridal magazines displayed on the magazine rack on the corner table when Sanjana walked in.

'Hi.'

She sat down with an audible sigh and leaned her head against the wall behind her. She looked tired, her skin grey and drawn. She closed her eyes as she caught her breath, her hands protectively splayed over her swollen belly.

'Sorry.' She opened her eyes, after a few seconds. 'It's just been a lot.'

'All OK at work?' asked Radhi, hoping that her job was at least part of why her friend looked so drained.

Sanjana ignored her question. 'I just met with Papa's old accountant.'

'And?'

'Not here, I'll tell you about it on our way home. Is Hetal still with her client?'

Radhi was just about to reply when the door to the waiting area opened and a visibly surprised Hetal entered the room.

'Hi.' She looked curiously at Radhi, then Sanjana, and then back again at Radhi, a small, uncertain smile on her face. 'My assistant told me you've been waiting. Sorry. This was an old but very fussy client.'

'No, no . . . *we're* sorry to come unannounced like this,' Sanjana said quickly. 'Radhi told me we should call first but I said we'll just wait. Hetal will spare a few minutes for us.'

'Of course, *didi*, come. Should we talk in the studio?'

Without waiting for a reply, Hetal turned, leading them out of the room. As she passed her assistant, she asked her to send in two cups of coffee and a glass of coconut water.

The studio smelled of clove and lavender. It was a pleasant, delicate fragrance that seemed to be emanating from an incense-oil burner in the corner of the room. Beside it, on a corner table, stood a tall flower vase with an elaborate arrangement of purple orchids.

Radhi glanced at Hetal's desk. It was a cluttered but tasteful jumble of files, picture frames, marker pens, rough pads with hand-drawn designs, and quirky stationery. As Hetal shuffled some papers and cleared up her desk, Radhi looked at her with new eyes, seeing her as more than Sanjana's chatty sister-in-law. Here was a talented, driven and ambitious woman. But the question was how far would she go to realize her dreams?

Hetal switched off a couple of overhead yellow spotlights, so that the room was more mellow and comfortable to sit in. She turned to them expectantly.

'So?' Her smile was uncertain. 'What's going on? And, *didi*, you aren't looking too well, would you like to lie on the sofa instead, with your feet up?'

Sanjana waved her away. 'I'm fine . . . This will hopefully not take too long.' She took a deep breath and forged ahead. 'Hetal, did you have an argument with Papa on the day he died?'

Hetal looked at them wordlessly, opening her mouth and shutting it. Radhi could almost see her brain grappling with the implications of lying or telling the truth. Finally, the woman answered. 'So what if I did? How does it even matter at this point?'

'It matters to me. If he was upset about something, I want to know,' Sanjana said.

'I'm sorry, *didi*. It was between me and Papa. It has nothing to do with you or Papa's death. Who told you about it anyway?' She threw Radhi an accusing look.

'Why did you need to order new latex gloves? What happened to your old ones?' Radhi asked levelly.

'What?' Hetal's expression had changed from one of anger to distress.

Radhi pressed on. 'Why did you lie about where you were at the time of his death?'

'I didn't!'

'You said you were at Worli Naka buying fruits that afternoon, after which you went to your tailor. But Worli Naka is shut in the afternoon between 2 and 4 p.m. So, why did you lie?'

'How dare you come into my office and call *me* a liar?' Hetal's voice was rising. It was shrill, angry and laced with unmistakable fear.

'This is rich coming from you!' She turned to Sanjana. 'Your father lied to us and almost ruined us in the process! And you have the gall to call me a liar?'

Sanjana raised her hand, a pinched expression on her face. 'Hetal, please—'

But Hetal was too wound up to stop now. 'We've become the talk of the town because of your father! And your brother? Don't even get me started on *his* lies!

'And you—' She turned her gaze on Radhi. 'I've heard all about *you* and your propensity for attracting trouble. I know your kind of people. So deeply troubled and unhappy within that they'll do anything to distract themselves from their own problems and focus on others . . . What good do you think you are doing? Encouraging Sanjana *didi*, in her delusions. Some friend you are—'

'Enough, Hetal!' Sanjana's voice was choked up, her face ashen. She whispered to Radhi, 'Take me to a doctor.'

Both Radhi and Hetal stared at Sanjana uncomprehendingly.

'I need a doctor,' Sanjana repeated weakly.

This time her words registered. Both women sprang into action, Radhi calling Ramzan *bhai* to be ready at the gate, Hetal helping Sanjana get to her feet. But as Sanjana turned towards the door, they froze. For at the back of the pregnant woman's white kurta was a bright red stain, the size of a fist.

* * *

The sky had changed colour almost without warning. One moment the sun had been out, in the next it had been swallowed whole by a sudden assault of hungry, dark clouds. It seemed purple and bruised now. Swollen, as if it had witnessed unspeakable acts. A lance of lightning pierced it again and then again. Ruthless, in its interrogation. Any moment now, the quivering sky seemed ready to spill its secrets. But not yet. Not today.

* * *

Kamal's knife hovered over the julienned celery and carrots on her chopping board. She watched the lightning slash the sky with sharp, jagged cuts, and wondered what it would be like to run the edge of her knife across her left wrist. She wasn't sure what she was most affected by, Bhawani's death, the manner of his dying, the thing that she had done or the terrifying suspicion that what she'd done had somehow led to his death.

* * *

Hetal looked out at the Arabian Sea from the window of her studio. To the world, it seemed livid. The water had turned dark, the colour of ash. The waves were pounding the shore, hurling themselves relentlessly against the rocks, raging without mercy. But Hetal knew what lay beneath the anger. What often lay beneath anger. Pain. The sea was hurting for the sky. Watching as the lightning tormented its beloved, unable to help, furious at its own impotence. What inspired such loyalty, she wondered? What begot such devotion? The persistent ringing of her phone snapped her out of her reverie. It was Jayesh. She wiped her sweaty palms with her *kurta* and answered the phone.

* * *

'How is she, *didi*?' Lila asked, as she handed Radhi the glass of water.

Radhi had just come home from the hospital and was sitting on the sofa smoking a cigarette and staring unseeingly at the Marathi movie playing on the TV. Lila took the remote and switched off the television.

'What is it, *didi*? Is Sanjana *didi*, OK? Is the baby fine?' Lila asked more urgently this time.

Lila's tone brought Radhi back to the present. 'Sorry, Lila. Yes. Yes. Sanjana is OK and so is the baby. Thank God. But Sanjana has a condition with her placenta. She's been advised to take complete bed rest. The doctor's told her not to work and just take care of herself.'

'OK . . . So, that's not too bad then, right?' Lila's tone was uncertain.

Radhi shook her head, her expression grim. 'She came very close to losing the baby today. The doctor didn't tell Sanju, but he told us.'

'Good heavens!' Lila wiped her forehead with the pallu of her sari before seating herself on the window ledge, her usual perch.

'You know,' Radhi continued. 'I can't stop thinking what if she had? It would have all been my fault, wouldn't it?'

'Your fault? What in the world are you talking about, *didi*?'

'Think about it, Lila! I am leading her on this wild goose chase! If not for me and my theory that Kirti Uncle was murdered, she would've got over her initial disbelief about his suicide and be so much closer to accepting his death. But because of all the doubts I've been raising, she hasn't even been able to grieve properly.

'She has so much to look forward to. But she isn't moving on. Rather than making plans for the baby, we're plotting about how to find a murderer! The doctor has told her not to work because he doesn't want her stressed. But we know it's not work, right? It's all of this that's got her so worked up—'

'*Phishh*! What hogwash, *didi*! How can you even think like that? Are you seriously telling me that it was a mistake to tell your friend that her father may have been murdered? You would rather let her believe that he didn't care enough to stick around and hold his grandchild? C'mon, some friend you'd be! Put yourself in her place. Wouldn't you want the truth?'

But Radhi didn't answer. She lit up another cigarette and went to stand by the window instead.

'I'm going to get you food. You need to eat.' Lila got up and walked away to the kitchen.

Radhi scanned the bloated, slate-coloured sky, amazed that it was so dark at just five in the evening. She heard the clap-boom of thunder. It was loud and ominous and yet not loud enough to drown out her thoughts.

Her conversation with Jayesh at the hospital was haunting her. How afraid the poor man had seemed, how desperate. After Hetal had left, he'd sat with Radhi and pleaded with her to stop this "madness".

'I know my wife can be very stubborn once she gets an idea in her head. And I know the two of you have some doubts about how Papa died. But surely there's a reasonable explanation for all of it? And if not, then just take it to the police. If they feel the need to reopen the investigation, they will. But Sanjana can't be running around the city meeting her dad's doctor and accountant and God knows who else! Her father's dead, for heaven's sake, but my child is on its way!'

A fork of lightning illuminated the world every few seconds and, along with it, stark reality. Radhi was guilty. She'd advised Sanjana to consider the consequences of all the questions they were asking, but had she stopped to think about them herself? Had she considered the risks? Had she looked closely at her own motives? Was this just another way for her to distract herself? The way she'd been doing all her life. Obsessing over people and things and situations, so she didn't have to pause and look within. Hetal's words came back to bite her. 'Some friend you are!' Had she not been a good friend?

Lila returned with a plate of a rice and lentil *khichdi*, a thick yogurt-based curry, and a bottle gourd sabzi sweetened with jaggery, which she placed on the dining table.

She stood there with her hands on her hips, until Radhi extinguished her cigarette. But Radhi couldn't eat. The burning sensation in her stomach was back again in full force.

* * *

It rained that night. And for the whole of the next day. It was the kind of downpour that could obliterate every doubt, worry and fear. Not because it was soothing, but because of how incredibly insignificant it made one feel. Problems seemed to diminish in the face of it, rendered inconsequential, shallow, impotent. The weather department had issued a twenty-four-hour red alert for heavy rainfall, and schools and businesses were ordered to shut.

Radhi gave Lila the day off, spending it by herself at home. She needed to think about the incredible mess that was her life. A month ago, the plan had been to return to India, to focus on herself and her career. How had she managed to get this derailed? True, she was helping her friend. But if she thought about it honestly, wasn't she a little relieved that she had an excuse not to write?

Two years ago, she'd been frozen when her last book was such a staggering hit. She'd been unable to write because she'd been petrified she wouldn't be able to repeat its success.

Then Mackinzey had disappeared from her life, and any guilt she'd had over not writing had dissipated. Surely, no one could expect her to think in the face of such a glaring loss? Now back in India, Radhi had latched on to this tragedy. Poring over every little detail of the situation, thinking about the Kadakias every waking moment, ensuring in the process that she had no headspace for anything else.

As Radhi contemplated her decisions, she moved restlessly about her apartment, putting up picture frames and paintings on the walls. She responded to emails and messages from friends, both in India and in New York, spoke to her business manager, who wanted her to sign off on a few investment decisions. And she read.

She made herself a creamy, mushroom risotto, opened up a bottle of Merlot and settled down to read Agatha Christie's *Crooked House*. About a murder in a wealthy, dysfunctional family.

CHAPTER 22

'Hi, Radhi? This is Jayesh. Can you talk?'

Radhi stopped, immediately concerned that he was calling her so early in the morning. 'Oh hi, Jayesh . . . All okay?'

'No . . . Well, yes, I mean the baby's OK . . . but Sanjana . . . she's just . . . I don't know. She's really out of it. Can you come over?'

Radhi hung up, promising him that she'd be there in ten minutes. She'd come to the park for a run. It had finally stopped raining, and the air was impossibly clean and filled with the fragrance of wet earth.

As she walked out of the park, she was about to light a cigarette when she noticed a van selling shots of fresh aloe-vera juice. For once in her life, she chose the healthier option, hoping it would be the first of many good decisions.

Jayesh opened the door before she could even ring the bell. Radhi was surprised at how haggard he looked.

'She's taking a nap.' His voice was low as he shut the door softly behind her.

Radhi followed him into the living room and waited until the maid had served her water and left the room.

'So? How're you guys?'

Jayesh shook his head wearily. 'She's a complete mess. She's been crying a lot. Not sleeping at all. I've never seen her like this. Not even when we had the miscarriages. Honestly? I'm a bit terrified. I told her I'd call Manju Aunty here for a few days to stay with us but she refused. Said she wanted to see you.'

Radhi was silent.

Jayesh sighed, then shrugged. 'I know it's about her father. She's obsessed with finding out what happened. I tried to dissuade her in the past because I was thinking about the baby. But I realize that this may have been selfish on my part. It's just that the timing is so . . . shitty.' He rubbed his eyes, looked away.

Radhi nodded. 'I agree. This isn't the time for her to be thinking about death, let alone murder. I've been equally scared since that day at the hospital. I know how badly she's wanted this baby. How much you both do. We can't allow her to risk it.'

Jayesh looked at Radhi, both surprised and grateful. He'd expected her to argue in favour of continuing their investigation. Now, she'd turned out to be an unexpected ally.

'Jayesh? Who're you talking to? Is that Radhi?' Sanjana's voice came to them weakly from the bedroom.

'Sanju, yes, it's me,' Radhi called out, as Jayesh and she both got up and made their way to the room.

'Radhi!' Sanjana clutched her tightly when Radhi bent down to give her friend a hug. 'Thank God you're here!'

Lying on the bed, her eyes sunken, her hair dishevelled, Sanjana looked pale and fraught. Radhi felt a sharp pang of regret at the sight. Instead of an expectant mother's glow, Sanjana's skin was tight and dull. She should have had baby books on her bedside table and been thinking about doing up the nursery, hiring a baby maid and making lists of baby things to buy. Instead, except for her pregnant belly, there was no sign of impending motherhood either in her room or in her eyes.

'Did Jayesh ask you to stay away? Is *that* why you haven't come to see me?' demanded Sanjana, as soon as Radhi had taken a seat at the edge of her bed.

'No, of course not. It was the doctor . . . He told us you needed complete rest. So I thought I'd give it a couple of days before dropping by.'

'I can't rest, Radhi! I can't discuss baby names with Jayesh like he wants me to!' She glared at her husband, who looked away unhappily. 'Not while the person who killed my father roams scot free! Let's find out who did this. After that I will stare at this stupid ceiling and knit mittens all day!'

Radhi looked at her friend sadly. 'What would Kirti Uncle have wanted for you, Sanju? If you're doing this for your father, surely you must think about what would've made him happy? Just look at you. Forget taking good care of yourself, you're not even being responsible. You're actually jeopardizing this pregnancy.'

Sanjana looked visibly upset. 'You've been talking to Jayesh, haven't you?' Then turning on Jayesh, she yelled, 'I'm so mad at you. You're ganging up on me!'

Radhi winced. 'Sanjana, you're taking this the wrong—'

Sanjana cut her off. 'Radhi, I would've thought you of all people would understand the pain of losing a parent before their time had come!' She threw off her blanket and began to get up. 'Never mind. If nobody will help me, I'll do this myself.'

'Stop, Sanju, please.' Jayesh rushed to her side. 'I'm begging you to calm down.' He tried to put his arm around her, but she brushed him off angrily.

'OK.' He raised his hands, palms facing outwards and took a couple of steps back from the bed. 'OK. Just listen to me for a second.'

Sanjana was still glaring at him but she sat back down on the bed.

'Will you please lie down?' Jayesh asked.

She shook her head stubbornly.

He sighed. ' OK. Here's the deal. If you lie down right now. And promise to take good care of yourself. I promise to help Radhi with whatever she needs in finding out who did this.'

Sanjana didn't budge. She looked at Jayesh, not sure whether to believe him.

'Please,' he whispered desperately. 'I swear. *I swear on my unborn child*!'

Sanjana stared at Jayesh for a few moments longer, then her anger seemed to fizzle out of her. Her shoulders slumped forward. Her eyes welled up with tears.

'Hush, darling.' Jayesh went to her and gently helped her back into bed.

There was a knock at the door, and the maid came into the room carrying a tray laden with food. She placed it on the window ledge and went back out to get another tray containing plates, spoons and forks. On the first, there were tall glasses of freshly squeezed sweet lime juice, a platter of apple slices, a savoury semolina cake stuffed with grated carrots and spinach, and steamed fenugreek nuggets seasoned with sesame seeds and coriander, accompanied by a bowl of thick, black date-and-tamarind chutney.

Sanjana's eyes were on the food. 'I'm suddenly hungry!'

Jayesh and Radhi exchanged relieved glances. He put out a raised tray in front of Sanjana and laid a napkin across her lap.

Looking at them, Radhi suddenly felt an intense longing for Mackinzey. Just a few months before he disappeared from her life for ever, he'd nursed her back to health from a terrible case of flu. How tender he'd been, how tolerant of her crabby mood.

She sighed and accepted the plate the maid was holding out to her.

'OK,' Jayesh said, after all three of them had settled in with their food and the maid had left the room. 'Sanju's told me a little bit about what you guys know. And I'll admit it sounds . . . off. My question is why not go to the police? My dad knows a few senior people. I'm sure we can get them to reopen the case. Do you want me to talk to Manju Aunty and the rest of the family?'

'I don't think that would be a good idea, Jayesh,' Radhi murmured quietly.

He stared at Radhi for a few seconds as the implications of what hadn't been said sank in.

'No!' He looked horrified. 'Surely you don't think that?'

Radhi didn't respond.

'You *seriously* think someone from the family is involved? Come on, Radhi . . .'

'We don't know yet,' she admitted. 'I believe Bhawani had something to do with it. And now he is dead. I don't think that's a coincidence.'

Over the next few minutes, Radhi and Sanjana filled Jayesh in on everything they knew so far. What Kamal had told them. How Mr Poddar was involved. How Hetal had been caught lying. And how she now claimed that Ranjan was lying too.

When he'd heard everything, Jayesh fell silent, mulling it all over. 'I don't know what to say . . . You're right. When you look at it all together, it does seem a bit *much*—'

'Oh, before I forget,' Sanjana interrupted. 'Remember that insurance policy Amit was talking about?'

Radhi nodded.

'Turns out that Hetal and Ranjan convinced Papa to buy this policy about four years ago. You know how I met my father's old accountant the other day?' Sanjana didn't pause for an answer. 'Well, he told me that the insurance agent is Hetal's cousin.'

There it was again. Another coincidence. Radhi filed this information away to chew it over later.

The three of them carried on debating what had happened and, by the time Radhi left, she was glad to see that Sanjana was in much better spirits.

* * *

The Temple Hill Gymkhana had a new name — The Caramel Club of Sports and Fitness, but nobody ever remembered to call it that. Not even the staff who worked there. Among the residents of Temple Hill, it was still the THG, a place of cliquish privilege that hadn't given out new memberships in the entire last decade.

Sprawled beside the sea, across four luxurious acres, the THG comprised two large buildings that accommodated the badminton, squash and TT courts, along with the gymnasium, the yoga studio and various other sports facilities. A third, stouter building housed banquet halls and ballrooms, where members of the THG could host weddings and parties, as well as a few floors of comfortable overnight rooms, which members could book for themselves or their guests.

Radhi hadn't been here since she was a little girl, when she used to come with her mother, who'd drop her off for her tennis class before going for a swim. As Radhi walked up to the building that housed the main reception area, she marvelled at how much everything had changed. Gone were the pastel-coloured cement structures with their large, overhanging eaves. Now, everything was sleek, made of glass and steel that gleamed in the sunlight.

Ranjan had said that after his session with Mr Ganatra, he had gone for a workout to the gym at the THG. But what if he hadn't? Or what if he had, just not at the time he'd said?

Radhi walked up to the reception desk, where the entry registers used to lay open with pens hanging from ribbons. Members had to flash their ID cards at the staff manning the desk and note the time of their arrival in the register, with a signature beside it. More often than not though, they'd just flash big smiles. The staff had been around for ages and recognized most of the regulars. At the reception desk, however, there were no registers.

'Where do I sign in?' Radhi asked the man behind the counter.

He pointed to a small scanning device on the desk. 'ID card.'

'So, there's no entry register anymore?'

The man at the reception looked at her curiously.

'Are you a member, madam?' There was obviously no point answering her question, if Radhi wasn't one.

'I am.'

The man nodded and didn't say anything. Radhi realized he was waiting for her to give him her card. Quickly she fished out her ID and handed it to him. He checked the photo on the card and looked at her. The photo was over a decade old. If she were being kind to herself, she'd say at least her hair was definitely different.

'It doesn't look like you, ma'am,' he concluded, after a pause.

'Well, it is me.'

'Would you happen to have another ID card?'

Radhi brought out her US driver's licence. This one had a more recent picture. Finally, the man was satisfied.

'You live in America, ma'am?' he asked, handing back her ID.

'Used to.'

'Well, you need the new RFID card, with the magnetic chip. You need to fill out an application for it.' He produced a blank form from a drawer beneath the desk.

'Thanks.' Radhi took the sheet of paper and folded it in two, before putting it in her purse. 'So there's no entry register anymore?' she repeated.

The man shook his head. 'The entries have all been automated. The feed goes straight to an internal security server.'

'Where's the server located? On the club premises, right? I'd like to see the visitor log.'

'We can't show it to members, ma'am. Those are the club rules.' He was looking at her suspiciously now.

Radhi sighed. She hated what she was about to do but decided it was worth a shot. 'You see the "Zaveri Reading Nook" there?' She gestured to the large library right next to the entrance of the lobby. 'That was made with a donation from my grandfather. He was one of the main founding members of THG.'

The man looked like he didn't much believe her, but he'd had a lifetime's training to be polite, nevertheless.

'It's not up to me, ma'am, but you can speak to the Chairman or someone on the committee to access the records.'

The committee! Of course! Why hadn't she thought of that before! Vrinda *fia* was on the committee and would easily be able to get Radhi what she needed. She nodded at the man, turned away and quickly called her aunt.

* * *

It occurred to Radhi, as she sat at a poolside table waiting for her aunt, that the THG offered a near perfect cross section of Temple Hill's close-knit community. She watched the kids rush from one class to another, skating to gymnastics, tennis to football, with their nannies in tow. Their mums, fitted out in the latest shapely sportswear, regardless of whether any sports had actually been played, sipped on green smoothies, their short time with other mums as nourishing for them as the drinks in their hands. The men would trickle in post work, some carrying their alpha streaks all the way from their boardrooms into the squash and tennis courts. Others would hit the bar to enjoy a game of cricket and a beer with friends — a prized pocket of time before wives, children and parents took charge of their evenings. While the THG was many things to many people, it was the retired uncles and aunties who enjoyed it the most. They met each evening for bingo games, bridge tournaments and film nights. And for precious conversation. Nobody at home had the kind of time they now found on their hands.

Radhi had just ordered a pot of cardamom tea and two plates of *vada paav*, a vegetable burger-like dish, when she saw Vrinda enter the poolside café and scan the tables. Radhi waved at her and Vrinda walked towards her with a smile. Radhi was always amazed at how elegant her aunt managed to look in her simple *mal* saris. While others in their social circle flaunted their diamonds, Vrinda always wore silver. Radhi had got her appreciation for antique silver jewellery from her aunt.

'Here you go.' Vrinda brandished a roll of papers at Radhi. 'The entries for the whole month.'

'Oh, I just wanted it for—'

'I know, I know,' Vrinda interrupted her. 'But I didn't want to draw attention to any particular day or any particular guest. It is better this way.'

Radhi had told her aunt everything she knew so far when she called. Vrinda had listened carefully, interrupting once or twice with a question or two, though she hadn't reacted too much over the phone. But by the way she'd promptly made the calls and acquired the logs that same day, Radhi knew her aunt believed she was on to something.

'So what date are we looking for?' Vrinda was already riffling through the papers.

'Last Wednesday, 28 May.'

'Here you go.' Vrinda handed Radhi six sheets for that date.

As Radhi began to go through the papers, the waiter arrived with the food.

Vrinda raised her eyebrows at the sight of the white buns stuffed with deep-fried potato patties. '*Vada paav*? . . . I can't eat this, love. I don't have the ridiculous metabolism that you and your sister got from your mother!'

'Come now, *fia*! Just look at how incredibly fit you are!'

Vrinda shook her head at the tempting snack Radhi was offering her. 'For a reason, love, for a reason.'

Radhi shrugged and took a big bite of her bun, before wiping her greasy fingers with tissue paper and turning her attention to the tedious-looking sheets Vrinda had handed her. The Gymkhana had almost 700 visitors on 28 May. And every day since, it seemed, from the look of the remaining sheets in *fia*'s hands. The log listed the membership number, the name of the member and the time of entry.

'Why are there no records of the exits?'

'Because when you exit, you don't need to swipe your card. There's no way to record exits, unless we install another set of electronic exit barriers at the gate. Which, the committee felt, and I agree, seemed like a waste of space.'

Radhi went back to the log. Luckily, it was listed chronologically, so she only had to scan the sheets that began after

3 p.m. There were two of them, and Radhi went through both quickly. Ranjan's name wasn't on either.

'It's almost as if I don't want to see it,' she muttered, as she went over the first sheet again more slowly, then handed it off to Vrinda to double-check.

When both of them had gone through the sheets twice, Radhi looked up eagerly. 'Seems like he wasn't here that day. My hunch was right, after—'

'Wait a minute.' Vrinda was looking at a sheet which Radhi had discarded because its entries began at noon. 'See this one, here? It's got a few entries between 3 and 3.15 p.m. right at the bottom.'

Both Radhi and Vrinda bent over the sheet. There on the second-but-last line, 3.15 p.m., was the name Ranjan Kadakia.

* * *

Radhi watched her aunt air kiss an acquaintance she'd just bumped into. Her aunt could talk to anyone. You could put her in front of a punk kid with pink hair and a skeleton tattoo on his face or an MIT professor of aerodynamics and she would find something in common with them. It was a quality Radhi admired greatly, having spent most of her life grappling with what she now knew was social anxiety.

They'd just finished their tea, during which time they'd discussed the Kadakia situation some more. Radhi was frustrated. She felt she was back where she'd started. She'd been sure that Bhawani was hiding something, but he was dead. She'd also been sure that Mr Poddar was hiding something, and he was — well, just not what Radhi had imagined. And she'd been positive that Ranjan was lying, but he'd turned out to be telling the truth. Now she seemed to have reached a dead end. For the first time since she'd started digging, she had no questions left to ask.

Radhi was craving a cigarette but the club was a non-smoking zone. She'd have to go all the way out to the main road to be able to smoke. She was waiting for the waiter to give her the bill, when she saw something that gave her pause. A woman with a large swim bag on her shoulder and two kids in tow was signing a register. She handed an ID card to the man at the counter, who entered the details into his computer. Radhi remembered then that all the various sports facilities maintained their own records of comings and goings, separate from the main entry log. And these, it seemed, were still recorded manually.

Radhi decided to head to the gym to check the register there. She messaged her aunt to wait for her, then headed up to the second floor.

It was relatively easy to get hold of the register there. The attendant who was supposed to be manning the gym desk had to rush over to the spa counter across the hall, because the attendant there had gone on her tea break. Quickly, Radhi turned the register to face her and flipped through the pages to the right date. She scanned the entries, once, twice and then a third time, looking over the single page, back to front, front to back.

There was no Ranjan Kadakia.

* * *

Heart pounding, Radhi rushed to find her aunt and told her what she'd learned.

'Is there any regular trainer or gym attendant we could speak to? I want to be sure that he really didn't come to the gym that day.'

'I'll do you one better. They've recently installed CCTV cameras in some areas of the club, and the gym is one of them.'

Together, Radhi and Vrinda made their way to the building where the senior administrators of the Gymkhana had their offices. They needed permission to access the surveillance footage. As Vrinda went in to one of the offices to speak to the person in charge, Radhi wondered what she would find on the camera. And what it would mean for the Kadakias.

CHAPTER 23

In the car on her way home that evening, Radhi's mind worked with a rapidity that had nothing to do with the three cigarettes she'd chain-smoked outside the Gymkhana premises after her aunt had left. She was stuck again. And yet, she also felt she was inches from the truth. She felt it in her bones. Ranjan couldn't have committed the murder. She couldn't see how. But if not Ranjan, then who? Was it possible she was looking for more than one person? Were there two separate murderers who had killed for two different motives? Or had they worked as a team? Unless, unless . . . was she looking at this completely wrongly? Perhaps it wasn't one of the family. Then what? She called Jayesh and told him she was coming up to see him and Sanjana. Radhi was now close, but for the last fifteen minutes her car had been stuck in traffic, as vehicles streamed out of the parking lot for the Sea Mist.

'What's happening?' she asked Ramzan *bhai*. 'Why are there so many cars coming out of our building?'

'It's the day of the *satsang*, *didi*. The attendees are leaving.'

After a few more minutes waiting for the car to move, Radhi gave up. 'OK, this is silly. I'm just going to walk, Ramzan *bhai*. You can head home after you've parked the car. I won't be needing it tonight.'

'Yes, *didi*.'

Inside the building compound, a large cluster of women were talking in animated voices near the lobby.

'*Maldives? For five days? Nice!*'

'*Taco? Where? In Parel? Good, good, I love Mexican food.*'

'*Bankrupt? No! The Sarafs? Really?*'

Radhi caught snatches of their conversations as she tried to manoeuvre her way through the throng of women waiting for their respective cars and drivers to show up to ferry them home. For a group that was just coming out of a *satsang*, their conversation was so far removed from anything spiritual that Radhi had to fight the urge to giggle.

As she passed the party hall, Radhi noticed two women standing at the exit handing out giveaways to the ladies who were leaving. Each woman was carrying a small transparent bag filled with almonds, large pieces of sugar and dried coconut.

She recognized several of her neighbours from the building as she wove her way through the crowd, nodding hellos to Mrs Maniar, Mrs Gandhi and Mrs Poddar, who gave her a frosty smile. Radhi felt a pang of guilt, even though she'd done nothing wrong. And the Poddars clearly had.

Radhi had a toxic relationship with guilt, and it had formed a major part of her work with her therapist back in New York. Over the years, she'd made some headway. For the most part, she could function with the guilt, without feeling the constant urge to overcompensate. But every now and then, it did tend to get the best of her.

It was in the lift of the B Wing, on her way to Sanjana's apartment, while she was still thinking of the Poddars, that Radhi knew for certain who the murderer was. The realization left her feeling cold all over. She reached Sanjana's floor but didn't immediately step out. She stood there for a few moments, willing her racing mind to slow down enough for her to arrange her thoughts coherently. When she felt ready, Radhi pressed the button to go down. Once outside the lift, Radhi left the building and continued down the hill, until she reached the café White.

'Masala chai,' she mumbled to the waiter, as she absently took a seat.

Radhi wasn't sure how long she sat there, staring out of the window, but there were two empty cups of tea in front of her when she was finally able to pull back from her thoughts and come back to the present. She got out her phone and called Jayesh.

'Hi, can you meet me at White, right now?'

'White? That same place that used to be Mama Jones?'

'Yes.'

'OK . . . but weren't you coming home?'

'Not right away.'

Jayesh walked into the café less than ten minutes later. They waited until the waiter had taken their order for a pot of lemongrass tea and a plate of spinach and corn-stuffed sandwiches, before Radhi told Jayesh what she'd discovered at the THG. And what she now suspected.

When he'd heard her out, Jayesh was quiet for several minutes, his expression hard to read. Finally, he asked Radhi gravely, 'And you're absolutely sure about all of this?'

'No. But I will be in a few hours . . . What about Sanjana? How is she?'

Jayesh sighed. 'After her conversation with you this morning, she's actually doing much better. She ate a big lunch, took a long afternoon nap and even asked me if we could look at pictures of cots.'

'You're worried this is going to throw her into another funk?'

Jayesh fell silent again. They sipped their teas while he processed what to do.

'No,' he sighed. 'I think she is stronger than you or I give her credit for. I think she's mentally prepared for the fact that the truth, whatever it is, is going to be unpleasant. And the sooner we can put this behind us, the better it's going to be . . . But what about the police? Should we say something now?'

Radhi shook her head firmly. 'That is not our call to make. Let the family decide.'

Jayesh looked relieved. 'In any case, it's not like we have any actual proof.'

'No, but I can think of a way we can get some.' A plan had already begun to form in Radhi's mind.

'That's, I don't know, like out of some Bollywood film,' Jayesh announced, when he had heard Radhi's idea.

Radhi shrugged. 'You know what they say — art is inspired by life, but life is equally inspired by art.'

They returned to Sea Mist, where they told Sanjana. Just as Jayesh had predicted, she took the news surprisingly well.

'So, now you need the entire family together here?' Sanjana asked, once she'd heard Radhi's plan. 'That shouldn't be too hard. Jayesh can tell them that I'm sick of bed rest and really down and out. That it would cheer me up to have them here to lunch.'

'Tell them to bring Kamal as well. You can say you need her to help in the kitchen.'

Sanjana nodded.

'And no kids,' Radhi added.

'Don't worry. I'll tell them we want it to be a quiet affair . . . I'll go and make the calls now.' Jayesh rose.

'Thanks, Jayesh, but there's just one more thing I need you to do.'

Radhi had long suspected that Bhawani's death wasn't an accident but hadn't quite figured what anyone would gain by killing him. Until now. She needed Jayesh's help to prove it.

When Sanjana's husband had gone, Radhi asked her friend one last time if she'd thought about the consequences of what they were about to do. Sanjana's almond-shaped eyes were filled with pain. 'No . . . But I *have* thought of the consequences of doing nothing.'

Radhi nodded. 'In that case, I need you to make two calls. One to your father's accountant and the other to—'

* * *

Back home, Radhi asked Lila to make them a large pot of ginger tea. Then they sat by the window. It was drizzling outside.

A soft and gentle rain, like a sort of reconciliatory gesture after the drama of the last few days. As they sipped their tea, Radhi told Lila what she suspected, what she intended to do and why it was important that they speak to Kamal.

* * *

Later that evening, Radhi stood outside Mrs Maniar's house, holding a steaming plate of *pitla*, a Maharashtrian delicacy. She rang the bell.

As before, a shadow could be seen in the gap between the floor and the door and an eye appeared at the peephole. Then the door was flung open. Mrs Maniar stood in a fuschia-coloured, flowy kaftan, her hair in two pigtails.

'Radhika!' she squealed in delighted surprise. It was one thing for her to coerce the younger woman into a breakfast and quite another for Radhi to show up at her doorstep of her own accord. And bearing food! Wait till she told the other neighbours about this!

Radhika smiled brightly at her.

'Sorry, it's taken me for ever to keep my promise.'

'Come in, come in!' urged Mrs Maniar, clueless about what promise Radhika was referring to, but anxious to get her inside, lest she changed her mind.

'I know I've come unannounced, but you have to try this—'

'*Pssh*! We are neighbours!' Mrs Maniar interrupted her. 'This is what neighbours do! They pop in. In the olden days, nobody ever shut their doors. We were in and out of each other's houses constantly. Borrowing flour, sharing a cup of tea, returning a vessel or a wandering child. The doorbell was reserved for guests and postmen. Now, of course, it's all changed. Even five-year-olds need to fix a "date" to play with each other! Anyway, look at me rambling on . . . Now, what do we have here?'

She peered at the fluffy yellow chickpea dish and the rice-flour rotis in Radhi's hand.

'This is *pitlu*. It's a Maharashtrian dish. My cook makes it very well.'

Mrs Maniar called for two bowls and spoons and asked her cook to make them tall glasses of thick buttermilk spiced with rock salt and green chillies. Then the two women settled in for a chat. One just happy to be talking. The other with one particular thing in mind.

CHAPTER 24

Radhi had suggested that they wait until after the lunch was done. She'd wanted to give Sanjana one last chance with her family, just in case she decided to change her mind. But Sanjana hadn't wavered. Everyone was still enjoying their post-meal betel-leaf *paans*, stuffed with *arcia* nuts and sweet, rose-petal preserve, when she'd called Radhi and told her it was time.

As Radhi and Lila walked to the B Wing, Radhi marvelled at herself. She hadn't thought she'd have the stomach for this. What was about to happen would be unpleasant, ugly and irrevocable. She was conscious of all the lives that would be changed for ever. And saddened at the acute human failing that the desperate act of murder represented. And yet, if she was being completely honest with herself, there was also a part of her that had treated the death of Kirti Kadakia like a puzzle to be solved. A purely cerebral exercise like the Rubik's Cube she'd managed to crack at the surprisingly early age of five.

As they stood inside the lift to Sanjana's apartment, Radhi experienced a surge of adrenaline. There was no denying it. She wanted to be here, in the middle of the terrible family tragedy that was about to unfold. To see the murderer's face when she'd proved their guilt. She wondered what that said about her. Something else to explore with a therapist, no doubt. Just not now.

When Radhi rang the bell and walked into the living room, the Kadakias greeted her with a friendly wave. Even Hetal seemed to have put their last encounter behind her. From the looks of the table, which still had to be cleared, they'd had a heavy meal of fried puris, a spicy yellow lentil daal doused in ghee, paneer cubes simmered in a spinach gravy and *basundi*, a creamy, saffron-flavoured, sweet dish made of reduced milk and topped with a generous sprinkle of cashews and almonds. The rich food along with the still afternoon air had made them drowsy, lulling them into dropping some of their normal bitterness and bickering.

Amit, Ranjan and Jayesh were on the sofa in front of the TV, chatting, the fate of the Indian cricket team on mute opposite them. Manjula was near the window, holding a pair of garden scissors. She was examining Sanjana's potted plants, snipping away the extra growth and airing the soil in the pots. Sonal and Hetal were on a long divan beside Sanjana, who was seated on a large, wing-tipped chair, upholstered in a rich Persian-blue velvet. Her feet were resting on a matching ottoman, as she listened to Hetal tell Sonal about her eighteen-hour labour.

At the sight of Radhika, Jayesh switched off the TV and got up. He was clearly nervous and anxious to wind up the pretend "happy family" lunch.

'Hey,' Amit protested. 'We were watching that!'

Jayesh gave him an apologetic look.

'Listen everybody.' He paused until he had everyone's attention. 'Radhi has something she wants to tell us. But before she speaks, I want to apologize to each and every one of you. I'm sorry this is happening in my home. I truly am. But it *is* necessary.'

A buzz of confusion spread through the room as everyone tried to speak at once. The sluggishness of the afternoon had suddenly evaporated, leaving everyone alert and curious.

Jayesh went to stand at the back of the room, and Radhi came forward to take his place. Lila crept quietly to stand beside Jayesh, to do what Radhi had instructed her to do.

'What is this?' Manjula Kadakia stared at Sanjana, who refused to meet her eyes or those of anyone else in the family. She looked straight ahead instead, a pained expression on her face.

'Aunty, please,' Radhika said firmly. 'Let me speak.'

Manjula silently took a seat on the wooden swing by the window.

'As all of you already know, Sanjana has had a hard time accepting Kirti Uncle's suicide—'

'Oh, come on. Not this again,' muttered Ranjan under his breath.

Radhi ignored him. 'Over the last week, I've been helping her find answers to what happened. What might have drawn Kirti Uncle to end his life? Was it his financial troubles, or something else? We've spoken to his doctor, a couple of neighbours, his work associates—'

'I don't believe this!' Ranjan interrupted, his voice louder this time. 'My father's dead! Let him go peacefully, I—'

'Ranjan.' Amit gave his younger brother a look. 'Let Radhika speak.'

Ranjan glared at Radhi but fell silent.

'As I was saying, we've been trying to understand why Kirti Uncle might commit suicide. Now we know the truth.'

A palpable ripple of tension passed through the room. Radhi paused to look at everyone in turn.

They all stared back at her, their bodies stiff with expectation. And something more.

'Well? Why did he do it?' Hetal broke the silence, her voice unnaturally shrill.

'He didn't.' Radhi announced this so softly that for a moment it seemed like no one had heard her.

'What did you say?' There was a shocked tremor in Manjula's voice.

'Kirti Uncle didn't commit suicide. He was murdered.' This time it was obvious everyone had heard, Radhi's voice loud and clear. 'Murdered by someone in this family.'

A death-like hush descended upon the room. Sonal turned to look at Sanjana, as if for confirmation, her eyes wide with horror. Hetal sat absolutely still on the sofa, her pudgy hand covering her open mouth. Manjula was holding on to the thick, jute rope of the swing, clinging to it as if for dear life. Amit seemed stunned, the wind knocked out of him, while the blood drained out of Ranjan's face, leaving him grey.

Sanjana looked at her family, her eyes full of tears and regret. And Jayesh was looking at Sanjana, a silent prayer on his lips for his wife to get through this afternoon safely.

'What absolute hogwash is this!' Ranjan erupted, then addressing Sanjana, '*Didi*, your friend needs help!'

The silence now broken, everyone began to speak at once.

'Sanjana, what's gotten into you?'

'Radhika, why are you hell-bent on causing trouble?'

'What is this? A Bollywood film?'

'Guys! Guys!' Sanjana shouted. 'Please. If you don't let Radhi speak, we are going to go to the police with what we know.'

That got everyone's attention, and a brittle and jittery silence settled upon the room once again.

'We started out by asking if Kirti Uncle had had any big fights or disagreements with anyone. A neighbour perhaps or someone he worked with? Turned out Bhawani and he had a showdown a couple of weeks ago because Kirti Uncle refused to lend him money for his daughter's wedding.

'Then we found out that Mr Poddar from the third floor had come to see Uncle the day he died, and they'd had a big argument, as well. But it wasn't him. No. The fight that led to his death was different, more bitter, more personal.

'As we dug deeper, we realized that instead of other people, we should have been paying more attention to his relationships with the people within his own home.' Radhi surveyed each person in the room, before adding, 'One of you has been very angry with him. One of you has been lying to us about where you were on the afternoon that Kirti Uncle died.'

'I didn't do it,' said a voice so softly that Radhi thought she'd imagined it.

Radhi turned to a visibly shaken Hetal. 'I didn't say you did.'

'I lied about where I was that afternoon, but I didn't kill him.'

Radhi stayed quiet, letting the woman unburden herself.

'Yes, I did have an argument with him that morning. And I said some things that I'm ashamed of. But I swear on my children, I had nothing to do with his death!'

Radhi waited to see if she would say anything more. But Hetal just sat there on the sofa, perspiring in spite of the air conditioning.

'I know you didn't do it, Hetal,' Radhi confirmed. 'There's someone else who has also been lying to us all along.' She looked directly at Hetal's husband.

'Ranjan, you told the police that you had a physio session that afternoon, after which you went to the THG to work out at the gym.'

Ranjan all but froze. 'Yes . . . Yes, I did.'

'Only you didn't. There's an entry that shows you arrived at the THG, but there's none in the gym register.' Radhi retrieved the printouts of the entry log from her purse and waved them in front of Ranjan.

'So? I must not have signed the register that day. They aren't very strict about it.' Ranjan scornfully dismissed the sheets.

'I thought you might say that, so I checked the CCTV footage in the gym as well. You didn't go to the gym at all that day. You entered the club but left soon after, knowing fully well that the RFID system only records the entries, not the exits . . . Why did you lie, Ranjan?'

'It doesn't matter why I lied. I didn't kill my father!' Ranjan cried.

Radhi ignored him. 'You know what's strange? You fought with your father and two days later, he ended up dead. Then you had a fight with Bhawani and that same week he ended up dead, too. Isn't that too much of a coincidence?'

'What are you saying?' asked Ranjan hotly, 'Is she insane?' He turned to Sanjana who stared back at him silently.

Radhi continued. 'You convinced your father to buy that insurance policy, didn't you?'

Ranjan stared defiantly at Radhi. 'What if I did? Everyone knows that!'

'But do they know that you paid his premium this year because you knew he couldn't afford to? That you knew about your father's financial troubles long before they did?'

'You knew?' Amit sounded shocked.

'No, I didn't!' Ranjan glanced nervously from Amit to his mother, who was looking equally stunned by Radhi's revelations.

'But you did. Mr Ganatra told me he asked you to speak to Kirti Uncle about his losses. So, in fact, you knew many months ago.'

Ranjan slapped his own forehead. 'Yes. Yes. But not to this extent! At that point, the losses were manageable!'

'That morning, you said your father called you to ask about his chequebook. It doesn't take ten minutes to talk about that. There was something else in that call that triggered his murder, wasn't there?'

'What are you talking about? This is rubbish!' Ranjan's face was now an angry shade of pink, and he was sweating profusely.

'Yes, Papa called me about something else. He wanted to borrow money from me. Said he owed someone and that he would pay me back. But I . . . I refused. I was a complete jerk about it. And I've been kicking myself ever since!'

'You know, Ranjan, that sounds so believable that I could almost think I'd got it all wrong. Only problem is that

Bhawani saw you in the house that afternoon. And began to blackmail you about it. And then you had to kill him too.'

'OK, this is now crazy! You can theorize all you want! I'm going home! I don't have to listen to this!' Ranjan picked up his phone and keys from where they were lying on the centre table and put them in his pocket. He looked around the room, as if daring someone to stop him. Nobody moved. Yet he remained rooted to the spot.

'But you do, Ranjan,' Radhi continued calmly, 'because Bhawani told someone about what he'd seen.'

'You're making this up!' Ranjan cried.

'I'm not.' Radhi raised her voice so that it could be heard beyond the closed door, in the kitchen. 'Kamal?'

Kamal came out of the kitchen. She was trembling. Radhi nodded at her, encouraging her to come closer, to the centre of the room.

The young woman took a few small steps towards Radhi.

'Kamal, did Bhawani tell you who he saw that day?'

The maid gave a small, almost imperceptible nod.

'Could you tell us who it was?'

Kamal gulped, then pointed a shaky finger at Ranjan.

'What? This is a lie! She is lying. Both of you are!' Ranjan looked afraid for the first time.

'Kamal, you may go home now.'

Kamal immediately scampered out of the room, visibly relieved.

'Why would I lie, Ranjan?' Radhi asked. 'What possible motive could I have?'

'I don't know! Why would I kill my own father?' he countered.

'The apartment, the insurance payout, an end to the debt he was piling up . . . It's the oldest motive in the world . . . Money.'

Ranjan looked wildly about the room, seeking support from his family. 'I didn't do it! Someone tell her.'

Radhi had been standing all this time. Now she pulled an empty chair towards her and sat down, one leg crossed comfortably over the other. 'You don't have to convince me. Just convince the police. They are on their way.'

'What?' The man's shock was obvious to everyone.

'Stop it! Stop it! He didn't do it! I did!' Manjula confessed, with an anguished cry.

A death-like stillness descended on the room as everyone stared at Manjula Kadakia, their faces filled with an identical stunned horror.

'No, Mummy, you don't have to protect me! I swear I didn't do this!' Ranjan erupted. 'C'mon, let's just get out of here.' He strode across the room, attempting to help his mother up from her seat on the swing.

Manjula looked up at Ranjan, then shook her head, her eyes brimming with tears.

'Don't worry, Mummy! I'll explain to the police. You don't need to do this. I'll tell them where I really was . . . I . . . We'll get the best lawyers.' He suddenly seemed to deflate, losing steam.

'*Didi*?' He turned to his sister. 'Do you really believe I killed our father?'

For the first time Sanjana met Ranjan's eyes. 'I know you didn't do it. Mummy did.'

Ranjan gaped at her, opening his mouth and shutting it again. He looked at his mother again, who for the first time in her life sat with her eyes downcast, her shoulders slumped. Her body language so unusual for her, it gave away more than anything Radhi or Sanjana could say.

Ranjan sat down heavily on the sofa. Bewildered. Stunned. The compass of his life suddenly broken.

Finally, Manjula began to speak.

CHAPTER 25

'I killed your father. And I am not sorry. I did it for you. I did it for us. Ranjan is not the only one who knew about his losses. I did too.' Manjula's voice was so low at first that they had to strain to hear her.

'About two months ago, I found a valuation receipt for some silverware in his shirt pocket. It was a long list of items including vases, trays and large *thalis*. I couldn't understand what it was for, but something, almost a sixth sense, stopped me from asking him about it.

'The next time I was alone at home, I shifted the mattress in my room to access the safe box we have inside my bed. I keep our important documents there.' She was now addressing Radhi. 'And also most of my larger silver items that don't fit inside the safety deposit box at the bank.'

She glanced at Sanjana. 'The silver wasn't there. Except for the folder of documents, the safe was completely empty. I was scared. That evening, I visited the store that had issued the receipt and learned that your father had brought all the silver there to be valued and mortgaged.

'Yes, Hetal.' She turned to her younger daughter-in-law, who had gasped involuntarily. 'I suspect he took your silver there too. I tried hunting for the valuation receipt so that I could get it back without you realizing what he'd done. But I haven't managed to find it yet. I am so ashamed. It was your wedding silver. How I wish I had known he'd asked you for it.'

'How could Papa do this!' Amit burst out. 'This is . . . this is stealing!'

Manjula looked at him sadly. 'He wasn't a bad man, just stubborn. He believed one of his other investments would eventually pay off and then he would be able to get it all back.'

'When you found out about the silver, didn't you confront him?' Sanjana asked. She adjusted the cushions behind her, wincing as she did so.

Manjula shook her head. 'Not immediately. God knows I wanted to. I found it impossible to sit in front of him and have dinner that night. I pretended I was unwell and slipped off early. Which wasn't that difficult because I was feeling physically sick just thinking about why he had felt the need to do this. First, I wanted to be sure about the extent of the damage.

'The next morning, I called your father's accountant, Mehta*ji*, and asked him to get me my bank details. I haven't really ever done any of my own banking work. Your father always took care of it for me.' She looked at Ranjan as she said this, as if willing him to understand, even if the others did not.

'Mehtai*ji* didn't call me back like I'd asked him to. So half-an-hour later I called him again. He said there seemed to be some mix-up. My account, which was supposed to have close to fifty-seven lacs in it, had just a few lacs left. He said he was on his way to the bank to straighten out the mix-up. I didn't say anything to him, but I knew then that your father had got to my account as well.'

'I don't believe it.' Sanjana looked angry. 'Papa would never do something like this.'

Manjula's expression was furious. 'You had no difficulty in accepting that *I* am capable of murder? But your precious Papa wouldn't steal? Well, he did! Not only did he wipe out our joint account but he even got to my personal account. Thirty years of working. And do you know what he left for my retirement?' She shook her head as if it wasn't even worth mentioning, then gave a bitter, broken laugh.

'But that's not even the worst part. No, no . . . it gets much better. I confronted your father that afternoon. He apologized for the losses and for wiping out my life's savings, but the stubborn, arrogant man he was, he continued to insist that he could make this right. He'd made one bad investment, but he was sure the other one would pay out!'

'Yes, that's what he told me as well when Ganatra Uncle asked me to speak to him,' Ranjan admitted. 'Of course, he hadn't racked up such a massive debt back then. But he was sure it would all work out. He told me to keep my nose out of his matters!'

'I wish you had told me when you found out!' Manjula cried. 'We could have stopped him in time and then . . . and then he'd still be alive—'

'He would still be alive, if you hadn't killed him,' Sanjana interrupted coldly.

'I haven't completed my story.' Manjula's voice was equally icy. 'The day after I spoke to him, I went to the bank to check my safe-deposit box. I had a terrible feeling that he had got to my jewellery, just like the silver. I opened it, petrified that it would be empty. But you know what? It wasn't. It was worse.' She paused, staring at Sanjana.

'He'd taken all of my jewellery but hadn't touched your mother's. He was married to her for eight years. Eight! And to me? Twenty-seven.' Manjula's eyes gleamed with the pain of betrayal. 'Twenty-seven years of standing by his side, raising his children, but in the end, he still chose her.'

Sanjana looked away, suddenly surprising herself by feeling sorry for the woman who had killed her father. Manjula's pain was palpable. Oppressive. Everyone in the room could feel it. The family were silent. Finally, Amit, his voice strangled from what Radhi suspected was an effort not to cry, asked, 'How did you do it?'

Manjula didn't answer him right away. But it seemed to Radhi that now that the older woman was finally talking, she wanted to tell them everything.

'I came home from the bank that morning, numb. Unsure for the first time in my life of what to do. How to save us from ruin. Because that's what your father had essentially done. Ruined us. Destroyed our lives. We'd have to sell our apartment and the office to cover his debts. Where would we move? Everything we know and love is here. Ranjan's practice. Hetal's studio. Amit's start-up. The kids' schools and friends, our extended families . . . our entire lives revolve around Temple Hill.

'Can you even imagine beginning again in some far-flung part of the city? At my age? Or continuing to work here once everyone knew why we had to sell out and move? The smell of failure is pungent. It would permeate everything we did. Every relationship, every interaction would be marred by it. You might be too young to understand this, and I hope to God you never have to, but failure changes how people look at you. Just look at the Poddars.' Manjula shuddered. 'I, for one, refused to live with their pity.'

'You killed my father because you didn't want people to feel sorry for you?' Sanjana said scornfully. But even as she said this, she knew that the anger she was feeling wasn't directed towards Manjula alone. She was furious at her father for his lies, his destructive pig-headedness, and for the situation he'd put his family in.

Manjula threw Sanjana a long, hard look. 'I killed your father because he betrayed me. I gave him and his family twenty-seven years of my life. And what did he give me in return? Second place. Always second. And as if that wasn't enough, he was going to take away the one thing that I could be proud of. That I had worked so hard to build.'

As much as Sanjana wanted to hate Manjula, she knew she was right. She could see the devastating ripple effect that her father's actions would have had on the family. Manjula's own school would've been the first to suffer. The cream of

Temple Hill flocked to Aspire High, not only for the quality of education it offered but also because there was a sort of prestige associated with it. Anywhere else, the Kadakias might've been able to start afresh, but Temple Hill wasn't so forgiving. People here had long memories and exacting standards, especially when it came to others. Manjula was right. The stink of failure would have engulfed their lives.

Radhi looked at the proud older woman in front of her and understood for the first time what this act must have cost her.

'Is that when you decided to do it?' she prompted gently.

Manjula nodded wearily. 'I didn't sleep a wink that night. I couldn't stomach his treachery. As I lay beside him, I was seething with anger. At the same time, I felt this debilitating kind of helplessness. All I could think was: how could I make it all right again? In the morning, I had a moment of absolute clarity.'

Radhi could see there was no anger or fear in Manjula's eyes. Just raw grief. Despite everything, she had loved the man she had killed.

'How did you know?' Manjula asked.

Ranjan had got up to get his mother a glass of water. Manjula looked up at him gratefully, her hand caressing his in a rare display of tenderness before she took the glass from him.

Radhi waited for her to finish before replying. 'It was your handbag. That day when you were searching for Kirti Uncle's obituary, you emptied out the contents of your bag on the bed. I remember thinking to myself about how remarkably neat your handbag was. No random receipts, papers, wrappers or pens, not even loose change. There was nothing superfluous. Except two things. There were two transparent packets of raisins and cashews.

'I didn't think much of it then. But yesterday, I entered the building when the *satsang* women were leaving. At the gate, each of them received a similar, transparent pack containing almonds, chunky sugar pieces and dried coconut. It occurred to me then that the two dried fruit bags in your handbag must've been giveaways from the *satsang* you attended on the day that Kirti Uncle died. Which got me thinking about why you would have two packets in your handbag.

'One possible explanation was that one of the bags was from the week before. But that didn't seem likely. Your bag looked like it was emptied out, cleaned and organized regularly, maybe even daily. Why would you keep a giveaway from a week before, especially food in this heat? Also how likely was it that the giveaways for two consecutive weeks were the same? This time, it was almonds and chunky sugar, while I'd seen raisins and cashews in your bag. It seemed like the giveaways changed every week. I checked with Mrs Maniar, and she confirmed they did. Which could only mean one thing. That day you got up, left the *satsang* midway and then rejoined it a while later. Receiving two packs of giveaways for the two times you exited the hall.'

There was silence as everyone processed what Radhi had said.

'I had to go up to tie the polythene bag around his face and scatter the empty strips of the sleeping pills on his desk . . . So much for joining a *satsang*. God has never helped me before, why did I think he'd start now?' Manjula's question hung in the air, naked in its anger and pain.

'But where did you get so many pills from? They aren't just available over the counter.' Ranjan looked stunned, still unable to accept this side of his mother.

'From her doctor, Kashmira Aunty,' Sanjana answered. 'Yesterday, Radhi asked me to call her up and say that Mummy was suffering from insomnia after Papa's death. I requested her to prescribe some sedatives on the phone. As Radhi had predicted, she sounded surprised and said that Mummy was already on sleeping pills. In fact, just a couple of weeks ago, Mummy had called up requesting a new prescription because she'd misplaced the earlier one. I asked her the name of the sedatives Mummy was supposed to be on.' Sanjana paused to look at her brothers. 'They were the same as the pills found on Papa's desk. Our guess is she didn't take any of the pills prescribed to her, just saved them up.'

'That was the easy part,' Manjula murmured. 'Giving them to him was the tough one.'

'You mixed it in with his food, didn't you?' Sanjana asked tonelessly.

The older woman nodded.

'But how?' Sonal, who'd been quiet throughout, finally spoke up. 'You weren't at home when he sat for lunch, and you couldn't possibly have mixed it in all the food, knowing that Bhawani and Kamal would be eating it too.'

'I think it was in the mango juice, the *aamras* that you prepared for Kadakia Uncle,' Radhi guessed. 'You added the crushed sleeping pills to it when you sent Kamal downstairs on the pretext of looking for your blouse. That is why you gave up mangoes.'

'*That* is why you gave up mangoes?' Sanjana repeated incredulously. 'You couldn't bear to eat them knowing what you'd done? And I thought it was out of love!'

'I'm done explaining myself to you,' Manjula told her. 'You have a very limited understanding of love. Maybe because you've only experienced it in its absolute sense. You've been fortunate. But love can be broken. Or half-hearted. Or born of guilt. And some of us only ever experience that kind.'

'My mother died when I was six. I was raised by someone who wasn't my mother. So don't tell me I know nothing about half-hearted love.'

Sanjana knew that she'd been deliberately cruel but she seemed unable to help herself. Manjula looked back at her, stung, surprised at the pain that had come from such an unexpected quarter. Sanjana stared back, defiant but increasingly ashamed of herself.

'That's enough now, *didi*.' Ranjan got up from his seat on the sofa. 'Mummy has already told us why she had to do what she did. Let me take her home now. She can rest. I'll come back and we can discuss this among ourselves.'

'There's actually one more thing, Ranjan.' Radhi hesitated, knowing that what she was about to say next would add even more pain to a room filled with disappointment.

'Bhawani.'

'Come on!' Ranjan looked shocked. 'Surely that was an accident? You don't actually believe someone killed him too?'

Radhi didn't reply, her silence more telling than words.

'Oh, God!' Ranjan ran his right hand through his hair, as he sat back down on the sofa.

'Bhawani was in the apartment that afternoon,' Radhi said quietly. 'He heard a sound in the study and went to check it out. He saw Manjula Aunty and what she was doing. And decided to use the information to his own advantage, so he blackmailed her. I'm assuming he did it more than once.' She looked at Manjula who nodded. 'Enough to make Aunty realize that he wasn't going to just take the money and disappear. That she would need a more permanent solution.

'That day, she knew that Bhawani was washing windows at the Solankis'. She also knew that the husband and wife would most likely be at work and the place would be empty, save Bhawani. She decided to use the Solankis' keys, which are always hanging on the key holder by your front door. She entered their apartment, approached him on the pretext of speaking to him, and pushed him out of the window. She came straight back home before anyone had even realized what had happened.'

'Do you even realize how insane that sounds?' an outraged Ranjan yelled at Radhi, before turning to his sister. 'Do you? *Didi*, I'm surprised at you. How easily you've believed the worst of Mummy!'

Sanjana didn't reply. Having already said what she had to Manjula, she seemed to have lost her appetite for retribution.

'Mummy, is this true?' Amit asked, but it seemed Manjula, like Sanjana, was also done talking. She sat on the swing, looking out of the window, refusing to react to the conversation in the room.

'How can you even know all this, Radhi?' Amit asked.

'It was because of something Kamal said. She mentioned Bhawani was skulking around the house a few days before he died and that one late evening, when everyone had retired to their rooms for the night, she saw him enter Aunty's room. It got me wondering what he could he possibly want from her at that hour. But I wasn't sure. Not until this morning.'

Radhi looked to Jayesh. He had been leaning against a wall, worrying about his wife and unborn child, but now he straightened, took a deep breath.

'This morning, when I came to your house to borrow the set of measuring spoons, I'd actually come to pick up the Solankis' keys. I sent them for fingerprint testing. My uncle knows some people in the police and forensics. The keys came back with Mummy's fingerprints.'

'Are you saying this is going to be become a police case?' gasped Hetal.

'Of course not! What a stupid idea!' Ranjan turned around to scowl at his wife. Then, he called out desperately to his mother, 'Mummy, will you please say something? There are dozens of reasons why your prints would be on those keys. They were in your house, after all!'

Manjula gave her son a small sad smile, then returned to her study of the sky outside.

Ranjan looked at Radhi and Sanjana. 'I'm going to take her home now. She's clearly not feeling well.'

He hurried to his mother and put an arm around her. She got up without protest. At the door, Ranjan turned around to see if Hetal was joining him. But she continued sitting there without meeting his eye. Finally, he stepped outside.

CHAPTER 26

'What now? The police?' Amit asked his sister.

Sanjana sighed and shook her head. 'I don't know. I've been thinking about this all night. Going to the police is going to affect all our lives. More devastatingly than the financial problems Papa created. None of us did anything wrong. Why should we have to suffer? Why should our children have to live with this all their lives? But there has to be some justice, not only for Papa but also for Bhawani. He didn't deserve to lose his life, however much of a scoundrel he was.'

Jayesh entered the room, carrying Sanjana's medicines, the maid following him holding a tray with some food. There was a plate with peanut brittles, a bowl of spicy, deep-fried, noodle-like *sev*, and steaming cups of strong, cardamom tea.

Radhi accepted the tea gratefully. Now that the initial adrenaline rush was wearing off, she suddenly felt exhausted. She had also been up all night, her mind furiously working out the various possible ways this afternoon could play out. It had all been dependent on her hunch that the only way to get Manjula to confess was through her sole weakness, her favourite son, Ranjan. But for that to happen, Ranjan had to appear deeply guilty. Piece by piece, a case would have to be built against him, one that would only be strengthened by his own rash reactions. He would have to be pushed just enough for Manjula to see the danger and come to his rescue. Any more, and he might have broken down and told his family where he really was. It had been a balancing act, and Radhi was relieved it was done. Now, she leaned back in her chair, eyes closed as she took a sip of the sweet tea. This was far from over for the Kadakias, but Radhi felt she'd earned a moment of respite for herself.

'What if we do something for his family?' asked Sonal, once the maid had left the room and everyone had settled down again. 'We'll receive a significant payout from the insurance policy. That'll take care of Papa's debts and we'll still have money left over. What if we set up a fund for his daughters?'

Sanjana nodded. 'That's a good idea.'

The others agreed, anxious to clear their consciences, and Radhi once again marvelled at how powerful guilt could be. Motivating or debilitating, depending on how it crept up on you.

'You know, I lent him money too,' Amit admitted quietly. 'Of course, I had no idea that he was making all those losses in the stock market. This was some six months ago. He just told me that he had liquidity issues, that his money was tied up in some investments and he needed to borrow twenty lacs.'

Sanjana frowned at her brother. 'So, you gave it to him.'

'Yes, he's borrowed from me before, but he's always returned it.'

'But not this time?' Sanjana guessed.

'Not a single rupee!' Sonal replied in place of Amit, 'Honestly, *didi*, we were very upset. This was money Amit took out of his start-up. His partners wanted him to pay up, but Amit couldn't bring himself to ask Papa. When I finally convinced him to, Papa said he wouldn't be able to return the money immediately. Said we would have to just wait for it and that he would give it back when he was ready. No explanations. No date. Amit quarrelled with him then. But to no avail. We finally had to break a few of our fixed deposits to put the money back into Amit's business.'

Sanjana's distress was obvious. 'I'm sorry. I had no idea—'

'I should have realized then that he was in trouble.' Amit shook his head. 'This was not like him at all.' Finally, he addressed the elephant in the room. 'What about Mummy?'

'In spite of everything she's done, I can't help feeling sorry for her,' Sonal murmured.

'I do too,' Sanjana agreed. She sighed heavily. 'But she took two lives. There has to be some justice.'

'She has to live with what she did,' Amit pointed out. 'And with the knowledge that we know too. Isn't that punishment enough? . . . You know how proud and righteous she is.'

'Well,' Sanjana said, 'she can't possibly be allowed to run her school. How can we let parents send their children to be educated by a murderer?'

To take the school away from Manjula was to take away the purpose of her life. And yet, they all realized, however harsh it sounded, that what Sanjana had said was true.

'What if she doesn't agree to step down?' asked Sonal. 'It isn't that easy to deter her from something she wants. That much we all know.'

'You heard Ranjan,' Hetal interjected. 'When it comes to his mother, he will fight all of us. Besides, it's not like there's any way to actually prove any of this to the police.'

'We can,' Sanjana said. 'We have a recording of her confession. She has no choice.' Radhi had asked Lila to stand at the back of the room and to hit Voice Record when Manjula began to speak.

'My, you really have thought of everything, haven't you?' Sonal looked at her sister-in-law wonderingly.

'Not me. Radhi. She's the one who figured everything out.'

'But what I don't understand is, how does Kamal fit into all this? Did Bhawani really tell her he saw Mummy in the study?' Amit looked confused.

'No. Bhawani didn't tell her anything. What he did do was steal the two lac rupees from Uncle's study, presumably once Manju Aunty had left.'

'The money Ranjan, in fact, accused him of stealing?' asked Hetal indignantly.

'Yes. You remember he was the one who Kirti Uncle sent to the bank. So he knew the cash was there. Once he'd taken it, he hid it in the kitchen, in that last cupboard under the platform, where you keep plastic cutlery and such.'

'Why there?' asked Sonal.

'I think he knew that eventually, when the noise over Kirti Uncle's death had died down, someone would remember the two lacs and search the servant room as well as the garage, where his belongings were kept.'

'That's exactly what Ranjan did,' Hetal confirmed.

'So he put it in the kitchen, in a cupboard that none of you were likely to open.'

'How clever,' Sonal said.

'He was. But he wasn't lucky. Kamal found the money, removed it and didn't tell him.'

'Oh!' Hetal sounded genuinely surprised. 'I didn't know that little thing had it in her.'

'Yes, but I suspect that proved to be Bhawani's undoing.'

'Meaning?' Amit asked.

'I think that's when he got desperate and began to blackmail Manju Aunty. Though, we'll never know for sure.'

Hetal frowned, 'So, who has the money now? Kamal?'

Radhi nodded. 'Yes. I told her we wouldn't hand her over to the police if she cooperated with our plan this afternoon.'

'But how did you know she had it?' Sonal looked perplexed.

'I didn't. Not for sure. Kirti Uncle was supposed to give that money to Hemendra *bhai* but *he* never received it. Mr Poddar visited him that afternoon, but he insisted that he had nothing to do with it either. Which left only the murderer. Or so I thought. But when Kamal told me that Bhawani had been in the house that afternoon, it got me thinking. He knew the money was there. He was the one who withdrew it from the bank. And I'd seen him scrambling desperately in that last cupboard, searching for something when he thought he was alone. He hadn't seemed happy to see me. I wondered if he'd hidden it there and, if so, who could've removed it.' Radhi leaned forward to put her empty cup of tea on the tray on the centre table and picked up another full one.

'Yesterday, I called Kamal and asked her. She denied it at first. But when we told her we'd hand her over to the police for obstruction of justice and her luggage would be checked and her parents summoned from their village, she confessed to finding the money there and taking it.'

Amit's phone buzzed. He silenced it, glanced at it, then sighed. 'We need to leave now, *didi*, the children are getting restless.' He got up slowly. 'I'll come over to see you tomorrow. We'll talk more then.'

Sonal got up to join him, but Hetal remained seated. 'I'll be home in a bit,' she informed them. She waited until her brother and sister-in-law had left the room. Then she quietly requested Jayesh give her a moment alone with Radhi and Sanjana.

'I'm sorry,' she murmured when they were finally on their own. 'Sorry, I lied to you about where I was that afternoon. And that I behaved badly the day you came to see me at the studio.'

She sighed heavily. 'You were right, I wasn't at Worli Naka that day. I was with my lawyer. I'm planning to file for divorce. In fact, the argument I had with Papa that morning was about that. He opened an envelope addressed to me from my lawyer by mistake.

'Papa called me in and asked me why I wanted to take such a drastic step. When I told him, he pleaded with me to reconsider. He said he'd talk to Ranjan and help us work things out. But when he realized that my mind was made up, he yelled at me and told me that I was being selfish and short-sighted. Inconsiderate of the impact it would have on the children and the family.

'I told him that my children were my business and, with regard to this family, I'd give it exactly as much thought as everyone had given me. Honestly? I was pretty mean. And I feel terrible about it. Especially, because he was the only one who took my side whenever there was an argument with Mummy or Ranjan.'

She looked at Sanjana and Radhi, as if she deserved to be judged but was hopeful for some compassion.

'This is because of Ranjan's affair, isn't it?' Sanjana asked gently.

'You knew about it?' gasped Hetal.

'Not until yesterday.' Sanjana looked to Radhi to explain.

'I was at the Gymkhana yesterday,' Radhi began reluctantly, knowing that what she was about to say would only hurt Hetal more. 'Ranjan's name was on the main sheet of club entries but not on the register outside the gym. Nor was he anywhere on the CCTV footage. At first, I thought that I'd found the murderer. But just to be sure, I decided to check all the other registers and entries. The one outside the pool, the tennis courts, the badminton courts, the TT rooms and even the bar. The more I searched the more certain I was that it was him. But then I found his name. It was in the register for rooms. You know the THG has rooms that visiting guests can book for the duration of their stay?'

Hetal nodded.

'He was signed into one of the rooms for that afternoon. With a guest.'

Hetal started to say something but couldn't for several minutes.

'I found out last month,' she finally admitted. 'Overheard him whispering endearments to her in Papa's study. He was telling her that he couldn't wait until the next time they were together and he could smell her hair. Her hair!' she scoffed.

'But do you know how I felt then? It was the strangest thing. I wasn't upset that he was in love with someone else. Just unbelievably furious that he was making such a fool of me! That's when I decided I would divorce him and that

I'd make it ugly! I would spring it on him, make him feel as foolish as I'd felt.'

'There's one thing still bothering me though,' Radhi admitted. 'Why did you lie about Ranjan's fight? You said it was a minor argument, when it wasn't.'

Hetal reddened at Radhi's question. 'I was the one who instigated it. I nagged Ranjan to bring up the topic of the apartment with Papa again that morning, even though we'd discussed it in the past and he'd refused. I knew Papa wouldn't agree to sell the apartment that easily. But I thought if Ranjan pushed him enough, Papa might loan us some money and we could buy our own. Which I could then kick him out of. Obviously, I didn't know about Papa's preposterous financial problems then.'

Hetal left soon after, making them first promise they wouldn't tell Ranjan about the divorce just yet. She would tell him in her own time.

'Do you think she knows who he is having the affair with?' Sanjana wondered, when it was just the two of them.

Radhi nodded. 'I think she might.'

CHAPTER 27

'So who was it? The woman Ranjan was seeing?' Madhavi added a dollop of sour cream to her burrito bowl before moving on to the fresh guacamole.

The table was groaning with all the food Lila and Radhi had spent the morning cooking up — an elaborate Mexican spread for the lunch Radhi had invited her sister and *fia* to. At one end, there were bowls of creamy black beans, cilantro rice, red and yellow peppers sautéed in olive oil, a green tomato salsa and another made of mango, besides an array of condiments for a burrito bowl. At the centre sat a colourful corn-and-pineapple salad, topped with nacho chips, along with a crunchy vegetable and bean lasagne with a spicy Mexican twist. For dessert, Radhi had prepared little shot glasses of Kahlua-flavoured tiramisu. When the table had been laid, Radhi thought they had probably gone overboard, but after the tense last few days, it had turned out to be relaxing.

Now, they were in the middle of lunch, and Radhi had just finished telling her sister and aunt a little bit more about the entire sorry affair.

'So, who was it?' Vrinda asked, gingerly removed the nacho chips from her pineapple salad to put them on Radhi's plate.

Radhi took a bite of a chip before answering. 'Kanika Ganatra.'

'Mr Ganatra's daughter-in-law?' Madhavi looked surprised. 'That pretty, young thing? . . . Really? Hmm, I can't picture them together. I wonder what drew her to him.'

'Probably, what always draws people together,' Radhi guessed. 'Loneliness.'

'How did you know?'

Radhi frowned. 'I didn't, not until much later. But I would've figured it out sooner had I been paying more attention.'

'On the day that Bhawani died, Kanika almost swooned when she saw the body. Instinctively, she reached out to grab hold of Ranjan, who immediately slipped his arm around her waist. It wasn't so much what he did, but how he did it. And how comfortably she leaned into him. There was a sort of ease, a familiarity in their body language with each other.'

'What about Hetal? Does she know?' Madhavi put her spoon down, dabbed her lips with a napkin and leaned away from the table with a satisfied sigh.

'She must have some idea.' Radhi remembered how she had looked up the day of Bhawani's murder and thought mistakenly that Hetal was staring at her. Now, with the benefit of hindsight, Radhi realized that Hetal had actually been looking at her husband with Kanika.

The three women moved from the dining table into the living room.

'Lila, a pot of your strong ginger chai, please.' Vrinda smiled at the younger woman clearing the table. Lila nodded.

'By the way, Radhi tells me you are quite the *khabri*, excellent at digging up information. She said she would never have figured it all out without your help.'

Lila blushed. 'I only did what *didi* asked me to do. She's got real talent for this stuff. In fact, I think, she should just forget this writing-shiiting and open a detective agency.'

'Ha ha ha, yes, that would be exciting, wouldn't it?' Vrinda laughed. 'Your *didi* needs some excitement in her life.'

Then, looking at Radhi, she asked, 'By the way, did that Nishant ever call you?'

Radhi gasped. '*You* gave him my number? I wondered how he got it. Why would you do that?'

'Why not? He seemed like a perfectly nice boy. I would've given him my number also, if he'd asked!' Vrinda grinned.

Radhi turned to her sister, holding up her hands. 'Don't worry, *di*, I'm going to say no. I know Mrs Bansal will throw a fit otherwise.'

'No! Please go out with him! If it means you can finally start getting over Mackinzey and moving on with your life, I'd be thrilled. Don't worry about my mother-in-law. I'll handle her. Besides, Nishant made it very clear that he wasn't interested in meeting Prachi for a second date. So, why shouldn't you see him?'

'Well, he *was* kind of nice,' Radhi admitted.

'Nice? He was a hunk! A delicious hunk of chocolate!' Vrinda proclaimed, and all three of them laughed.

Then Vrinda suddenly sobered. 'I forgot to tell you, Radhi, I met Mrs Poddar in the lift on my way up here and she gave me the iciest of hellos.'

'Yes, unfortunately that relationship is collateral damage.' Radhi told them about how she and Sanjana had confronted Mr Poddar about why he had visited Mr Kadakia.

'So it was about the society tender then?'

Radhi nodded. 'The building and the terrace need some significant repair work. Mr Poddar picked a builder and pushed for the contract to be given to him. Later, Kirti Uncle found out that the builder had given Mr Poddar a big kickback in exchange for the contract. He confronted Mr Poddar and threatened to tell the building committee. They had a big row over it.'

Vrinda shook her head. 'I'm sorry to hear that.' She'd known Mr Poddar in his heyday and was saddened to see his reduced circumstances.

Lila returned with tea and biscuits. She poured each of them a cup.

'I hear the Kadakias have put their apartment up for sale.' Madhavi said.

Radhi nodded. 'They want a fresh start.'

'And Manjula?' Vrinda asked.

'She's moved to Bhagwandhaam.'

'That *ashram*? Really? She's never struck me as the religious type. But I suppose there's a lot she needs to introspect about.'

Vrinda looked at Radhi. 'Were you comfortable with Sanjana's decision not to hand her over to the police?'

Radhi had spent a lot of time thinking this over. Not the legality of what they'd done, but the morality of it. They'd spared Manjula a life in prison. But what gave them the right to offer mercy? Would Bhawani's family agree with the kind of justice they'd meted out, if they knew? And was it really mercy that they'd offered anyway? Could a purposeless existence away from everyone and everything one valued ever really be called that?

'Honestly? I feel Bhawani's children should've had as much say in the decision as Kirti Uncle's. But I don't blame Sanjana. In her place, I'd have done the same for my family.'

'Well, I think you did a good thing there.' Vrinda squeezed her niece's hand. 'Everyone is answerable for their own karma. And your intent is as important as anything you do. You know that, right?'

Radhi nodded.

'Stay accountable for your own thoughts, words and actions. Beyond that, leave it be,' she continued.

'Speaking of thoughts and words,' Madhavi grinned, 'any plans to put those on paper?'

Radhi smiled back. She *did* have a plan. She'd written a long email to George telling him how the entire story had played out. And he'd responded with just one line, 'You know that's your next book, right?'

When she read his words, Radhi had felt a tingle run down her spine. George was right. She'd write a murder mystery next.

THE END

ACKNOWLEDGEMENTS

I owe much gratitude to the many people who've helped bring this book to life. A heartfelt thank you:

First to Maulik, my husband, who somehow saw exactly what I was trying to do with the book, almost as if he'd read my mind. And who continued to believe in the idea and me, even when I had trouble believing in either.

To Kanishka Gupta, my literary agent, for championing the book so fiercely and doggedly.

To Emma Grundy Haigh for taking a leap of faith and putting her trust in a completely new and unknown voice.

To Emma again and Aruna Vasudevan for their sensitive and gentle editorial inputs.

To both, my friend Navaz Irani and Dr Rukumani Krishnamoorthi for answering my strange questions on how best to murder people!

To my brother Sahil, and my friend Niraj, for taking the time not only to read the initial drafts but to sit me down and tell me everything I could do better. And for doing it with kindness, so that I wouldn't just stop and give up.

To Swati and Deepti, for not only reading the initial drafts and giving me their precious feedback — I expected no less from them — but also for the sustenance I draw from our conversations about books, motherhood and life. And for being the kind of women who lift other women up.

And finally, always and for ever, to my mum, because of whom, I am who I am.

THE JOFFE BOOKS STORY

We began in 2014 when Jasper agreed to publish his mum's much-rejected romance novel and it became a bestseller.

Since then we've grown into the largest independent publisher in the UK. We're extremely proud to publish some of the very best writers in the world, including Joy Ellis, Faith Martin, Caro Ramsay, Helen Forrester, Simon Brett and Robert Goddard. Everyone at Joffe Books loves reading and we never forget that it all begins with the magic of an author telling a story.

We are proud to publish talented first-time authors, as well as established writers whose books we love introducing to a new generation of readers.

We won Trade Publisher of the Year at the Independent Publishing Awards in 2023. We have been shortlisted for Independent Publisher of the Year at the British Book Awards for the last four years, and were shortlisted for the Diversity and Inclusivity Award at the 2022 Independent Publishing Awards. In 2023 we were shortlisted for Publisher of the Year at the RNA Industry Awards.

We built this company with your help, and we love to hear from you, so please email us about absolutely anything bookish at feedback@joffebooks.com

If you want to receive free books every Friday and hear about all our new releases, join our mailing list: www.joffebooks.com/contact

And when you tell your friends about us, just remember: it's pronounced Joffe as in coffee or toffee!

ALSO BY MEETI SHROFF-SHAH

TEMPLE HILL MYSTERY SERIES
Book 1: A MUMBAI MURDER MYSTERY
Book 2: A MATRIMONIAL MURDER

Printed in Great Britain
by Amazon

44885187R00148